Praise for The

"*The Alamo Bride* is an exciting, romantic tale of the early days of the Texas Republic. The spunky, determined heroine is a perfect match for the handsome, mysterious hero who holds a secret that could either make or break Texas' fight for independence. Great conflict, a strong faith element, and Kathleen Y'Barbo's extensive research skills and knowledge of Texas history make this book a fascinating read."

–Vickie McDonough, bestselling author
of forty-seven Christian romance books and novellas,
including The Texas Boardinghouse Brides series

"Kathleen Y'Barbo is a Texan through and through and a gifted storyteller on top of that. Her love of the Lone Star State has come through in so many of her books, but in *The Alamo Bride*, she brings all the legendary Texas mystique and history together in a story that readers won't be able to put down. As a native Texan myself, I still honor the cry of 1836— Remember the Alamo—and I know historical romance lovers will long remember *The Alamo Bride*."

–Kristen Ethridge, author of the bestselling Christian romances
in the Port Provident series

"Kathleen Y'Barbo knows how to write adventure-filled historical romance that will keep the pages turning! This book was packed with action, danger, adventure and of course, a bit of romance! I loved it! *The Alamo Bride* kept me on the edge of my seat, yet still managed to have plenty of warmth and humor from the characters. Fantastic read and a great addition to the Daughters of the Mayflower series!"

–Ashley Johnson, book blogger and reviewer at BringingUpBooks

The
Alamo
Bride

The
Daughters
of the
Mayflower

KATHLEEN
Y'BARBO

BARBOUR BOOKS
An Imprint of Barbour Publishing, Inc.

Print ISBN 978-1-68322-820-2

eBook Editions:
Adobe Digital Edition (.epub) 978-1-68322-822-6
Kindle and MobiPocket Edition (.prc) 978-1-68322-821-9

All scripture quotations are taken from the King James Version of the Bible.

Cover Photograph: Malgorzata Maj/Trevillion Images

Published by Barbour Books, an imprint of Barbour Publishing, Inc., 1810 Barbour Drive, Uhrichsville, Ohio 44683, www.barbourbooks.com

Our mission is to inspire the world with the life-changing message of the Bible.

 Member of the
Evangelical Christian
Publishers Association

Printed in the United States of America.

DEDICATION

For Mary Beth Patton and Ginger Tumlinson
Cousins and keepers of the family flame

And to Linda Hang, polisher of prose and copy editor extraordinaire
Thank you all for doing what you do so I can do what I do.

Daughters of the Mayflower

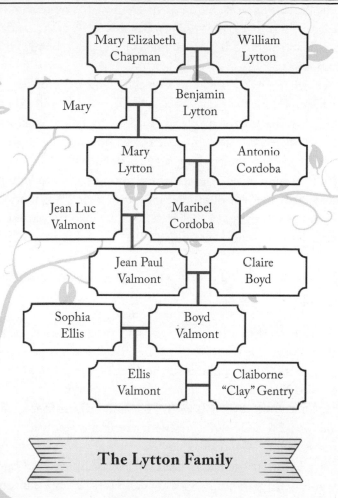

Mary Elizabeth Chapman — William Lytton

Mary — Benjamin Lytton

Mary Lytton — Antonio Cordoba

Jean Luc Valmont — Maribel Cordoba

Jean Paul Valmont — Claire Boyd

Sophia Ellis — Boyd Valmont

Ellis Valmont — Claiborne "Clay" Gentry

The Lytton Family

William Lytton married Mary Elizabeth Chapman (Plymouth, 1621)
Parents of 13 children, including Benjamin
Benjamin Lytton married Mary (Massachusetts 1675)
Born to Benjamin and Mary
Mary Lytton married Antonio Cordoba (Spain 1698)
Only child was Maribel
Maribel Cordoba married Jean Luc Valmont (1736)
Only child was Jean Paul Valmont
Jean Paul Valmont married Clarie Boyd (1770)
Children included Boyd Valmont
Boyd Valmont married Sophia Ellis (1807)
Children included Ellis Valmont
Ellis Valmont married Claiborne "Clay" Gentry (1836)

Dear Reader,

Though *The Alamo Bride* has been in progress for quite some time, I began the actual writing of the story exactly 182 years after the day William Barret Travis penned his now-famous letter from behind the walls of the Alamo.

President Andrew Jackson and General Sam Houston had a long history as friends from their days back in Tennessee as well as a mentoring relationship that might have led Houston to follow Jackson to the White House. When Houston made choices that sent him in a different direction, Jackson continued to support his friend with advice and occasionally political support or employment. Although, as president, Jackson could not officially help his old friend Houston when Houston took over control of the Texian army, it is believed he continued his pattern of aiding the general by not only providing advice but seeing to much-needed funding.

Most likely that funding occurred through secondary channels where allies of Jackson were encouraged to send money to the cause. These were not the only donations the army received. Sometimes the influx of cash came from entities and businesses, and other times it came from individuals or governments of other nations. Basically any person or government who disliked the politics of the Mexican government or saw a benefit in Texas becoming its own republic contributed.

Thus, people from diverse backgrounds and citizenships gave to the cause. A fictional New Orleans Grey with a desire to gain a little political stature and the right connections to do so—namely an uncle who was the first governor of the area gained in the Louisiana Purchase and a grandfather who sailed with Jean Lafitte—could definitely parley his information in regard to buried treasure to achieve that goal.

In October 1835, a group of men came together to form two companies of soldiers called the New Orleans Greys. The sole purpose of the Greys was to come to the aid of those fighting for freedom from Mexico. The Greys were a military organization, so named because of the grey wool uniforms they wore. Though members of the Greys came from all over the world, they were united in the cause of freedom for Texians and Tejanos. Before the Greys were disbanded two years later, many died for this cause.

And in case you're wondering whether I misspelled the word *Texian*, rest assured, I did not. While no one knows for certain how this term originated, it refers to citizens of the lands that would eventually become the state of Texas. This word remained in use for quite some time, but once Texas achieved statehood, its citizens were most generally referred to by the same term we use today: Texans.

As an aside, my mother's family came to Texas in exactly the same way as my fictional Ellis Valmont's family. Setting off from New Orleans with three hundred of Stephen F. Austin's settlers—now referred to as the Old Three Hundred—they were given land on the Gulf of Mexico at Velasco, and some of their descendants still live on that very land. Thus, this is a personal favorite story of mine as well as a tale of Texas and the Texians.

Enjoy!

He that dwelleth in the secret place of the most High shall abide under the shadow of the Almighty. I will say of the LORD, He is my refuge and my fortress: my God; in him will I trust. Surely he shall deliver thee from the snare of the fowler, and from the noisome pestilence. He shall cover thee with his feathers, and under his wings shalt thou trust: his truth shall be thy shield and buckler. Thou shalt not be afraid for the terror by night; nor for the arrow that flieth by day; nor for the pestilence that walketh in darkness; nor for the destruction that wasteth at noonday. A thousand shall fall at thy side, and ten thousand at thy right hand; but it shall not come nigh thee. Only with thine eyes shalt thou behold and see the reward of the wicked. Because thou hast made the LORD, which is my refuge, even the most High, thy habitation; there shall no evil befall thee, neither shall any plague come nigh thy dwelling. For he shall give his angels charge over thee, to keep thee in all thy ways. They shall bear thee up in their hands, lest thou dash thy foot against a stone. Thou shalt tread upon the lion and adder: the young lion and the dragon shalt thou trample under feet. Because he hath set his love upon me, therefore will I deliver him: I will set him on high, because he hath known my name. He shall call upon me, and I will answer him: I will be with him in trouble; I will deliver him, and honour him. With long life will I satisfy him, and shew him my salvation.

PSALM 91

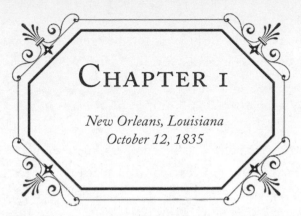

CHAPTER 1

New Orleans, Louisiana
October 12, 1835

He was the nephew of a governor and statesman and the grandson of a pirate who sailed with the infamous Jean Lafitte, but tonight Claiborne William Andre Gentry was merely one of the many anonymous souls who walked along Magazine Street in the Vieux Carre.

Back in Tennessee, his sisters had teased him about the dark hair that was so different from their blond braids and yet so similar to the pirate whose name was forbidden in their home. Here in New Orleans, Clay's resemblance to the grandfather his family never spoke of had caused him to fit in rather than look out of place. And when a man was carrying a secret on behalf of the president of the United States, looking out of place was not the goal.

The night was warm, unseasonably so for October, and the air was thick. Like as not, there would be storms before daybreak.

Clay moved swiftly down Magazine Street, keeping to the shadows and avoiding the glare of the gas lamps. Though the full moon overhead turned everything it touched a dull silver, murky darkness was never far away in this city.

He knew from experience that the darkness did not merely extend to the streets and alleys. It also lay deep in the hearts of men who dwelled here.

In the last few months, he'd discovered the names of some of those men. His mission tonight was, in part, to discover if what he'd learned was true. The remainder of his task for the evening—the duty he held and the favor the completion of that duty would incur—weighed heavy on his mind.

"He shall cover thee with his feathers, and under his wings shalt thou trust."

A verse first memorized at his mother's knee because it made him laugh to think of the Lord covered in feathers, now these words gave him strength. With the verse in mind, Clay picked up his pace.

Just yesterday, news of the battle in Gonzales had reached the city. A squabble over ownership of two cannons very likely had launched what would become a full-blown war.

The general who would lead his troops in that war needed funding if he was to be successful. Funding that the Mexican government would very much wish to intercept.

For that reason, he'd spoken to no one since his arrival in New Orleans. In times of war, not all friends were truly friends. And, sadly, not all family escaped the title of enemy.

Though he kept the evidence of who he was—the papers that named him as a citizen of Louisiana by virtue of his uncle's position—tucked into his boot, he would not make that evidence public. Better to remain a stranger than to be targeted because of an alliance that came from an accident of birth.

As he walked past Banks Arcade, he thought of the battle for Texas brewing here in New Orleans. A war of words had been waged for months between the owners of the Creole mercantile houses who supported the Mexican Federalists and the Americans who populated the Faubourg St. Marie. Recently the Americans had declared victory and celebrated by raising a quarter-million dollars in funds for two companies of men to go and join the fight.

One week from tonight these men would meet to have their names added to the rolls. To Clay's understanding, one company would be headed north to Nacogdoches while the other would be setting sail for Velasco.

His grandfather held a special fondness for Velasco. So much so that he'd left a substantial amount of the fortune he earned during his years at sea buried there. Father wanted nothing to do with what he deemed ill-gotten gains, but Clay had been fascinated with the idea of someday digging it all up. Over the years, he had begged his grandfather to show him the map that led to the location of this treasure, but the old man never would.

Then after his death, a letter came for Clay. Inside was a map and a two-sentence warning:

> Commit this to memory and then destroy it. With great riches comes great responsibility, so you must only retrieve this to use it for a cause greater than yourself.

Someday he would fulfill his grandfather's request and find a use for that treasure, a cause greater than himself. Tonight, however, he had other issues to handle. Thoughts of Velasco would have to wait for another day.

For another cause.

Clay pulled open the ornate door and stepped inside the building situated at the corner of Natchez Street then climbed the stairs. Below him the market sold everything from china to ships to humans—a detestable trade—but one floor up, the atmosphere was decidedly different.

As on most nights, Jim Hewlett's dining establishment, known here by some as Hewlett's Exchange, was doing a brisk business. He tipped a nod toward the owner without slowing his pace.

Clay slipped past the privacy screens that kept this part of the structure hidden from prying eyes and paused beneath one of the four massive chandeliers that lit the expansive room. To his left was the wood and marble bar backed by row upon row of French glassware. Straight ahead, the silver-haired man he was to meet awaited him in an alcove beneath an ornately framed but poor copy of a Caravaggio still life painting.

His companion for the evening was a man he knew as Reverend Smith—who, given his close attention to the ladies in the room and his thick French accent, was surely neither a man of the cloth nor in possession of that surname. Smith was thick around the middle and of average height, just the sort who would not call attention to himself in a crowd.

The older man barely acknowledged Clay as he approached, preferring to turn and stare up at the painting. "A pity the money that is won at the tables above us cannot be spent in part to decorate the tables here."

Ignoring the reference to the gambling that went on upstairs, Clay merely nodded. "I suppose."

"You suppose?" Smith's thick brows rose as if Clay had insulted him personally. "I assure you that your grandfather not only would have an opinion but also would likely own the original." A grin surfaced. "Or know how to acquire it."

If Smith's expression was meant to chastise Clay, the sentiment missed its mark. "No doubt he would. But the subject of my grandfather is not what we are here to discuss."

The supposed reverend drummed his fingers on the table, calling attention to the signet ring on his right hand that bore the coat of arms of a prominent French family. "It is he who speaks for your character, my boy. Without your provenance, you'd not be undertaking this endeavor."

His temper rose. "My provenance also includes a Louisiana governor and more than one man who merely made a quiet living and took care of his family."

"So I have heard. Still I stand by my previous statement."

Something inside Clay snapped. "We are here because I have proved myself worthy of this endeavor and for no other reason."

More than proved himself, Clay had become indispensable to President Jackson in his cause of aiding his old friend Sam Houston. He let the statement hang in the thick air between them.

His outburst caught the attention of the trio of gentlemen at the next table, among them Samuel Jarvis Peters. The banker tipped his head in a polite greeting and then went back to his conversation.

His temper was what got him into this situation. He could not allow it to make things any worse.

The Frenchman broke out in a broad smile. "I jest, my friend. If you were not worthy, you would not be here, yes?" He paused to cast a covert glance around the room before returning his attention to Clay. "I see that you know the Peters fellow. I should not be surprised. What I wonder is whether it's through old William or Andre, rest his soul."

Again Clay bristled, but he made an effort to keep his expression neutral. While his uncle, William Claiborne, a statesman and governor of this state, was a worthy relative, in Clay's mind so was Andre Gallier. Both sailed seas of turmoil to claim victory, Claiborne's over political causes and Gallier over the law itself. Neither was held in higher esteem than the other in his mind.

"He is a family friend," Clay said, leaving the stranger to guess on which side of the family the alliance fell. Clay reached for his pocket watch, more as a show of his impatience with the wasted time than any hurry to be elsewhere.

"Of course you have managed to keep your ties to this city. Odd, don't you think?"

"How so?"

Smith paused to grin. "Seeing as your father hid his family away in Tennessee to keep you from any taint of scandal. In any case," he began as he retrieved a document from his vest pocket and slid it across the table, "I have this for you."

Clay turned the document over and noted the presidential seal. He'd had plenty of communication with the president or his aides, but never had anything been in writing. Nor would it ever be, per the president's orders. The subject of Texas was a tricky one, fraught with issues of states' rights and already the source of much contention among the ranks in Washington and elsewhere. Clay's mission was personal and not at all connected with the position President Jackson held.

This had to be a trick.

Slowly he returned his gaze to Smith and found the older man watching him closely. "Who gave you this?"

The smile became a blank expression. "The same man who set the original plan in motion, Mr. Gentry. Surely you do not wish me to speak his name aloud in such a public place."

Clay broke the seal without looking away. The wax crumbled beneath his fingers. Finally he turned his attention to the letter.

Would that this finds you well, Claiborne. I offer my fondest wishes to you. I have authorized the bearer of this letter to receive the item you have guarded so well. Please accept my thanks for a job well done and rest assured those who will now take over for you have only the best interests of the mission at heart.

It was signed with the formal signature of the president himself.

Only it wasn't signed by him because Andrew Jackson did not write this letter. Not only was the signature slightly different, but the man who'd practically been family for as long as Clay could remember had never once called him Claiborne.

Further proof of deceit.

Clay folded the paper and settled it into his jacket pocket and then let out a long breath. "Have you read this?" he asked Smith.

"I have not."

Again Clay studied the man across the table as he calculated his next move. Somewhere between Andrew Jackson and Reverend Smith the plans to deliver aid to the Texian militias via their leader, General

Houston, had been discovered. The perpetrator of this fraud could be anyone. Clay's best guess was the source came from Mexico. There were many there who would pay well to put an end to the resistance on their northern border. And yet there were also those on this side of the border who could profit.

Clay kept his attention on Smith. He had pledged a vow on his own life that he would see that the money that had been quietly raised arrived at its intended destination. If he had to give that life for the cause, the money would arrive safely.

A strong desire to get out of this place and back into the shadows bore down on him. He needed time to think. Time to formulate an alternative plan.

"What does it say?" Smith asked.

He shrugged as if easing into the idea even as his eyes covertly scanned the room in search of any possible accomplices. "I am to make the delivery to you." He paused. "Tonight."

Smith leaned forward. "Those are the same instructions I received. I understand it is a change of plans, but given the current situation, it is the only way."

"What is the reason for this change?"

Another shrug and then Smith reached for his coat. "I was not told. So shall we go now?"

He ignored the question as he caught the attention of Hewlett. The older man offered a nod and Clay returned the gesture. Was Hewlett friend or foe?

At this moment, he could not say for certain, though before this day, Clay would have thought the relationship the exchange owner held with Grandfather Gallier and his associates meant that Clay could feel safe in this place.

Now every face that turned his direction could be a man looking to stop him from carrying out his mission. Again he considered the fact that any friend could be a foe.

"Unless of course you've decided not to do as he has asked. I'm sure our mutual friend could be made to understand, although I doubt your father would."

"What does my father have to do with this?" Clay managed through a clenched jaw as he swung his attention back to Smith.

"Everything and nothing," the Frenchman said with a casual lift of one shoulder. "I worry for the safety of your family, is all. However, that is a conversation for another time, for we are likely being watched. I suggest you offer me a smile as we leave this place. I would hate to think those who had an opinion as to the business we are conducting here might consider taking action."

Clay rose and stared down at Smith from his superior height. "I find it odd that you would threaten a man who is on the same side as you, Reverend Smith."

"Do you now?" Smith stood and shrugged himself into his coat. "Look into your heart, Mr. Gentry, and then look around this room. Just as you are looking to serve your needs, so are they. Do not think you're above it."

The statement jarred him more than Clay would have liked. It was a simple thing to consider himself part of the noble cause of aiding General Houston to bring freedom to Texas. A bit more complicated were Clay's other reasons for doing so.

Was he following a path leading to his own benefit, or had he truly chosen a nobler way?

The question chased him as he descended the staircase, trading the elegance of the dining establishment for the fetid chaos of the exchange below and then finally for the damp night air of Magazine Street. As he'd expected, a slow drizzle of rain had begun.

With Smith on his heels, Clay ignored the rain to lead him in circles through the dark streets at a brisk pace, formulating a plan as he went. With their destination finally in sight, he stopped and whirled around to watch the older man hurrying to catch up.

Out of breath, Smith shook his head. "If your plan was to lose me on the way here, you failed, sir. Besides, it is common knowledge that you took rooms on the third floor of Banks Arcade."

Common knowledge. Hardly.

Still, Clay forced a laugh. "If my plan had been to lose you, I would not have failed." He paused. "But this is where we part ways for now. I will make the delivery as planned, but on my terms." His expression went serious. "In one hour at the Place d'Armes."

Smith took a step back to look beyond him. "No, Mr. Gentry. The exchange has already occurred. I'm afraid you are no longer needed."

And then everything went dark.

Clay opened his eyes to find the last of the stars overhead being chased away by the dawn. With his head throbbing and the horizon unsteady at best, he stumbled to his feet and made his way to his rooms.

As he expected, they had been ransacked and the money was gone. Cursing himself for a fool, Clay fell back onto the narrow cot and stared up at the ceiling. Every detail of the mission had been committed to memory just as he'd done as a child with Grandfather Gallier's map.

Less than six weeks from now he was expected to arrive at the agreed meeting place and transfer the funds. To fail was not an option.

He studied the crack in the plaster ceiling and allowed his mind to consider all the options available to him. His own personal assets could never match the amount of the missing funds.

Or could they?

Clay sat bolt upright, ignoring the jolt of pain and the spinning room as he laughed out loud. Of course. The Gallier treasure. According to Grandfather, the value of what lay beneath the Texas soil was much more than what had been stolen last night.

He stood and began to pace, holding on to the walls until the room slowed its turning. Years of practice allowed him to call up the image his grandfather made him memorize. All that remained was how to make the trip there without drawing attention to himself.

For as crafty as the Smith fellow was, he couldn't possibly have hit him on the back of his head while standing in front of him. There was at least one accomplice in this endeavor, likely more.

A smile rose and laughter once again followed as an idea occurred. Why bother to make a covert escape and risk being followed when he could sail out of New Orleans in plain sight?

His passion for the plight of Texas was well known, as was his intention to do what he could for that cause. Thus, no one who knew him would find it odd when one week hence he attended the meeting downstairs in the very building where he now sat and presented himself as a candidate for the roster of the New Orleans Greys.

He would muster in with Captain Morris's battalion and be delivered to Velasco before the end of the month without anyone lifting an eyebrow. The only wrinkle in what was a nearly flawless plan was the question of how he might slip away to retrieve the treasure. That, he decided, would be left to God's own provision. If need be, he could invoke the name of Andrew Jackson himself should he be caught and questioned.

Once his mission was complete and the funds were transferred to Sam Houston's representatives, the president would surely excuse him from his duties as a Grey and call him to Washington. There Clay would be given the place in the Jackson administration that he had been promised. The appointment that would make everything right that Clay and his temper had made wrong.

Clay smiled. Yes, this would work. It had to.

The only question remaining was whether to alert the president to the situation. With nearly six weeks until the date of the exchange, there was no reason to worry the man.

If all went well, President Jackson would never know that the stake Clay had in seeing the mission complete was now a very personal one.

CHAPTER 2

Quintana, Texas
October 22, 1835

Despite the fact that her feet stood on Texas soil, the blood of Spanish noblemen and French privateers ran through Ellis Valmont's veins. Her family tree was populated with brave souls who fought and died for a cause greater than themselves. Even though she'd married into the Valmont family, Mama could recite their stories as if calling back memories fresh enough to see with her eyes closed.

As a child Papa heard tales of his noble-born Cordoba grandmother who survived a childhood orphaned on a Caribbean island and then married a privateer whose goal was to rescue treasure much greater than gold and silver, the treasure of enslaved souls. Grandmother Valmont told those same stories to Mama when she joined the family, as much to see that the tales were passed down as to explain why Papa sometimes got lost in a book or caught the wandering fever and picked up stakes to travel bold paths others might shun.

Had Papa not inherited that penchant for adventure passed down through the generations, this branch of the Valmonts might have continued to reside in some well-appointed home along the Rue Royal or another grand address. Ellis had given up counting the number of aunts, uncles, and cousins they'd left behind when Papa took them to Texas.

These same family members proclaimed Papa to have lost his mind. To this, Papa would tell them he'd finally found it. Had found a home here on the banks of the river and a cause for which he was willing to lay down his life.

Until war came to the shores of her coastal Texas home, Ellis had never given serious thought to what it might be like to make a choice to die for a cause greater than self. Now she thought of such things constantly.

Too often an unfamiliar sail on the horizon cast fear into her heart, and now she could not blame the ancient crumbling books Mama preserved from her New Orleans home and carried to Texas. Books that once entertained Great-Grandmother Maribel Cordoba on Isla de Santa Maria now lay covered in quilts in a trunk beside Mama's bed, only to be removed by Mama and turned with care lest the fragile pages be ruined.

Of the two, Mama was the one who always looked to preserve the past, while Papa was always looking to the future. As the only daughter, she had learned much from both of them.

From her mother, Ellis learned the ways of healing using plants that grew near their coastal Texas homeland. As deep as the roots of these healing herbs grew, deeper still grew Ellis's roots in the Texas soil.

She drew her *rebozo* close and gave thanks her mother insisted she take the colorful Mexican scarf along on this morning's mission to deliver a remedy for Grandfather Valmont's persistent cough. She had arisen well before the sun to mix the herbs and now carried them down the familiar path to where the canoe was kept. On the other side of the river in his Velasco home, Grandfather was likely sipping chicory coffee while the sky bled from deep purple to pale blue.

Though war waged elsewhere, there had been little cause for worry lately in Quintana and Velasco. Still, no citizen of this disputed land could rest easy with Mexican forces unwilling to give in to those who sought freedom.

Thus, she was always on her guard wherever she walked, and she never went anywhere without a watchful eye and a knife hidden in the pocket of her skirt. And, of course, with an escort of some sort, though generally it was one of her rowdy and most unhelpful younger brothers or the elderly farmhand they called Mr. Jim.

The boys' absence today, caused by misbehavior that Mama had punished by sentencing them to cleaning out the barn starting well before daylight, meant she would make the trip without them. Mr. Jim had been called down the road to help the Widow Callahan by cutting up a tree that fell on her chicken coop, so he too was unavailable.

Thus, she was alone. Not that she minded, for the quiet solitude that came from walking the path, crossing the river, and then making her way to Grandfather Valmont's home was something she liked very much.

The canoe was where she last left it, well hidden in the reeds on the far end of their property at the river's edge. Ellis quickly crossed the deep brown waters and secured the canoe out of sight on the other bank. Grasping her basket of herbs, she climbed out and made her way down the path.

A few minutes later, she rounded a corner and Velasco appeared in the distance. The city was situated at the eastern shore of the Brazos River, the dark thread of water called the *Rio de los Brazos de Dios*—River of the Arms of God—by the Spaniards. Huddled against the river's banks all the way down to where the Brazos met the bay, the collection of buildings spread in both directions away from the shipyard and the impressive Valmont home. Ships bobbed at anchor here as well as along the coast, some of them built by Grandfather and his men.

It was a source of pride to both Papa and Grandfather that Valmont Shipbuilders was bigger than any other enterprise in Velasco other than the military outpost of Fort Velasco. Now that the skirmish at Gonzales appeared to portend more than just an ongoing disagreement with Mexico, likely both the fort and the shipyard were destined to expand to fill the needs of protecting Texas.

Ellis shook off the thought with a shrug of her shoulders. That the Valmont family was well-off financially compared to others in the city held little place in her thoughts. Even though the shipyard would profit from war, the Valmonts prayed only for peace.

Built adjacent to his place of work, Jean Paul Valmont's grand home sat as near to the shoreline as he could place it without getting doused when the spring rains fell. The love of the open water had been passed down through the generations, but unlike those before him, Grandfather built boats rather than sailed them.

Ellis had made this walk more frequently since Papa and her brother Thomas went to fight with Major Burleson and the militiamen at Gonzales last month. With the men away—she refused to believe the rumor regarding casualties that reached them several weeks ago—it was up to Ellis to see that all was well with the senior member of the family.

She found her grandfather right where she expected, but she had not anticipated that he would have company at this hour. Voices rose in conversation that seemed to border on disagreement, causing her to stall on the stone path that led to the back of the home and the porch facing the river.

"I'll not believe it until there's proof," Grandfather said in the French language he rarely used here in Texas. "They're alive and would never do what you claim."

"The proof will come soon enough." The speaker was male, but beyond this Ellis could discern nothing further. "I warn you only because the friendship between our families goes back longer than either of us have been alive."

"And your jealousy of me and my family goes back to our own parents, does it not?" Grandfather paused to allow a fit of coughing to pass. "I thought I'd be rid of you when the Lord took my Claire home, but it appears the vendetta you swore against me did not die with her."

Laughter that held no humor reached Ellis's ears. She craned her neck to try to spy something of the stranger's identity.

"The fact that Claire did not deserve you has nothing to do with this.

Although, perhaps had she chosen me instead of you, none of this would have happened. Now I merely wish to offer an opportunity that will make us both very wealthy."

Ellis edged closer at the mention of her namesake grandmother, Claire Ellis Valmont. Who was this man?

"You came to gloat at what you wish me to believe is my loss and nothing else," Grandfather said, his voice almost unrecognizable in the anger this usually soft-spoken man's tone showed. "Boyd and his son are neither traitors to our cause nor dead and buried. You, however, are known to shift loyalties to follow what benefits you."

"On that we agree. However, you must consider the fact that your son may be clever enough to preserve his life and the lives of his family by doing things that he might otherwise find abhorrent."

Silence crackled between them. Ellis's temper rose. How dare that man accuse her father of doing abhorrent things?

Whatever that meant.

"Henri," her grandfather finally said, "go back to whoever sent you and tell him it did not work."

"Be reasonable, Jean Paul," the man said, switching to English. "Just outside your door is Fort Velasco, a Mexican garrison until four summers ago. Soldiers from New Orleans have only just arrived to join the fight. But look what they fight against!"

"Seems I heard the same arguments back in '32, and yet we sent General Ugartechea and the Mexican army away on ships we had waiting for them."

"General Santa Anna is no Ugartechea. There's no surrender in him, I promise you," Henri said. "And unlike the previous commander, the general and his superior army will kill us all unless he has assurance of our loyalty."

"And so you wish me to throw my support your way so that we might join a cause that you claim has taken my son and grandson? Which of us would be the fool then, Henri? You for asking or me for allowing fear to rule my decisions when the Lord is the One clearly in charge?"

She thought she heard the stranger chuckle. "Will your Lord save you from Santa Anna and his men?" he said, returning to Acadian French. "I think if you believe that, you are the fool."

"Henri," Grandfather said gently, "this is how you lost Claire to me."

"Had she chosen me, she might still be alive."

The words hung in the air between the men, neither responding for what seemed like an eternity. With two years gone since cholera took Claire Valmont, the family had yet to recover from the loss. Grandmother Valmont had been the essence of home and family, and the mention of her brought tears to Ellis's eyes.

She quickly swiped them away. How dare this man say something so horrible to Grandfather?

"The Lord, He honors those who have faith in Him," Grandfather finally said. "I believe He will keep watch over me and my family. I cannot say the outcome of the coming war just as I could not have predicted the loss of my beloved wife, but I can say that much for certain."

"You have a successful business and a name that is well known," the other man said. "Do you not think the general will wish your shipbuilding enterprise for his own and your head on a platter so he may gloat to his enemies?"

"Let him then," Grandfather said.

"Mark my words. He is coming for you by land and by sea. Can you not see past your foolishness to at least protect what remains of your family before they are all murdered in their beds?"

Ellis covered her mouth with her hand to stifle a gasp. In the process, the basket tumbled from her arm and scattered herbs on the ground at her feet. She knelt down to pick them up only to hear the clatter of boots on the stones.

Grandfather arrived first followed by a rather menacing man of a similar age. Where her grandfather's hair still bore traces of the dark hair of his youth, the stranger's hair was pure white.

"Who is this?" he asked, his tone almost wistful. "I believe I know that face, although I did not expect to see it here."

Grandfather took Ellis's basket and set it aside and then reached for her hand to help her climb to her feet. "What are you doing here, and where is your escort?" he asked, ignoring the other man's question.

"I came to bring a remedy for your cough. The boys have been assigned tasks that kept them from accompanying me."

She almost added "Grandfather" to that statement, but something in his eyes caused her not to indicate their relationship. He would explain later, of this she felt sure, but for now her grandfather was wordlessly imploring her to leave. She gave him an almost imperceptible nod.

"Please thank your mother for me. Hurry home to her now, and in the future do not come alone." He reached for the basket and then nodded for the stranger to follow as he turned his back on Ellis.

"Have I just seen a ghost?" the stranger demanded as he remained rooted in place. "This woman, she is the image of the painting in the parlor, and yet that is impossible."

Grandfather cast a glance over his shoulder to meet her questioning stare. "Go on home now," he told her. And to the stranger he said, "Our discussion is not done, Henri, but my time is limited. What is it to be?"

The man her grandfather called Henri gave her one last long look and then turned to follow. At the corner of the building, he paused once more.

"Your name," he called to Ellis. "Is it also Maribel?"

"Do not answer this man," Grandfather called. "And should he persist in his questions, he will regret it."

The man called Henri turned to argue with Grandfather, leaving Ellis to show the pretense of returning to the canoe that would take her back to Quintana. In truth, she merely found a less visible place from which she could observe the goings-on.

A short while later, the silver-haired stranger stormed past her hiding place with no visible indication that he knew she was close by. Ellis stalled a few moments to make sure the man did not change his mind and return. When she stood up and stepped back onto the path, Grandfather was waiting for her.

"How did you do that?" she said, startled. "I was watching the path for anyone who passed by."

Her grandfather chuckled and linked his arm with hers. "Ellis, dear, you were watching the path where you expected someone would be. You must never be blinded by what you expect. Always allow for the unexpected." He paused to give her a sideways look. "And always have a lookout. That's why you should never travel from Quintana alone."

"I am observant," she argued.

"Observant enough to let an old man find you without being detected."

"I do see your point," Ellis said as she matched her step with his. They made their way past the spot where she dropped the herbs and around to the wide expanse of porch that shaded the ocean-facing side of the Valmont home.

"Who was that man?" she asked as soon as they had settled side by side on the bench her father had built last winter from a felled log.

"No one you wish to know," he told her.

"And yet he knew you. And Grandmother." She paused. "And he thought he knew me."

"Ellis," he said on an exhale of breath, "it is so easy to forget you've reached the age of a grown woman when I so want to respond as if you were still a child. The thing that makes me unsure as to which you truly are is the fact that you could only know these things if you were eavesdropping." He paused to slide her a sideways glance. "Which is something a well-brought-up young woman would not do."

She shrugged. "I beg to differ. I am well brought up, and yet when someone I love is being threatened, I go to whatever lengths necessary to protect them." It was her turn to pause and meet his stare. "Including eavesdropping."

Grandfather Valmont chuckled again. "Yes, I suppose you were doomed to inherit that from both sides of your family. You are both Ellis and Valmont."

"Hence my name?" she said with a grin that matched his.

Her grandfather's statement had been a joke at its inception, with Grandfather warning his son not to make the mistake of naming his firstborn daughter after two strong-minded women. Going against that advice, her parents had christened her Ellis Maribel Valmont, and according to some members of the family, her fate had been sealed.

Thus, between her Valmont heritage, which included her great-grandmother Maribel, and her Ellis heritage from Claire, she had indeed descended from strong stock. Mama would call it stubborn.

"I will have your promise that you do not make this trip alone again. And at the first opportunity, I will speak with your mother regarding my reasons."

She turned to look at him. "As you say, I am a grown woman. Why not speak with me regarding your reasons?"

"Because my reasons are not what matters." His expression softened. "Your safety is what I care most about. And while it may be perfectly safe to visit me in the light of day, I have grave concerns regarding what happens along the river between Quintana and Velasco under the cover of darkness."

"Oh," she said as she contemplated his meaning. "Then I do promise."

He patted her hand and nodded. "Thank you. I look forward to a day when that promise is no longer necessary."

"As do I."

CHAPTER 3

Ellis and her grandfather fell into companionable silence as the activity down at the docks increased. With the sun now fully overhead, some of the ships had begun to disgorge themselves of cargo and persons. Others were doing just the opposite.

Ellis, however, was still trying to piece together the puzzle of the overheard conversation. She had already considered several scenarios and decided how she would respond depending on what her grandfather was willing to admit.

"So this man, Henri," she finally said with her arguments ready, "he was your rival for Grandmother's affections?"

"Oh child, I should have known you gave up too quickly. Have you an entire conversation planned out in that brilliant mind of yours? Perhaps with answers to arguments I have not yet made?"

She shrugged. He knew her too well.

Wrapping a protective arm around her, Grandfather Valmont sighed. "All right, if you must know, I did indeed win your grandmother's affection despite his pursuit of her. That Henri was not her first choice has long plagued him."

"You seem much nicer," Ellis said as she snuggled into his embrace. "I'm glad she chose you."

"Well, thank you, but I'm not so sure I was all that nice back then. Still, Claire had a mind of her own, and nothing would sway her from her decision to make a life with me, even when the Lord led us to places where no lady of good standing would have willingly gone."

"She had good standing," Ellis protested. "She just wanted to be where you were."

"She did at that." He paused. "As to his mention of the painting, I suppose you're also curious?"

"I am."

"Well, that's a story I will leave for another day, except to say that when Henri and I were boys, we thought it great sport to sneak into my mother's parlor and play our games there. My mama, she was quite certain rowdy boys did not belong amongst her precious things, so we were not supposed to enter that room."

"But you did," Ellis supplied.

"Of course," he said. "What Valmont has ever been able to resist a challenge?" At her smile, he continued. "The most memorable thing about that room, which was filled floor to ceiling with books of all sorts, was the painting of my mother that hung over the fireplace."

"Maribel," she said.

"Yes, Maribel. The portrait was done when she was just about your age."

"And she favors me?"

"My child," he said slowly, "if she stood beside you today, no one could tell the difference. Henri certainly could not."

"That man, Henri. He threatened you. And he made claims about Papa and my brother." Though Ellis had planned to be quite strong when she broached this topic, the legendary Valmont and Ellis strength failed her as tears began to flow.

"Child," Grandfather said gently as he cradled her in his arms. "Dry your tears and pay no heed to the words of a fool. He cannot know half of what he claims. Do you trust your papa to bring himself and your brother home safely?"

"Much as it is in his power to do so, yes, I do," she said. "But—"

"No buts," Grandfather said. "Trust does not allow for any buts. We pray for their safe return until the Lord shows us proof that was not His will."

"So it is possible Henri knows something about them."

"About as possible as it is for that sun to turn around and go back the direction it came," he said with a shake of his head.

"But just as he said, there is a vessel from New Orleans in the harbor," she protested. "I heard talk of it in town. Men from New Orleans fitted out in grey uniforms have come to join the fight."

"Well, yes, but did you ever consider he might have gotten his information from the same source?"

"No," she said softly.

"The Greys have been expected for weeks. It would be no trick to know they are here." Grandfather motioned to the shimmering body of water the Spaniards called the *Seno Mexicano*—the Gulf of Mexico. "See that ship there docked at the end of the pier? The one with the three masts? That's the *Columbia*, the ship with the Greys aboard. They'll be marching off soon, I'll reckon. Should be a sight to see."

Ellis looked up at him, her interest renewed. "Then let's go see them."

"You go along without me," he said. "I've got enough to do at the shipyard. Although it is likely you've got things to do at home."

She had plenty to do, of course. With Papa and her older brother away, their work fell to Ellis and Mama. The little ones were as helpful as they could be, but their age kept the two boys from offering much aid when men's work needed doing.

Grandfather Valmont covered her hand with his. "It is a great regret of mine that your father brought you children here."

Once again, Ellis gasped. Not once in all the years since the Valmonts had arrived on Texas shores had her grandfather stated anything close to this sort of sentiment.

"I know," he said with a chuckle that held no humor. "I suppose you're quite shocked."

"I am. You love Texas," she protested. "I've lost count of how many times you've told me this. So I don't understand."

"No," he said gently. "I don't suppose you would."

Grandfather Valmont paused to allow a wry smile. "For me, Texas is home. It is the place I belong." He gave Ellis a sweeping glance and then shook his head. "But you, my child? I am not so certain. Here you sit wearing a simple cotton dress and rebozo. Were it not for the quality of your scarf and the red color of your hair, no one would know you from any of our Tejano neighbors. Even then perhaps not, for they have much Spanish blood amongst them."

"And there is nothing wrong with that," she snapped. "My clothes are suited to the heat here, and there is nothing wrong with dressing in a similar way to neighbors who have been so good to us. Not all persons of Mexican descent are the enemy, Grandfather."

"Of course not," he said. "I employ many good men of Mexican citizenship, and count many more Tejanos than that among my dear friends. For that matter, we are all citizens of Mexico until the question is finally settled with war. But none of this is what has given me cause to speak as I have."

"Then what is the cause?" she said, looking up into kind eyes that were dark like Papa's.

"When I see you, my only granddaughter, my thoughts go to my mother—your great-grandmother—Maribel. My mother was a woman who highly approved of great adventures, but I wonder if she too might prefer that you were back in New Orleans preparing for a wedding rather than here in Velasco praying against the coming war."

She gave a moment's thought to his statement and then shook her head. "I never knew her, but you did. Wouldn't she approve of a cause so worthy?"

"I suppose she would, though there is a big difference in approving of a cause and approving of a loved one living in danger due to that cause," he said. "I would much prefer to see you living a comfortable life back in New Orleans. You would be the belle of every ball and would have dozens of the city's most eligible bachelors lined up at the door to court you."

"Grandfather, really," she said.

"Hear me out, my dear. You would exchange your sandals for slippers of the finest kid leather, and you'd certainly be clothed in silks rather than plain cotton." He shrugged. "That is the life I wish for you. Not this one."

Just for a moment, Ellis allowed herself to try to imagine what that life might be like. The best she could do was think back to the days before they arrived here in Texas, to call up vague memories of cool marble floors and impossibly high beds with yards of fabric flounced around them and canopies that reached almost to the sky.

"I see you agree," he said sadly. "And for that I ask forgiveness."

"I do not agree," she said. "First, it was Papa who led us here, not you. You followed because you love us and, like my papa and your mother, you enjoy a grand adventure."

Her grandfather's expression lifted. "That is a fact."

"Much as the comfort of New Orleans would likely be tempting, I only remember it fondly and nothing more. Given the choice, I will take sandals and cotton to slippers and silks any day."

He peered at her. "I'm not sure I believe you."

Ellis shrugged. "It is the truth. I am where I was meant to be." A movement in the harbor caught her attention, and she nudged her grandfather. "Look there. I see a boat setting off from the vessel that has brought the Greys. Do you think they are coming ashore now?"

Grandfather grinned and stood. "There's only one way to know for sure. You watch that boat and see where it is going while I fetch my spyglass."

He disappeared inside the house only to return a few minutes later with a shiny brass spyglass. Ellis recognized it immediately as the spyglass he had inherited from his mother, Maribel Cordoba Valmont.

Legend had it that Maribel Cordoba carried this spyglass with her aboard the privateer Jean-Luc Valmont's ship when she served as a lookout for pirates in her youth. After marrying the privateer and taking to sea with him to serve a greater mission antagonizing slave ships, she once again employed the spyglass, at least until the arrival of the Valmont children sidelined them both.

Until now, none of the Valmont children had been allowed to touch the precious item that Grandfather kept under lock and key. Ellis gasped as a shaft of sunlight shone across its golden surface, illuminating fingerprints that were too small for Grandfather to have made.

"Are those hers?" Ellis asked.

"I believe they are. I should have the brass polished but I believe her marks belong there, don't you?"

"I do," she said on a whisper of breath.

Grandfather handed the spyglass to her with care and then showed her how to lift the small end to her eye. "Close the other eye and it'll all come into focus," he told her, and to her surprise, it did.

"I see them," she said as the distant scene suddenly became crystal clear.

"Tell me what you see, then," Grandfather said.

"I see a boat coming ashore with men dressed in grey."

"Hence the name, I suppose," he said. "What else?"

Through the spyglass she scanned the faces of the men. Eyes facing forward and backs straight, most wore the blank expressions of men headed toward a task they'd settled their minds upon. Then her gaze landed on a dark-haired man seated near the front of the vessel.

Unlike the others, this man's attention was constantly shifting. Had he not been dressed in the same manner as the others and seated among them, Ellis might have taken him to be their leader.

When his attention shifted her direction, Ellis jolted. It was as if he was looking directly at her.

"Well, what is it?" Grandfather asked.

A coughing fit prevented any further words between them. Ellis lowered the spyglass and regarded her grandfather with a practiced eye. How had she missed the signs that lack of rest showed?

"After I administer the herbs for that—" She paused to choose her words carefully. "Shall I also prepare a remedy for sleeping and leave it with you for tonight?"

"Heavens, no," he said when he regained his speech. "If I were to succumb to one of your mother's sleeping remedies, which I assume is the recipe you use, then I'd be hard-pressed to fight off anyone who caught me abed."

Of course.

Ellis sighed. Grandfather needed to be watchful, not only due to his position as a prominent citizen of Velasco but also because the shipyard would likely be the second place after the fort that the enemy would strike.

"It is my mother's recipe. And I do see your point." She handed him the spyglass, his safety now weighing on her mind. "Have you protection here?" she asked casually. "Watchmen or guards during the night?"

Grandfather chuckled. "For what purpose? So that an old man can get some sleep? There are greater causes than that and fewer men to perform them."

She nodded toward the boat moving toward the docks. "With more men arriving, wouldn't you think one or two of them might be spared from whatever duty calls them here to protect the good citizens of Velasco and those of us on the other side of the river in Quintana?"

"We all have the fort for our protection, Ellis," he said a bit more sternly. "I understand your concern for me, but do not let it go to your head. Texas is the only cause worth protecting right now. I am well and able to protect myself." He patted her hand. "Though I do worry about your mother and you children. Quintana is farther from the fort, and your father's land is isolated. I wish Sophie would listen to me and move you all into my home until these current troubles are over."

"Papa left the job of taking care of the land to us in his absence," she said. "And my mother will not be found shirking those duties."

He shook his head. "True, she will not, but I do hope she will consider that preserving the lives of her children is worth letting some of those responsibilities go."

Ellis's eyes narrowed. "Do you think it will come to that?"

"I certainly hope it will not," he said, his voice now reassuring. "If troubles come to us, the Lord always brings help, does He not?"

"He does," she said, knowing this to be true and yet realizing she was human enough to hold on to more than a tiny bit of doubt.

"And this morning as we sit here we are safe, are we not? We awakened today just as we did yesterday."

"We did," she said with a smile.

"Then thank the Lord for that and set other concerns aside." He nodded toward the spyglass and then looked out at the water. "As in life, we can observe or take part."

"What do you mean?"

"Those men you see arriving are not like us. They have no land here, no stake in what has become a deadly game between two rivals. I will admit their sponsors have more than our cause on their minds, but they have raised the money all the same to send these soldiers to us."

"What is more important than our cause, Grandfather?"

He shrugged. "Money, my child. There are some who would benefit greatly if we succeed in our quest for freedom from Mexico. For others, our loss would bring more profit."

She returned her attention to the boat now tying up at the dock. A crowd had gathered there, and even from where she sat, Ellis could hear cheering.

"Then I am glad our freedom was worth sending these men."

"As am I," he said. "Perhaps you'll leave me to my work and go down to join those who are letting them know we are grateful for their arrival."

Ellis grinned. "Yes," she said. "I'll do that, but only if you promise to doctor that cough. Otherwise I'll be forced to return alone through dangerous waters to care for you."

His smile faded. "Do not joke about such things." Then he shrugged. "But yes, I promise. Now off with you."

CHAPTER 4

Velasco at last. Clay allowed his gaze to follow the coastline to the east, scanning the broad expanse of river and then landing on the tumble of buildings that made up Velasco's sister city of Quintana.

Somewhere within his sight was the treasure that would solve everything. All he had to do was find a way to get to it.

He braced himself as the vessel slammed against the dock. After a struggle against the rising waves, the men secured the ropes, and the order was given to depart. He rose and joined the ranks as they made their way toward dry land.

Their trip from New Orleans aboard the schooner *Columbia* had been uneventful, though quarters were tight. Rather than sleep shoulder to shoulder with his comrades, Clay had chosen to place his blanket under the stars when it was not his turn to take up watch. Though used to sleeping under such rough conditions, he would welcome the cot that awaited him tonight at the fort.

Clay easily found Fort Velasco among the collection of buildings that hugged both sides of the river. The massive round structure would be their headquarters for the time being, and it was in that direction that the Greys would soon march.

"All in favor of electing Morris as captain, say aye," one of the men called. The troops shouted their agreement, and Clay joined them.

In short order the leaders had been chosen, and Captain Morris stepped forward with a well-dressed fellow at his side. The men closed ranks on either side of Clay, leaving him standing in the front of the group.

At Morris's nod, the man began. "Welcome, men of the Greys. I am Judge Edmund Andrews, and I will be swearing each of you in as citizens of our great land."

Citizens. All around him cheers went up.

Clay's breath froze. Nowhere in his plan had he allowed for pledging away his rights as an American to become a citizen elsewhere.

As the judge continued to speak, Clay weighed his options. He was this close to the treasure, and the only thing that stood in his way was a promise.

A promise once made was always kept—this had been his father's belief and his father's before him. The value of a promise was greater than gold, or was it?

Clay let out a long breath and fell into line. With each step toward the judge, he weighed the cost. Could the president appoint a man to any position within his government after that man swore allegiance to another country?

He narrowed his eyes and thought about that. True, in most cases the answer would be a resounding no. But Texas had not yet gained its freedom, so was he truly swearing an oath to a country or merely to a cause?

This was not the first time Clay had hired out to fight for a cause that was not his own. His own father had termed him a mercenary. While he had hired his services to others, what he could not tell his father was that he never sided with a cause he did not believe in.

By the time he reached the front of the line, he had determined an answer.

Texas might someday be its own country, but for now freedom was the cause for which he would fight. And Clay found nothing wrong with swearing an oath for freedom.

Once Judge Andrews had administered the oath, Clay looked him in the eye and responded with a bold and clear "I will."

"Welcome, citizen," the judge said with a smile and a firm handshake. "We are very glad you're here."

"As am I," he said, moving on to wait his turn in the next line. There he received a certificate attesting to his oath as an immigrant entering this new country.

Tucking the certificate away, Clay stepped over to sign the roster making him an official member of the First Company of Texian Volunteers from New Orleans. When he finished, he looked up into the most beautiful green eyes he'd ever seen.

"Thank you," the flame-haired woman said.

Clay Gentry, the man who had never been at a loss for words in his life, suddenly found himself completely mute. Though her dress and colorful scarf might have marked her as one of the local women of Mexican or Spanish descent, there was something about her that seemed familiar.

As if he had seen her before. Perhaps not in person, but elsewhere.

The idea was ridiculous, of course. And yet it felt like the truth.

Before Clay could find his voice, the soldier behind him nudged him along. And though he crossed a gauntlet of grateful Texians all offering him and his fellow New Orleans Greys a word of thanks or encouragement, the green-eyed woman's words were the only ones he could recall when he finally reached the end of them all and stepped inside the fort.

The remainder of the day was taken up with those things that were required to prepare the company for their coming duties. Finally, when the sun dipped below the horizon and their bellies were full, the company rested.

Tomorrow they would all be heading upriver to Brazoria where thankful citizens would greet them. At least that was what the judge claimed. Clay figured there might be cheers, but there would also be politicians making speeches.

There always were.

He shifted position on his cot and covertly glanced around to see whether any of the other members of Captain Morris's company still stirred. Once he was certain they did not, he rose and slipped away carrying his boots.

Staying to the shadows inside the fort, just as he had in New Orleans, Clay got all the way to the exit before he spied two watchmen who had been posted. Backtracking, he found his way around to a wall on the opposite end where his attempt at climbing would be less likely to be observed.

After several tries, Clay hefted himself up and over. His feet landed on sandy soil where he was able to easily catch his balance. With a glance back to be certain he had not been seen or heard, he hurried away to find a secluded spot to slip into his boots and determine his exact whereabouts.

Grandfather taught him the skill of navigating by the stars when Clay was a small child. Likely his father had no idea he and the old man would slip off to the lake near the Claibornes' Tennessee home to practice. With Clay at the tiller and his grandfather calling out the commands, they traversed the tiny lake until the first signs of light.

Father always wondered why Clay would fall asleep at breakfast when Mama's father was visiting. Mama, however, never had to guess. She too had learned the skill back when being the daughter of a pirate was a social concern she was yet to have.

His grandfather loved to tell tales of sailing under a new moon with no light overhead save the speckles of stars. In his tales, Mama was a girl who plied the seas with pirates who had only good in their hearts. Clay smiled at the memory.

Lest Clay believe his mother was beyond those days, he found more than once that the boat he'd left in one place had been moved to another. Other times he would spy her walking toward the lake after he'd been tucked in for the night. He would listen for the splash of the boat in the water, and sometimes he swore he heard it.

Of course, he had no proof that his mother still sailed the vessel across the lake during the wee hours of the morning. Still, he liked to believe she did.

Someday perhaps he would ask her. Maybe he would buy a boat and take her sailing himself, not on the little Tennessee lake but on an ocean with vast horizons.

First he had to survive this mission.

Clay made his way along a path he forged through the thicket so as not to be seen. Leaving sight of the fort, he slipped out of the underbrush to walk along the sandy shore. Here and there a candle burned, but otherwise the buildings showed no evidence of inhabitants.

At least none who were awake at this hour.

At the sound of coughing, Clay froze. Slowly he looked to his right where the whitecaps from the surf drifted to shore beneath the sliver of a moon. Then to his left where only darkness greeted him.

"What are you doing here?" a man said, though the sound of the waves kept him from determining exactly where the man might be.

He looked behind him only to find himself alone. "Show yourself," Clay responded as he turned back around.

"I've been here all along." A man of similar height stepped out of the thicket, the glow of his pipe leading the way. "Saw you coming toward me but then you headed down here. I wondered what you were up to."

The fellow stopped a few steps shy of Clay, close enough for him to see a man of similar age to his own grandfather, his dark hair sprinkled generously with silver. Though of similar height, this man was much thinner.

"Just taking a walk," Clay said with a casualness he did not feel.

"Beautiful night and I've been cooped up on a ship for days."

"You're a Grey."

The statement hung between them. "I am," Clay finally responded.

The older man made a move toward him, and Clay stood his ground. Then the fellow stuck his hand out. "Jean Paul Valmont, formerly of New Orleans and now a Texian through and through," he said. "Thank you for coming to our aid."

Clay relaxed and shook the man's hand. "Name's Clay," he said. "Glad to be here."

"I've got good chicory coffee on the fire," he said. "My sister sends it to me when she can. I'd be pleased to offer you a cup."

"Thank you but no," he said. "I don't want to be gone too long from the fort."

The truth, and yet it felt like a lie when he said it to the old man. What he didn't want was for Jean Paul Valmont to remember him or the fact that he'd been seen out here on the beach. And the best way to do that was to make a quick exit.

"Then good travels to you," Valmont said.

"Thank you, sir." Clay tipped his hat and made his way around the old man, picking up his pace as he headed to the spot where the river met the shore. There he headed off to the right and began his trek upriver, counting his steps as he went.

The purpose of tonight was to find the place where the buried treasure was. With just over a month until the meeting was to take place, it was far too soon to retrieve the coins. Rather, he would locate them and then return to get them at a time nearer to the date of exchange. In the interim, he would scout a location to relocate the treasure for safekeeping.

That much of the plan he'd already worked out. The rest would come.

His boots treaded lightly as he continued counting steps until he reached the number Grandfather's map required. Then a turn to the east and there it was.

Clay retrieved the short-handled spade he'd brought with him in his bag from New Orleans and dropped to his knees to dig. After a few minutes, the sound of metal hitting metal rang out. He kept digging until a small box appeared.

Yanking the box out of the ground, he used the spade to break open the lid. Rather than the mound of gold coins he expected, inside there was a folded piece of oilcloth. With trembling hands, he unfolded the oilcloth to find another slip of paper with a map on it.

"What the. . ." He sat back on his heels and then stood. "All this way and risking court-martial to find a map?" He kicked the box back into the hole and buried it again. Now what? He could not fail.

A sound caught his attention. Oars in water, perhaps, or was it something else?

Clay crouched down in the brush and tucked the folded paper into his boot alongside the traveling papers from Louisiana that identified him. He waited, barely breathing as he pressed his palm against the pocket where he kept his knife.

Yes. There it was again. Definitely oars. Either the old man had decided to follow via the river or a stranger was headed his way.

As the boat drew nearer, he could hear voices. Two men. Murmurs at first and then more clearly. Their language was Spanish. Whether they were friend or foe remained to be seen.

He thought to let them just float past. Then he heard clearly the substance of their conversation.

"The Texians at the fort will never know we've been here," one said to the other. "They are fools."

"With the number of men who will soon be gathered, we could kill them all while they sleep," the other said. "A pity our instructions are to wait upriver."

"Quiet," came the response. "I feel we are not alone."

With care not to make a sound, Clay retrieved the knife from its sheath and held it at the ready. He'd left his pistol at the fort, reasoning that he would not wish to use something as a weapon that would make enough noise to call attention to his absence.

If only he had that revolver now.

The knife would have to suffice.

CHAPTER 5

The sound of oars against water ceased, leaving only the night sounds of chirping birds and the croak of frogs. Though Clay could not yet see the men, he knew they must be very close.

Then he heard the soft *thud* of what must be the hull of a boat, followed by what sounded like coughing in the distance. Of course. No wonder the old man was watching tonight. He was waiting for the Mexicans.

For what purpose, Clay could not say. Nor could he say with any assurance on which side the old man's allegiance might lie.

With three men theoretically making their way toward him from two different directions, Clay had to think fast in order to decide what to do. The underbrush behind him was too thick to make an escape without being heard, but staying where he was meant risking discovery and being outnumbered.

Going north served no purpose other than to escape. At some point he would have to retrace his steps and come back this direction to return to the fort.

A good soldier knew when to advance and when to retreat. Until he had sufficient weaponry or assistance, any rational man would consider retreat the best option. Clay should either move north up the trail and leave these three to whatever they were up to or cross the river and go south to Quintana.

But of all the things Clay Gentry had been accused of, being a rational man was not one of them. He took a deep breath, let it out slowly, and then began quietly making his way toward the river's edge where he could see exactly where the two Mexicans had landed their boat.

He found the craft, a crude dugout canoe much like the pirogues the people in Grandfather's part of Louisiana used, but it was empty. Seizing his chance, he slipped into the river. Despite the warm October temperatures, the water was almost icy.

Stifling a gasp, he set to his task. Something that looked very much like a black snake zigzagged in front of him. Still he continued to move toward the spot where the strangers had departed their craft.

With care to keep absolutely quiet, Clay grasped the rough wood and gave it a strong pull in an attempt to haul it away from the bank. When that failed, he tried again.

"Did you hear that?" came the whispered Spanish words that signaled the men had not gone far.

Clay froze, his fingers still curled around the pirogue. The black snake slithered past again, this time closer than before. He closed his eyes and ignored it. Ignored the need to flee.

"He shall cover thee with his feathers, and under his wings shalt thou trust."

"You're imagining things, *jefe*," the other said. "I will show you."

Footsteps moved swiftly toward him. Clay took a deep breath and ducked under the water. The snake once again found him, this time swirling so close that the scales of its tail brushed Clay's cheek as it swam past.

When his lungs burned with the need for air, he slowly resurfaced. Apparently the man's point had been made, for neither of them was in sight.

Going back to his work, Clay tugged the pirogue free of the mud on the second try, and then gave it a shove that sent it toward the center of the river. Without their means of escape, the duo would be landlocked. There would be no returning to whatever location they set off from, at least not by means of the river.

Rather than risk meeting the Mexicans or the old man on the path, Clay swam as far as he could downstream and then cautiously climbed onto the bank. Teeth chattering and soaked to the bone, he hauled himself up to a standing position and listened for any signs of life. The surf roared to the south, and all along the banks frogs croaked softly.

A cracking noise split the night, echoing as white-hot fire slammed Clay's shoulder and sent him reeling back into the river. Icy water covered him as another shot sizzled into the river just shy of him.

Breath failed him as he struggled to find air. An image appeared of a hand that reached toward him, but was this friend or foe?

Clay shoved away the hand and kicked against the current. The action caused him to bob to the surface, but he did not dare remain there. Instead he gasped in a deep breath of air and tried to think.

The best he could determine, the shot had come from downriver. Whether it came from a person on the riverbank or a vessel headed his way, he could not say. In either case, the only way to escape was to swim against the tide.

And so he did. Or tried, anyway, for only one of his arms seemed to be of any use.

Another shot rang out, once again landing too close. He was moving slower now, having to lift his head above water more often. Thoughts were becoming more scattered. Difficult.

"He shall cover thee with his feathers, and under his wings shalt thou trust."

That much he could recall, though he heard it now in his mother's voice and not his own. In this moment, the God of feathers did not seem so silly. Did not seem so far-fetched, even if escape from this impossible situation did.

Clay tried to pray. Tried to form a thought that would give the Lord glory while also asking Him for help, but the words wouldn't come.

A solid object slammed into him. Out of instinct, Clay reached for it with his good hand and felt wood.

The pirogue. Climb in.

The first clear thought in what seemed like an eternity. Somehow he managed to slump over the edge of the pirogue and fall in. The landing was hard and painful, but he was no longer fighting the muddy river water for each breath.

Clay lay on his back and closed his eyes. His shoulder throbbed and his mind still refused to rest on more than the simplest of thoughts.

Breathe in. Breathe out. Stay very still. Ignore the pain.

These things he did as the craft jarred to a halt. He opened his eyes to stare up at the clusters of stars overhead. Though the water swirled past, the vessel remained as if rooted in place.

The shouts of men drifted over him, but his brain refused to determine what language they spoke. He tried to turn in their direction but saw only wood.

The sides of the crude vessel were low enough to offer very little protection, this much he could determine. Something zinged past.

Wood splintered. A searing pain scratched across him, though he was too numb to determine where.

Clay remained perfectly still for what seemed like an eternity. Finally the shouting and the shooting ceased.

"Unless you wish to swim out to the sandbar where it is lodged, the boat is lost," someone said, and this time he recognized the language as Spanish. "Though you can continue to waste your time shooting at it if you wish. I'm sure the soldiers at the fort would thank you for leading them directly to us."

"I do not, jefe," the other said. "And I had not thought of the noise bringing the soldiers."

"Then we go afoot and do not tell anyone how the canoe was lost, yes?"

If the other fellow responded, Clay did not hear it. There was no sound of footsteps retreating, only the rush of water on all sides and the distant sound of night creatures.

He might have closed his eyes, could have even slept, but when he awoke, the stars were still scattered overhead, only now they were not in the same location.

It did not take someone skilled in navigating by the stars to know the pirogue had moved during the night. Still, what he saw overhead made no sense. Rather than drifting southward downstream with the swift current, he had somehow gone north upstream.

The sky began to spin. Clay closed his eyes and then opened them again, though it felt like hours in between the two.

A slight lift of his head confirmed the vessel was no longer stuck on a sandbar in the river. Instead he was completely surrounded by the thick reeds that grew at the edge of the river.

Movement of any kind cost him with a pain that took his breath. Clay ignored it to look down at his right hand and saw his fingers wrapped around an oar.

Blood stained his left arm and pooled beneath his closed fist. When he opened the fingers of his right hand, a tiny feather rested there.

Tucking the feather into his pocket, Clay dropped the oar, sucked in a deep breath, and forced himself to attempt to rise into a sitting position. On the third try, he managed it. A look down sent the world spinning again.

So much blood.

Clay took in a shuddering breath and forced himself to assess the damage. Two direct hits. Something lodged in his left shoulder. The second had gone clean through his left arm. Blood trailing a line on his abdomen meant a third had come far too close to doing more damage.

But he was alive. Clay held on to that thought until it too disappeared into the fog that surrounded him. He swayed but caught himself.

Sleeping could come later. For now, he had to keep his wits.

It was impossible to see where the river ended and the riverbank began. A reach with his good hand touched only water reeds. And yet he must find land.

"I will not die here," he said under his breath as he tried to make sense of his options.

The oar. He swiped at it only to fall forward and land on his face. The pain pinned him in place, but his fingers found what he was reaching for.

Now he could use the oar to move the boat. But first he had to find his way into a sitting position again.

Using the oar as a crutch beneath his good arm, Clay shifted position. He was almost upright again when a cracking sound split the silence of the night.

The oar crumbled beneath him, and Clay jolted backward. With his gaze focused upward, one by one the stars went out.

Then there was only darkness.

"Is he dead?" asked Lucas, the older of Ellis's two little brothers.

Mack, the baby of the family, kneeled nearby. At barely six years old, he did not need to see such a gruesome sight. Thankfully, he was too enamored of a frog to notice.

Ellis Valmont looked down at the tattered sleeve of a uniform that might once have been a shade of grey. Crimson stained the cloth and the fingers that curled beneath it.

Still, she could see enough of the fabric to know this man was with those who arrived at Velasco just yesterday. What was he doing here?

The dark-haired soldier lay in the pirogue as if he was sleeping, though his face was pale and his lips nearly blue. Had Ellis not seen the uneven movement of his chest as the stranger struggled to breathe, she would have thought him dead.

"Who's dead?" Mack called as he forgot about the frog to hurry over in their direction.

"No one is dead. Lucas, go and get Mama and Mr. Jim."

"What if they're busy?" he asked.

"Tell them I need their help and that it is more important than anything they're doing. Can you do that?"

"Sure," eight-year-old Lucas said with a lisp caused by his missing two front teeth.

"All right, then. Get on with you, and hurry." As Lucas trotted off, Ellis moved to shield the youngest Valmont from the gruesome sight. "And take Mack with you."

"I don't want to go," Mack whined. "I want to see who is dead."

"No one is dead," Ellis said in a tone she hoped would indicate she no longer wished to argue the point.

She turned the little boy around by his shoulders and gave him a gentle push. Of all the Valmonts, she might have the reputation as the stubborn one, but little Mack would likely soon surpass her.

Mack hated to be told what to do and despised the fact that the honor to do things first generally fell to older siblings. As much as he hated these things, however, there was one thing he hated more: He hated to lose. At anything.

Ellis knelt down beside him and looked into the little boy's eyes. With his flame-colored hair and green eyes, he was her carbon copy. "Mack," she said gently. "What if you were to beat Lucas back to the house? Then you would be the one to fetch Mama, not Lucas."

His eyes widened. "I would, wouldn't I?"

"See how slow Lucas is walking? I bet if you hurry you can beat him."

Those wide eyes narrowed and his smile returned. "I am gonna beat him. You just watch me."

"You run fast now," she said as she stood. "I'll watch."

Off he went, easily catching up with Lucas. A moment later, he headed into the thicket with Lucas trailing behind.

Ellis waited until both boys disappeared down the path. The house wasn't far from here. Still, she ought to wait for Mama and Mr. Jim.

"I can't just stand around doing nothing," she said under her breath as she turned back to the river.

The pirogue where the man was lying looked very much like the Cajun-style dugout pirogue that had been stolen from a neighbor a few weeks ago. She made a note to check and see if that vessel had been found. If it hadn't, this man might be the culprit.

Perhaps the Grey changed his mind about his service to the cause of Texas. That would certainly explain why a man who was assigned to a regiment quartered at the fort would be wandering the river during the night.

Whether or not he was a thief, the man was in need of medical care. She took a step to the left to see if she could determine a way to pull the flat dugout vessel onto dry land. The pirogue had been lodged on a sandbar in the reeds for what appeared to be a few hours, for the sand was already collecting on the downstream side.

Worse, the thing was wedged right into the place where Papa swore the black snakes nested. Ellis looked around for a stick but found nothing she could use to move the pirogue.

Praying Papa was wrong, Ellis knelt down and reached across the distance to give the pirogue a tug. The soldier inside made a soft groan.

"I'm sorry," she told him, "but you cannot stay out here in the water. Whoever you are, we've got to get you out before the snakes come out at dusk."

The black snakes that hid in the reeds and slithered along the river's edge after sunset where Ellis's worst nightmare and greatest fear. She'd been bitten once, but once was quite enough. As the story went, Mama's cure was the only reason she survived.

Another tug and Ellis decided she would never be able to budge the pirogue from the bank. Ignoring her fears, she lifted her skirts just enough to edge out beyond the bank to where the muddy brown water swirled around her legs and ruffled the reeds.

From her vantage point she could see the soldier's face. And, though splashed with streaks of blood and marred by a nose that appeared to be broken, it was a handsome face. A memorable face.

Ellis gasped. She had seen this man before.

CHAPTER 6

Of course. Down at the docks just yesterday.

He had been among the soldiers to whom she had offered a welcome and a word of thanks. There had been something different about this one. Something that did not quite fit with the others who sailed with him.

She hadn't quite been able to identify what it was then, and she certainly could not now. He hadn't said a word. Just stared like he'd lost his powers of speech, then moved along.

Perhaps he was mute.

The man in question moaned, his eyelashes fluttering just long enough to give promise that he might open his eyes. "You again," he whispered, completely ruining her theory that the soldier was mute. "You're welcome."

An odd response. At least he was able to talk. Ellis leaned closer.

"Who did this to you?" she asked, but his eyes had drifted shut and he seemed once again beyond the ability to respond.

With a watchful eye toward the reeds where snakes could be hiding, Ellis cupped river water in her hand and poured it over his forehead in the hope that the chill might awaken him. When that failed, she used the hem of her skirt to dry his face and then allowed the bloody fabric to fall into the water.

There appeared to be no injury to his face, but the spread of blood on his cap and the wood behind his head indicated some sort of head wound. Though she would not do any further examination without Mama here, it did not take a trained healer to know that this New Orleans Grey had been shot at. Repeatedly.

A glint of something moving through the reeds made Ellis jump. Her heart pounding, she willed herself to calm down as she watched for whatever it was. Seeing nothing else, Ellis returned her attention to the soldier.

The blood on his left shoulder came from a wound that appeared to be the worst of them all. A few inches lower and his heart would have been the target.

"Ellie, Ellie?" Lucas called. "Where are you?"

She stepped away from the reeds and onto the bank in time to see her little brother racing toward the river. "Ellie, Mama and Mr. Jim . . . ," he called.

Ellis hurried to meet the little boy. "Where are they?"

"I went to fetch them, I truly did," he said, breathless. "But Mama is up at Miz Lyla's place and can't leave her until the baby comes."

"What about Mr. Jim?"

"I couldn't find him, so I sent Mack to hunt for him some more. I thought you ought to know though."

She ruffled the little boy's hair and smiled. "Thank you," she said as her mind reeled with the possibility that she would have to care for this wounded soldier alone.

"I can help," he said. "I've watched you and Mama and know what to do."

Ellis considered the thought of an extra pair of hands and then shook her head. There would be plenty of time for the boy to see wounded soldiers, especially if this war continued. Until that day when it could not be avoided, Ellis intended to keep those things from her innocent brothers.

"I do appreciate your offer, and I know you would be a huge help," she told him. "But for now I think it is more important to find Mr. Jim since he is big and strong and can help us get this man out of the river. Don't you think so?"

Lucas appeared to consider the question and then nodded. "I do think we might need help with that part of it. Plus Papa says there are snakes and we should stay out."

"Yes, he does, so perhaps you could go and see if Mack is truly looking for Mr. Jim. He does tend to forget sometimes and wander off." She paused to offer a broad smile. "If you were to find Mr. Jim, you would be my hero."

That did it for certain. If there was one goal in this child's life, it was to be a hero. This time he hurried off without bothering to respond. With Lucas the hero on the job, Mr. Jim would be here soon.

Ellis sighed as she straightened to watch the little boy disappear down the path. He so wanted to be like his father and older brother, and yet she couldn't help but ask God to slow down time and keep him just a little boy. To keep both of her younger brothers little boys.

For once they grew into men, she might lose them just as. . . Ellis shook her head. No, she wouldn't think of it. Wouldn't give heed to the rumor that Papa and Thomas were not coming home.

Men!

The sound of distinctly male shouting drew Ellis back to the riverbank where a vessel of some sort was churning upriver toward her. Soldiers dressed in the same grey uniforms as the wounded soldier populated the deck of the flat-bottom steamboat making its way upriver.

"Stop!" she called as she stood on the bank and frantically tried to signal to anyone who might see her. "One of your men is here, and he is wounded!"

As the paddle wheel slapped against the water and the engines churned, a bell rang out. Several of the men saw her and she waved, but none seemed to understand what she was trying to tell them.

"Help me," she called, gesturing to the reeds. "A Grey has been shot."

Those who had seen her continued to wave, but the steamboat never slowed as it approached. Apparently they hadn't understood a word she said.

If only they could see the pirogue and the man it contained. Though she hadn't managed to move the pirogue before, Ellis knew she had to give it another try.

This time she would wade into the reeds. It was the only way.

Saying a prayer for safety from the snakes, Ellis moved toward the pirogue as quickly as she could. The soldier lay so still and pale that she jolted toward him to press her palm against his chest to see if he still breathed.

He did. Ellis breathed a sigh of relief.

Then something under the water brushed against her leg and she screamed. Her heart racing, she stood stock-still and looked all around but saw nothing.

"I need to move this out into the open right now," she said, in part to herself and in part to the Lord, who could manage such things if He chose. "Those men need to know one of their own is here dying for lack of help."

And I do not want to be bitten again.

Ellis gave the pirogue another tug, and it seemed to budge, though only slightly. Another tug and she realized the action was futile. Taking one last desperate action before the steamboat moved out of reach, she waded around to the other side of the pirogue.

The water was deeper here, nearly halfway to her waist. It soaked her skirts, but from this angle she just might have a chance of getting the pirogue out in the open where the soldiers could see the injured man.

If only she wasn't terrified of the stupid snakes.

A bell rang out on the steamboat, reminding her of her purpose. "I cannot do this, Lord, but You can," Ellis said under her breath as she shoved and tugged to try to get the pirogue to move. A moment later, the soldier's eyes fluttered but did not open. "It certainly would help if you would wake up and help," she told him.

But he did not wake up, nor could she get the pirogue to budge. Frustrated, she kicked it.

It floated free.

Ellis let out a most unladylike whoop and shoved the pirogue toward the center of the river where the steamboat was now passing by, all the while gesturing toward the man in the pirogue. Out of the corner of her eye she spied what she knew was a snake just floating in the sun.

Imagining the vile thing dead and floating rather than merely sunning itself helped, but only slightly. Knowing this man's life depended on her set her in motion, however.

Waving frantically, she called out for the men to have the captain turn around. She pleaded. She jumped up and down and acted like a fool.

The men on deck seemed to enjoy her performance. They certainly rewarded her with laughter, whistles, and shouting.

Despite her efforts, the steamboat continued to churn the waters as it headed upriver at a brisk pace. As the vessel grew smaller, so did her hope that this man could be saved.

She continued to wave toward the vessel even as it churned out of sight upriver. Finally she gave up. There would have to be another way to get this man help.

Resting her head on the rough wood of the pirogue, Ellis refused to cry. Refused to be beaten at this.

Then she felt the swish of something with scales slither past her leg. Something that felt far too much like a snake for her to remain where she was.

With all her strength, she pushed the pirogue toward the riverbank and continued pushing until the crude wooden canoe slammed into the trunk of the massive pecan tree that shaded the trail and a good portion of the riverbank. Only then did she realize what she had done.

Ellis sat back on her heels with her skirts soaked and every muscle in her body exhausted. And then she laughed. It made no sense, for she was still afraid for the life of this stranger. But she had done what she did not believe she could do, and she hadn't been bitten by the snake.

"Thank You, Lord," she whispered as she swiped at the tears that gathered.

Tears of joy mixed with frustration and anger and settled deep inside her. A bird screeched in the top limbs of the tree, jolting her back to the present.

And to the man who needed her.

With the pirogue on dry land and the tree shading them from the sun, Ellis set to work. Peeling back his grey jacket and shirt, she examined the shoulder where blood was still seeping. The wound appeared deep and did not extend through to the other side; thus whatever hit him would have to be removed.

That was a job better suited to Mama and to a location other than lying under a pecan tree. For now she could only administer pressure to try to slow the bleeding.

First she gave a cursory look at his abdomen where something had sliced across him, likely a bullet that might have killed him if it had been aimed only slightly better. Then she pulled the sleeve of his jacket down to reveal another wound, this one thankfully gone clean through.

Much as she wanted to remove his hat to see what sort of damage had been done, no fresh blood flowed there, so she did not. There would be time to clean the wound later, if he survived, and the cap might actually be acting as a temporary bandage.

Ellis spread her soggy skirts out around her in the dappled sunlight, then returned her attention to the soldier. Thick dark lashes dusted high cheekbones that were draining of color. Who was this man? Ellis studied his face as if that might bring the answer.

It did not, of course, but she did know that this was someone's son, someone's brother. Perhaps someone's husband. She sighed. He also might be a deserter or the thief who stole the neighbor's pirogue.

Or both.

Ellis searched his pockets for some clue as to his identity. In his jacket pocket she found two things: the certificate he received when he took the oath of allegiance to Texas and a feather. Unfortunately, the ink on the certificate was smeared with blood and completely unreadable. She tucked both back into his pockets and continued her search, only to find nothing else that would help.

The Grey was broad of shoulder and easily as tall as Papa and Thomas. His face had once been clean-shaven but now his jaw bore a dusting of dark stubble, and his dark hair curled just shy of his collar. His hands bore no calluses, which told he had not made his living in the field or at sea.

Other than a knife, he carried no weapons. Odd for a soldier newly arrived. But then, it was odder still that he was here in this condition rather than on the steamboat headed upriver.

"Such a mystery, you are," she said to him. "Are you a thief? Hard to imagine since you've only just arrived and that pirogue, or one very much like it, was stolen well before yesterday. Is someone waiting back home for you?"

Ellis let out a long breath and let her imagination wander. A man like this surely had a wife and family. Or perhaps it was the lack of those things that sent him down the path to becoming a Grey.

She shrugged. Mama would say she was woolgathering again. Her imagination did tend to wander. But here under the pecan tree, as she waited for Mama and hoped this man stayed alive, the thoughts that escaped to fly free were the very thoughts that kept her calm.

Then she heard noises, the crackling of brush and the sound of foot-steps coming her way. Either help was coming or whoever shot this man had returned to finish the job.

CHAPTER 7

"E llis! Ellis!" Lucas's little voice made her smile.

"Right where you left me," she called. "Or nearly so."

The little boy appeared on the trail with Mack following a step behind. A moment later, her mother was visible.

Her heart soared. "Mama! Thank goodness."

Regal as always, her mother had covered her dark hair with a bonnet that matched her dress. Though she was often called upon to exercise her abilities as a healer, she rarely arrived with a hair out of place.

Ellis rose to meet her. Mama looked tired. It must have been a difficult birth. "I'm so glad to see you. Are mother and baby faring well?"

"The baby has not yet come," she said as she knelt beside the soldier to begin her examination. "But Lucas had me concerned when he said you were with a dead man and he could not find Mr. Jim. I was afraid Mr. Jim was our corpse. I left Lyla in her husband's care. I'm afraid if the baby does come, poor Jonah—as big and strong as he is—will faint dead away, so I cannot leave her for long."

"I cannot help in locating our farmhand," Ellis said, "but the soldier is not yet dead."

"No," Mama said, looking up from her work. "And he just may live, but he cannot remain out here under the tree." She nodded toward Lucas and Mack. "Lucas, go fetch one of the mules. Mack, open the door to the small barn."

Once the boys were gone, her mother motioned for Ellis to join her beside the pirogue. "What can you tell me about this man?"

She started by explaining where he was found and then offered her observations on his condition. Finally she told her mother what she found in his pockets and how she had been in Velasco to see for herself when he received the certificate that was now covered with the man's blood.

"He was in the river," Mama said. "Did you check for snakebites?"

"I only looked at his head and chest," she said. "I was waiting for you."

Mama gave her an appraising look. "Propriety has its place, but not when a patient cannot tell you where his pains are. Go and see if the baby is near to arriving. If he is, then you'll help with the delivery. Or you can stay here to finish the examination and I will go. I leave that choice to you."

"I will go," she said as she saw the boys returning with the mule. "Why did you send them for the mule?"

She smiled. "In the absence of strong men, we will use a strong mule to pull the pirogue. And since we know nothing about this man, he will stay in the small barn while he heals. You go along now. The boys and I will get him situated."

Ellis hurried off to take over for her mother. By the time the little one made his way into the world and she was certain the child's mother was in good health, the day was gone and night had fallen. She stepped out into the fresh night air and breathed a sigh of relief. Often she assisted Mama in these situations, but rarely did she go alone.

She arrived home to find the little boys already sleeping and a plate of cold fried chicken covered by a dishcloth awaiting her. Until that moment, Ellis hadn't realized how hungry she was. Moving the plate to the table, she spied a light in the small barn.

The soldier.

In the excitement of assisting in the birth, she forgot all about him. Ellis returned her plate to the sideboard and covered it once more, then hurried outside. She found Mama sitting beside the pirogue, which was shored up with straw and situated in the corner of the barn where it was being used as the substitute for a proper bed. In place of the oar, blankets appeared to make the rough wood more comfortable, and a small pillow had been placed beneath his head.

Her mother leaned against the wall beside her patient, her eyes closed. When the barn door slammed shut behind Ellis, her mother jolted awake.

"The birth was successful?"

"Yes," Ellis said. "A big beautiful boy who cried as soon as he was born. When I left, he was nursing just fine."

"And his mama?"

"I observed no complications, and she attested to feeling tired but otherwise fine. When I left, her sister had arrived and was caring for her. Jonah was sitting outside looking quite confused."

"Confused?" Mama said. "Whatever for?"

"Something about having seen plenty of farm animals born but never a baby." She shrugged. "He seemed quite pleased with his child, though."

"As I am with mine," her mother said. "Your first birth and you handled it beautifully."

"I was terrified," she admitted.

"I'm still terrified every time," Mama said. "But I do what I know to do and pray the Lord will handle the rest. He always does."

"I must have prayed too, but it all happened so fast I don't recall the words I used. Only that He did what I could not."

As Mama chuckled, Ellis looked down at the soldier. His color had not improved, but it did appear Mama had managed to control the bleeding on his shoulder. The other wounds were covered in a poultice and bound with cotton strips. Another strip of cotton had been wound around his forehead.

"I didn't move him to look at the head wound," she told Mama. "Though I would have if I hadn't known you were on your way."

"It will pain him, and it did bleed, so I bound it, but I think the concern there will be what it does to his thinking when he awakens," Mama said.

"What do you mean?"

"It is possible he may recollect nothing of how he came to be in that boat. That is common enough with any injury of this kind." She paused to look down at the soldier and then back up at Ellis. "Sometimes it also means that the patient may be missing more than just the immediate past memory."

"So he could awaken to not know why he is here or possibly more than that?"

"It is possible."

"Forever?"

Mama shrugged. "In the cases I have seen, the patient rarely remembers the accident if he does not remember it immediately upon awakening after treatment. As to any other complication of memory, that is something that only the Lord knows. He could always forget, or he could eventually remember. As to this man, we are not done yet."

Ellis returned her attention to the patient. The fact that Mama had not yet bound the shoulder wound meant one thing: there was still a bullet to be removed.

"Oh, I have bad news," Mama said as she looked up sharply. "We will be without Mr. Jim for a few weeks."

"Why?" Ellis settled down beside Mama on the straw-covered floor.

"He's had an accident. He was on his way back from Columbia early this morning when he came upon two men on foot who were looking to take away his horse. They succeeded and left him bleeding and unconscious. Had he not been found by a Methodist circuit rider, I hate to think what might have happened."

"Oh no," Ellis said. "Should I go and see to him?"

"The circuit rider took him to Columbia where a doctor there has patched him up and is watching out for him. He sent word through a friend who was riding this way for us not to worry and that he would see that Mr. Jim gets back as soon as he's fit to ride."

Ellis let out a long breath. What would they do without the old man's help in keeping things running here? She shook off the thought with a roll of her shoulders and returned her attention to the soldier.

"That shoulder wound?" she said. "It's not bandaged."

"No. I waited for you," she said. "It must be cleaned out first. We will do this together."

White-hot pain. Searing. Pain that made him scream.

Must get away.

Can't move.

Pain. Such pain.

Darkness.

Silence.

Then green eyes watching over him. Something cool brushing across his face. Once, twice, three times.

The soft sound of singing. A hymn perhaps. Soothing but with a power he could feel radiating around him. A power stronger than whatever had taken hold of him.

Then the pain again.

The darkness.

And silence.

Time floated around him but would not stick, nor did the words he wanted to say. He knew of plans made in secret involving important men and causes. He knew dates when appointments must be met and places where things of great value must be retrieved and exchanged.

Thoughts formed, spoken in the language of the Acadians. People he knew but could not recall how. Yes. An old woman who loved him. An old man too.

People with secrets. People who told tales in the old language so the secrets would be safe.

He spoke to them now and then but only through the darkness. Through the pain and the cold and the heat. And through the visits of the green-eyed woman.

She too wove through time and his thoughts, sometimes leaning over him, while other times he could only feel her presence nearby. There were others—children, an older woman, and at least one grey-haired man—but he only cared to see the woman.

Willing his mind to produce a reason why they were there proved impossible, as did thinking about anything other than the few facts he could string together. A date and a time, a location, and an important reason to exchange treasure for. . .

Yes, that is where reason and recall failed. The green-eyed woman told him it did not matter. She spoke soothing words and held his hand when fear attempted to rule him. She smiled and said that none of these things upon which he worried so much mattered at all.

She read to him from a book and brought cool water. Today her words had struck him to the core. *"He shall cover thee with his feathers, and under his wings shalt thou trust."*

He knew those words. The same words she knew. Thus he knew the woman spoke truth and that he was safe. If only he knew more than this.

Like where those words had come from or how they both knew them.

"You cannot stay another night out here," Grandfather Valmont said, causing Ellis to jolt fully awake. "It isn't seemly."

She had assumed her place beside the soldier's bed—now a proper bed borrowed from the house rather than the pirogue—almost a week ago now and had rarely left except to help Mama with the chores. With Mr. Jim not yet returned from Columbia, the number of duties he had so easily performed was becoming staggeringly clear. Two women and two children were hopeless against the long list, but she and Mama did try.

Ellis looked up at her grandfather with as gentle an expression as she could manage given the level of her exhaustion. The small barn was bathed in pale sunlight and the lamp had not yet been lit, but whether it was nearer to sunrise or sunset, she could not say.

"For your information, the patient is fully dressed in one of Papa's nightshirts under that quilt, and I do not do an examination without Mama present except in the case of an emergency—which has not yet been the case." She paused. "Thus, unless Mama has informed you that she has revoked her permission for me to keep watch over the patient, then I am going to have to respectfully disagree as to whether this arrangement is proper or not."

Her grandfather looked away and then shook his head. "She has not. But I wonder if your spending time here isn't making things harder on your mother now that she has no other help with the chores."

"I help," Ellis protested.

"That explains why you look so exhausted. Can you both help your mother and see to this man's care?"

"I can," she said, though she would never admit that the attempt at doing both had her wondering where she was and what she was supposed to do next most of the time.

He gave her another appraising look. "Perhaps you can, but given the fact this man could be a thief and deserter from the Greys, I fail to see why you are so devoted to him."

"Devoted?" She shook her head. "Why do you think that?"

"Because I see it on your face when I challenge whether you ought to spend every free moment of your time at his side in this barn."

Ellis took a deep breath and let it out slowly. "I am devoted only as a healer is to her patient. Any of those other things can be sorted out when he is well enough to defend himself against the charges."

"I saw him walk away from the fort," he told her, his voice rising. "I followed. I heard conversations in Spanish with at least two men."

"Who could have been the men who shot him," she snapped.

He let out a long breath. "Yes," he said slowly. "They could have been. But there is no proof that this man wasn't in league with the enemy. I told you before, we must be always on our guard. The war that seems so far away is not that far away at all. What steps are you and your mother taking to protect my family from this man?"

"Look around," she told him as she gave her best attempt at tamping down her temper once more. "The door locks from the outside. When Mama and I are not with him, the door remains locked. The boys are not allowed inside the barn at all. There are no windows that can be reached without a ladder. And as you can see, there is no ladder to be found in here."

He made a show of looking around the small barn and then shrugged. "All right, I see how you have secured this building, but what will you do when he awakens and threatens you?"

CHAPTER 8

Ellis rose from the chair she had placed next to the bed and set aside the Psalms she had been reading to the soldier before she fell asleep. "I have a weapon, and he does not. Between the sleeping remedies, his fevers, and the fact he has but one useful arm even if he were to overcome the other two hindrances, I doubt the man could successfully threaten anyone."

"I am doubtful," he said, though the expression on Grandfather Valmont's face told her he had much more he wished to say.

"Then we shall have to see, won't we?" She glanced down at the sleeping man and then back up at her grandfather. "I take it you have not been successful in identifying him?"

"Not yet," he said. "If he's indeed a Grey, then his name would be on the roster. Since the Greys decamped almost a week ago for Columbia, there's no one here at the fort who can say which men got on the steamship and which did not. If he is missing, his absence was not discovered before the Greys boarded to go upriver, or a search party would have been organized."

"And that did not happen?" she asked.

"It did not."

"Well, I know he is a Grey," she told him. "I saw him sign the roster down on the beach at Velasco the day the men arrived. Remember? I was with you and we watched them arrive, then you told me to go and welcome the soldiers." She paused. "As proof, he was carrying the certificate showing he is a citizen of Texas. I saw him sign it along with the roster."

Grandfather Valmont sighed. "So you've said. And yes, I do recall it was my idea you go down to the beach to welcome the soldiers. However, there were so many. How do you know this is one of them?"

"I know what I saw," she snapped again, though this time she was instantly sorry. Ellis certainly did not want to explain to her grandfather that the moment that had passed between her and the soldier on that beach had been imprinted on her mind well before he was found in the river. "Please forgive me. I am overtired."

"As is your mother. I've come to see what I can do to help here, but unfortunately I've got to be back at the shipyard soon. With so many going off to join the cause, I am left with fewer and fewer men willing to stay in Velasco with me and sadly none I can send here to assist." His expression brightened. "However, I do have good news. Your mother just received word that Jim will be returning soon. Apparently he is sufficiently healed to travel."

"That is good news." She leaned against the chair. "Is it awful that I hope he is well enough to work when he returns?"

Grandfather Valmont wrapped his arm around her and smiled. "Not so awful that I disagree. If only your father and brother would return. I pray every day that they will. I know in my heart they are alive and making their way back here."

Ellis leaned her head against her grandfather's chest. "As do I. Do you think. . ." She dared not say it. Instead she kept her silence.

"Oh child," her grandfather said, holding her at arm's length. "Every day we continue to expect that they will walk over the hill and surprise us all. We cannot stop expecting that, nor can we stop praying for it. The Lord, He hears us. He has them in His care, and He will return them to us in His own perfect time. Do not forget that."

"Yes," she said as she blinked back tears. "He does."

The door opened and Mama stepped inside. She wore a tired expression but quickly put on a smile when she spied Grandfather Valmont. "Jean Paul," she said with genuine affection. "The boys told me you had come to till the garden. Thank you so very much."

He released Ellis to offer Mama a shrug. "It is nothing. You needed the soil tilled up before winter, and I needed to see my family. We both are happy. Might I speak to you alone?"

Mama gave Ellis a questioning look and then nodded to Grandfather Valmont. "Of course. I've just made coffee. Come and join me."

Grandfather Valmont kissed Ellis's forehead and bid her goodbye, then followed Mama out into the sunshine. When the door closed behind him, she returned to her chair and the Psalms.

Hard as she tried, she found that her mind refused to stay on the words written on the page. Instead exhaustion took over and she allowed herself to close her eyes for just a moment. When she opened them again, the room was bathed in moonlight.

The darkness served to further disorient her, though the familiar soreness in her back reminded her that she had once again slept sitting up. Had she been called out to aid Mama and then been sent to rest in someone's darkened parlor?

As her wits gradually returned, Ellis realized someone was holding her hand. The soldier.

Of course. She was in the barn attending to the man who'd been found in the river almost a week ago. Ellis shook her head as if to dislodge the cobwebs that were slowing her thoughts.

All around her the barn was bathed in silver moonlight. Ellis swiveled in the chair and looked down at the hand still covering hers, the hand that rested atop the old borrowed quilt.

For days the soldier had suffered fevers that caused him to thrash about and speak without opening his eyes. His words made little sense, and his language was that of the old Acadians, leaving her to surmise that he, like her, was of Louisiana heritage.

The man's fevered talk had been almost indiscernible at first, and then he had begun to speak about the most outlandish things. Through the long nights when Ellis sat at his side bathing his fevered brow with cloths dipped in cold water from the spring, the Grey spoke to someone yet unnamed about treasure and the cause of Texas freedom.

Or at least those were the words she managed to discern among all the rest.

With eyes that were open but appeared unseeing, he spoke of secretive meetings and muttered names that made no sense. So insistent was he on repeating these things over and over that she had taken to writing them down in the back of her book of psalms.

Was he recalling things that were true, or as Mama suggested, had he forgotten due to the head injury and was conjuring up things that were merely dreams? Given the current condition of his health, it was impossible to know the answer.

Ellis gently removed her hand from beneath the soldier's fingers and then leaned down to reach for her book. He stirred, his lashes fluttering, but otherwise the stranger remained asleep.

She rose, leaving the book of psalms behind on her chair to cross the barn and light the lamp on the old oak table where Mama used to dry her herbs. Lingering there, she noticed that the two items from the Grey's pocket were still where Mama had put them on the beam of wood that ran the length of the barn's north wall.

Bypassing the feather, she picked up the certificate of citizenship that she had seen the soldier sign just a week ago. If only she had thought to look down at the name he was signing rather than up at his handsome face.

And he was handsome, even now in his weakened health. Every day that he lived, Mama gave greater odds for his survival. Still, his condition was grave. Ellis prayed that whoever waited for him back in New Orleans—and a man who looked like this one certainly had someone—would not be waiting in vain.

Placing the certificate back on the beam, Ellis stretched her arms and then her neck, allowing the tension to release. After a roll of her shoulders, she returned her attention to the certificate that proclaimed the Grey a citizen of Texas.

"I cannot continue to call you the Grey," she said to him, although she knew he likely couldn't hear. "You need a name."

She picked up the certificate and held it up to the lamplight. Blood had dried to near-black smears that obliterated all but a few letters of his signature. The first three were c-l-a. Ellis shifted position and turned the document around, all to no avail. There was only one letter left that she could see accurately, and that was a *y*. Though there were obviously other letters in between what appeared to be a rather long signature, she could only go with what she saw: c-l-a-y.

Clay.

Ellis smiled. Yes, until the soldier told her otherwise, she would call him Clay.

Returning to her place beside him, she retrieved her book and then looked down at the sleeping soldier. "Hello, Clay."

He stirred, causing the quilt to fall away from his shoulder. The bandage that held the poultice in place needed changing, but she'd hoped to wait until Mama arrived to supervise. Though she had argued with Grandfather Valmont about there being no impropriety between patient and healer, she felt the odd sting of something akin to it while looking down at the man's bare shoulder.

She reached down to carefully return the quilt to its place. Out of nowhere his hand clamped her wrist. Eyes only half-open looked up at her.

"Are you friend or foe, woman?" he asked in the language of the

Acadians, the only language he'd spoken.

"Friend," she managed, her heart now beating in her throat. "Who are you?"

"Cannot be late," he said, obviously ignoring her question. "The funds must arrive at the meeting point or. . ."

Ellis leaned in. "Or what?"

His eyes locked on hers. "Or we fail."

"Fail at what?" she said as she eased her wrist out of his grip.

Clay's eyes were closed now, but his body was tense and his jaw clenched. "The mission. Houston needs me and. . .I must be there. . .I. . ."

Houston again. Ellis turned to the back of the book where she had taken notes on the soldier's ramblings. He had said something about a meeting with Houston just two nights ago and then again yesterday morning. The recollection of it also reminded her how agitated he'd been yesterday as he insisted he must go see Houston.

"General Houston?" she asked him, just as she had yesterday morning.

Again his lashes fluttered, but he said nothing further.

Frustration set in.

"Who are you," she said softly, "to have known these men? If indeed you do know these men."

Though Ellis had little experience with the fevered talk of a patient, Mama had admitted that often a man or woman would speak the truth under these conditions when that same truth could be deeply hidden when the individual was in good health.

Ellis rose and pushed the chair away and then settled on the edge of the mattress facing him. "How did you come to be here?" she asked gently. "And what is your name?"

When she got no response, Ellis tried again. "All right, soldier, what is it you need to do? Tell me and I may be able to help you."

No response.

She gave one more attempt, this time asking the same questions in the Acadian language of her grandparents. The soldier's eyes jolted open, and he looked at her as if he had only just realized she was there.

"You understand, don't you?" he said.

Ellis nodded. "I do understand. Tell me how I can help you."

"Need boots. Must have. . ."

She shook her head. "Why? Is there something in your boots?"

Eyes once again closed, he had already returned to that place where her questions did not reach him. She rose and went to the corner of the barn where the soldier's bloodstained boots awaited a cleaning.

Mama had already taken the soldier's uniform away to wash it, but removing the stains had proven difficult. At present, the man's jacket was soaking and his trousers were laid out to dry on the porch.

She picked up the soldier's footwear and returned to where the lamp-light was strongest. Once again she could see nothing extraordinary about the Wellington-style knee-high boots. The dark leather was of good quality and the boots obviously well made. Inside was a maker's stamp that indicated them to be the work of a boot maker on Royal Street in New Orleans.

The soles showed no wear, so they must be relatively new. And they were definitely not the footwear of a poor man.

She ran her hand over the soft but sturdy bloodstained leather that made up the shaft of the boot, pausing at the matching indentions she and Mama had discovered when the blood was wiped away. Based on the size and location, the indentions were the mark of a snake aiming at the soldier's leg. The mark caused no harm because the leather did not allow the snake's fangs to reach skin, this much Mama confirmed during her original examination.

These boots had likely saved the Grey's life. Even so, what could be so important about the footwear that Clay would call out for these?

Ellis picked one up, held it up to the lamplight, and examined it closely, then returned it to its resting spot. She repeated the process with the other and then took a step backward.

Something was different. Off. What it was, she couldn't quite say.

Moving forward, she turned the boots around so that the toes were facing the wall and then took a step back again. Yes, there. She saw it now.

Ellis grasped the right boot. The curve of the leather that was supposed to be a close fit to the man in the bed did not match the left boot.

It might be argued that the soldier's legs were not perfectly symmetrical. And yet, she felt they were close if not exactly the same. But these boots were not.

She turned the right boot upside down and shook it. When nothing happened, she turned it right-side up again and brought it closer to the light.

Odd.

Viewed down into the boot, this one appeared to be exactly the same size as the other. She grabbed the left boot and held it against the right. Yes. They were the same.

"Which means you've got something hiding in this one, Clay, or whoever you are," she said as she returned the left boot to its place. "The question is, what is it and how do I get to it?"

Ellis ran her hand across the top of the boot where the seam was perfectly done. There had to be some hidden way of. . .

She gasped. There it was.

As she reached the inside of the top of the boot, her finger slid into what appeared to be a pocket. With a little more pressure, she managed to open the pocket enough to see that there was indeed something hidden inside.

"Well now, what do we have here?"

Her finger touched something crisp. It appeared to be documents of some sort, maybe, or perhaps a map.

"You clever man," she said as she glanced over at the sleeping soldier. "Now let's see what you've got hidden in your boot."

With a tug, Ellis managed to pull out the folded papers. The barn door opened and Mama stepped inside. She dropped the documents inside the boot and put it back next to the other one.

"What were you doing?" Mama asked as she made her way over to the patient.

"Just looking for clues about our patient."

Ellis joined her mother at the soldier's bedside. There would be plenty of time to tell her of her find, but for now there were dressings to be changed. She helped with that chore and then moved out of Mama's way until she was finished with her examination.

"He is healing." Her mother stood. "But the fever is troublesome."

"It comes and goes," Ellis said.

"Anything else?"

"He seems restless." She paused, reluctant to elaborate then deciding to speak the truth. "Sometimes he speaks, though he doesn't make sense."

"It's the fever." Mama walked over to the light and doused it, leaving the barn in darkness. "Or it could be the head wound. It is impossible to know at this point. Come, Ellis. He will be fine until morning. You will sleep in the house with the family tonight. It is time."

"But, Mama, I think perhaps given the fact he still—"

"You will sleep in the house," she said in that tone Mama used when she would brook no argument.

"Yes, Mama." Ellis followed her mother out and watched her bar the door.

"Given that he's healing," Mama said, "I want you to be on your guard. If he seems combative, we will increase the sleeping remedy and tie him to the bed if we must."

"Do you think he's dangerous?"

Her mother linked arms with her as they followed the familiar path to the house. "I don't know, and that is why we must assume he is."

CHAPTER 9

This time the darkness was different. Not like the deep ebony nothingness he'd grown used to. The sizzling heat and depths of cold did not come as often, or at least it seemed that way.

But where was the green-eyed woman?

He might have lifted his head to see if he could find her, but it refused to move. All he could do was use his eyes to look around as best he could, allowing his focus—blurry as it was—to fall on the shadowy things around him.

Nearby was a chair with a book on it; that much he could see because the silver light fell stronger there. Behind it were only shadows of things that might be. Or things that weren't there. He couldn't tell which.

A sound echoed in the space, a soft drumming noise that he couldn't place. Was it rain?

Again he tried to move, and again he found himself useless for anything other than lying still and watching the shadows for the green-eyed woman.

She would return. She always did.

So he would wait.

There was more. Something he needed to do. A place he needed to be. But where? And when?

The more he tried to remember, the more he seemed to forget. What he could not forget was the green-eyed woman and how she made him feel. If only he could speak to her.

The soldier was speaking again. Ellis could hear him before she removed the bar to the barn door and stepped inside.

The sun had not yet risen, but she had already raced through all her chores then made breakfast and set it aside for Mama and the boys. Mr. Jim would be home today, so she added extra bacon in case he arrived early enough to dine with the family.

Ellis set the plate of bacon and eggs on the chair and then found her way through the murky darkness to light the lamp. As the light filled the room, she saw that the patient had indeed been fine without her there. Or at least he appeared to be.

"Good morning," she said as she reached over to feel his brow.

Fever.

She sighed. "You're supposed to be getting better. I even brought breakfast for you. I guess I was a little too hopeful."

His eyes opened. "Green-eyed woman," came out in a deep and breathy voice.

Ellis smiled. "Yes, I suppose I am. How're you feeling this morning? Are you hungry?"

No response.

Instead he stared up at her. "November 18th at Béxar."

Ellis froze. "What do you mean? What is happening that day?"

He stared, once again mute. Then his eyes closed and remained that way until well after sunrise.

By then she had moved the breakfast plate to the table and written the date and location he'd given her in the back of the book of psalms. When taken separately, the Grey's ramblings had not made sense.

But now that she had this additional information, a story was emerging. It appeared the Grey was supposed to meet a representative of General Houston at Béxar on November 18 to deliver funds that were needed by the Texian army. Something had been buried, possibly the gold, and that could be found where the pecan tree split thirty-three paces from the river.

Information regarding just where along the Brazos this tree might be had not yet been mentioned. Nor had he identified the name of who sent him on this alleged mission to aid the Texians. These were the questions she would ask if she had the opportunity.

If only there was another way to. . . *Oh. The boots!*

Ellis scrambled to set the book aside. Grabbing the right boot, she slid her fingers inside and retrieved the folded papers. She set the boot back in place and moved closer to the lamp to spread out the documents on the table.

The first scrap of paper—not much bigger than the size of her hand—had what appeared to be maps drawn on both sides. She traced what must be a long road of some kind on the first side and saw where it noted the number of steps from something called *Ventana de Rosa* up to a split tree. There was another set of steps due north to where an X had been marked. Nothing was identified on this map, but it had to be the directions to where Houston's gold was hidden.

On the other side of this paper were directions from Columbus to Béxar and a notation of the specific place where the meeting would be held: Mission San Jose.

Now she had a location to go with the date. What she thought was the outlandish mumbling of a fevered man was becoming something that could be all too real.

Ellis set the map aside. The next document was smaller, and had fit so easily inside the first one that she could have missed it. Unfolding the page, she recognized the document immediately as identification of a citizen of Louisiana, because all the adults in the Valmont family had been in possession of one before they came here to Texas.

Her eyes scanned the page until she found what she was looking for. "Claiborne William Andre Gentry." She glanced over at the soldier and smiled. "No wonder there was so much space between your first name and last on your certificate. I suppose I can still call you Clay until you tell me otherwise."

She folded the pages back together, but instead of returning them to their hiding place, she tucked them into the hidden pocket that Mama had sewed into her rebozo. Until she could be certain just whom this man was working for, she had to do as her mother and grandfather warned. She had to believe him an enemy until he could prove himself a friend.

Though he claimed to be meeting General Houston or one of his men, what if he was delivering funds to the Mexican army to defeat Houston? That was certainly possible. With battles raging elsewhere and the price of Texas freedom being paid in the blood of its citizens, anything was possible.

Ellis returned to Clay Gentry's bedside and looked down at the sleeping soldier. "Who are you working for, Clay Gentry?" she said softly.

He mumbled something, his lips moving but the sound barely audible. She repeated the question, leaning closer.

"Jackson," he told her.

Ellis sat back, stunned. "Andrew Jackson? The president of the United States?"

For a moment she did not think he would answer. Then he whispered, "Yes," on an exhale of breath.

"Why?" she asked, but he remained silent. "Clay, wake up," she told him. "I want to know why Andrew Jackson would ask you to deliver money to the Texians. Why you? And why contribute to that cause when the president has so many other interests he could support?"

True, there had been talk that the president would somehow make

Texas a state, but that had only been talk. No politician wanted to be the one to initiate a war, apparently, so the subject of statehood had been lost in the cries for attention elsewhere.

Ellis shook her head. Of course. It was all so ridiculous that it had to come from a mind that was damaged from the head injury. The poor man couldn't help what he thought to be true, not in his condition. And yet, how did the excuse that the story was outlandish explain the papers in the hidden compartment of his boot?

Clay's eyes opened and he stared up at her. Ellis couldn't tell whether he was truly seeing her or merely looking past her. "I owe him," he said as his eyes slid shut. "And he owes Houston."

She settled on the edge of the bed in the hope of hearing him better. Though his lips continued to move, no more words emerged.

Ellis pressed her palm to his forehead. He still was burning up. Only then did she realize she had not yet administered the herbs that would reduce the fever. No wonder he was speaking such nonsense. She quickly took care of that and then bathed his forehead with a damp cloth.

Though she continued to pepper him with questions, Clay said nothing further on any subject. Finally she snatched up a slice of bacon and devoured it. She was about to reach for another slice when Clay's eyes opened again.

"Thirsty," he said.

She dipped the cloth into the bucket and dripped the water slowly onto his tongue. When she repeated the process, he began to choke.

"Enough for now," she told him. "Get well and I will bring water and breakfast."

His eyes fluttered open, and it almost looked as if he might smile. Then he fell into a deep sleep again.

Mama came and went, declaring today to be the day they decrease the sleeping remedy. Though she too was disappointed with the continued fevers, she was not surprised.

"He's not guaranteed a recovery, especially considering the severity of the shoulder wound," Mama reminded her. "Don't get your hopes up."

They'd left together then, she and Mama, for there were chores to be done. By the time Ellis managed to return to the barn, she found Clay lying very still but without fever.

"This is good news," she told him.

She leaned back in the chair, preparing to close her eyes for a brief rest, when she noticed his lips moving again. Shifting to the mattress, she leaned close.

"What is it, Clay? Are you trying to tell me something?" When he did not respond, she dipped the cloth in the bucket and let a few drops of water land on his lips.

He smiled.

"Do you want more?"

Clay opened his mouth just enough to allow her to give him a tiny bit more water. This time he did not choke, but she dared not offer any more.

However, as long as she was getting a response from him, maybe he would be willing to answer more questions. There had to be an explanation for the papers in his boot, and she was determined to find it.

"Why Mission San Jose?" she asked.

"Allies," he told her. "Easy to meet. No one will know."

Interesting. Still, a far-fetched story. "What time is the meeting?"

"Sunset," he told her, as always in the language of the Acadians.

"Do you speak English, Clay?" she asked him.

His eyes opened again and he looked up at her. This time she knew he saw her. "Clay?"

Ellis hid her smile. "I'm sorry. That is what I have been calling you. Perhaps you prefer Claiborne. Or Claiborne William Andre Gentry. It is a grand name. Very impressive."

He continued to hold her gaze, his eyes barely blinking. "Who is Clay?"

"That is you. It is your name, or rather all of those names are your name. I shortened it to Clay and then, well, never mind." She gave him a sideways look. "Or is it?"

She stood and took a step away from the bed. Was it possible, if he was indeed speaking truth and not nonsense, that the document in his boot had been forged?

Possible also that the man lying injured under her grandmother's quilt was not Claiborne William Andre Gentry from New Orleans, Louisiana? That he was a spy sent from Santa Anna to somehow do harm to the Texians at Béxar?

Or worse, to deliver the funds to the Mexican army? Indeed, anything was possible in a time of war.

Consider him a foe until he is proven a friend.

Ellis went to the table and mixed the herbs that made up the sleeping remedy and then returned to the patient. He allowed her to administer it without protest, though his eyes never left hers. After a while, the remedy did its job and the soldier—whoever he was—fell into a deep sleep.

That's when she sprang into action. Using ropes from the supplies in the barn, she tied his hands. Then she wrapped another rope around his feet. When she was done, she covered him with the quilt and then stood back to catch her breath.

His chest rose and fell in an even rhythm, attesting to the depth of his sleep. Questioning him now would likely not provide any answers, but she had to try.

"What is your purpose for going to Béxar?" she whispered against his ear. "Who are you meeting?"

"Houston," he said. "Important to meet Houston."

"Houston himself or someone representing him?" she asked.

"Himself, though no one is to know it is him."

Ellis shook her head. "So you're telling me General Sam Houston is going to meet with you at Mission San Jose on November 18th for the purpose of receiving money for his troops?"

"No," he said softly. "Gold coins."

"Gold coins," she echoed. "All right, then tell me how the most famous Texian in the army will be able to hide his identity."

"Dressed as a padre," he said. "Both of us."

She reached for her book of psalms and turned to the back page. Adding this information to what she had already written there certainly completed the story. But again she had to wonder how much of it was the truth.

She sighed. How could a man in his condition manage to lie consistently? It was impossible, wasn't it?

There was only one unanswered question. "Do you intend to harm General Houston?"

The Grey's eyes opened and then fluttered shut again. Apparently this was a question he did not intend to answer.

Consider him a foe until he is proven a friend.

And so she would, though she would defer the accusation that he meant harm to the general until she had further proof.

CHAPTER 10

When Mama arrived, she viewed the new situation with the soldier without comment. Ellis rushed to explain.

"He was making statements that frightened me. I do not know if he is recalling truth or speaking out of his mind."

When Mama raised her eyebrows, Ellis rushed to clarify. "He wasn't threatening us, Mama, if that's what you were thinking. I just. . ." She struggled to find a way to tell her without giving details she wasn't sure were true. "I feel like he is hiding something. Whether that is his loyalty to Texas or to someone in a position of power trying to help Texas, I do not know."

"So you think keeping him restrained is necessary?"

"That or keeping him asleep," she said.

"This is a temporary solution," Mama reminded her. "Eventually he will heal and awaken. Then what do you propose to do?"

"I have no proposal," she said with a sigh. "He is making claims that cause me to wonder whether he is a spy for someone else or an ambassador sent to bring aid to General Houston. He has been saying some truly outlandish things."

"Do you care to tell me any of these outlandish things in specific?"

"There is nothing specific to tell yet," she said, "but I am keeping track of them. I wrote them all down in case the information is needed. Both you and Grandfather Valmont have said we should be watchful and consider anyone we are not certain is a friend to be our enemy."

"These are difficult times these past few years," Mama said as she nodded in agreement. "But be careful about making pronouncements in regard to someone who cannot speak up in his defense."

"Agreed," Ellis said. "So I propose we keep him either asleep or restrained until he can speak in his defense."

Her mother seemed to consider Ellis's proposal. "For today, I will agree to him being restrained but not to giving him something for sleep. Healing requires he return to normal sleeping patterns."

"I understand," she said, knowing Mama was right.

"Even in times of war, a man should be given the right to speak in defense, don't you think?" At her reluctant nod, Mama continued. "Perhaps Mr. Jim can be convinced to stay here with him at night so that you do not have to feel afraid. He would, of course, need a bed of his own. I doubt he'd be willing to shirk his daytime chores in favor of staying awake at this man's bedside."

Or both do the daytime chores and still stay awake to provide care to the patient, she thought but did not say aloud. "Has he returned?" Ellis said instead.

"Not yet, but I expect him anytime now. I had word the circuit rider is bringing him himself." Mama nodded toward the soldier. "How much of the sleeping herbs did you give him?" Upon Ellis's answer, her mother continued. "Then I expect he will have a good long rest. Come, I have plenty for you to do while our patient is sleeping."

A few hours later, Ellis looked up from her work in the field to see a horse with two riders coming down the road. "Mama," she called as she hurried toward the road. "We've got company."

As the horse drew near, she spied their beloved Mr. Jim riding behind the Methodist circuit rider. The preacher urged the mount forward, hurrying their arrival at the gate.

"Welcome," Mama said, beating Ellis to the chore of opening the gate. "We are so thankful you've brought our dear friend home."

The circuit rider echoed the greeting as he rode through the now-open gate. Mr. Jim grinned broadly, showing his lack of teeth and his joy at being home once again.

No one—not even he—could remember when Antonio Jose Jimenez arrived on the property now owned by the Valmont family. Known by his preferred name of Mr. Jim, the old gentleman had worked for the previous owner, and though that family moved on, he did not.

Rather, Papa was happy for him to stay. Strong as an ox and able to do the work of a man half his age, Mr. Jim had been an asset to the family during the years before the war began and a godsend once the men went off with the militia to Goliad.

Had Papa not begged Mr. Jim to stay behind and keep watch over the women and children, the older man would have marched away with the rest. His allegiance to Papa was so strong, however, that he would do anything Boyd Valmont asked of him, even if that meant leaving the fighting to the others in favor of helping with everything from farming to mending fences to aiding in the laundering of clothes on occasion.

Lucas and Mack met them on the porch and hurried to take the horse's reins. As the preacher climbed down, it became apparent that the old man was not as well as expected.

"Bring the horse alongside the porch," Mama told the boys. "I think we are going to need to help Mr. Jim get on his feet."

The Valmont home, like others in the area, was built in the dogtrot style with two square structures united by a common roof that created a covered porch between them. The style was so named because a dog could trot happily between the parlor and the sleeping areas without going inside.

In the case of the Valmont home, Papa's success had allowed for a second story to be built over the first. Two large bedchambers upstairs housed Ellis's brothers as well as any cousins, friends, or trusted workers who needed a place to stay. Downstairs were two more bedchambers on one side of the open porch—one for Mama and Papa and the other for Ellis—with a narrow hall dividing the two rooms. A suite of parlor furniture and Grandmother Valmont's massive table and chair set from New Orleans filled out the other side.

Standing close enough to watch every move, Mama looked doubtful as Mr. Jim proclaimed he was just fine. Nodding to Ellis, she made sure there was help when that proclamation proved to be false.

His knees buckled, and it took her and the preacher to get him inside and situated in the rocker by the fireplace. Mama performed the duties of a hospitable hostess until she found a way to excuse herself. On her way outside, she motioned for Ellis to join her.

"He does not need to be here," Mama said when they'd left the porch. "He may believe he has the stamina of a young man, but his age is showing in how he is healing from his injuries. Did you notice his pupils were uneven?"

Ellis nodded. "And he appears to be slurring his words just slightly. Since he was hit with something on the back of his head, that would be an expected symptom, wouldn't it?"

"Yes," her mother said. "With one injured man to care for, I do not see how you and I can add another to our list of duties."

"But Mr. Jim will be fine soon, won't he?"

Mama leaned against the bark of the pecan tree and then looked away toward the river. "I hope he will." She slowly returned her attention to Ellis. "But I have seen people with this injury who did not recover. There is no way to know whether he will be helping us with the chores next week or. . ."

Mama did not continue. She didn't need to. Still, the pain of what went unsaid jabbed Ellis's heart. Mr. Jim was family, and they had already lost so much family.

Not lost, she corrected. For Papa and Thomas would be home. She knew it. That loss was merely a temporary absence.

"Oh Mama," Ellis said softly. "He's got family in Velasco. To be cheated of their last days with him, if that is indeed what these are, would be awful."

"You think very much as I do," her mother said. "He needs to go home to them for a visit. If he recovers, all the better. If he does not. . ."

Again she left the rest unsaid.

"How do you propose we get him there? When we left him just now, he was telling the preacher how he planned to fix those uneven rows Grandfather Valmont tilled in the garden as soon as he could get changed into his work clothes."

Mama chuckled. "Yes, I did hear that. It seems to me the only way to get him to Velasco is to convince him that I need him to help get us there."

"You mean all of us? Someone has to stay with the soldier."

"I've thought of that, and I think I may be able to find a neighbor to check in on him," she said. "It's the only solution. We must get Mr. Jim home, and there's no time to waste."

"I will stay with the soldier," Ellis volunteered. "You'll only be gone a short while, but he does still have a fever that refuses to stay broken. I can manage this."

"Only just this morning you told me you were afraid of him and wanted him kept asleep indefinitely. Now you expect me to give you permission to stay behind here and keep watch over him?"

"It is only a day's journey there and back, and that allows for a lengthy visit with Grandfather Valmont. I will be fine."

Mama seemed to consider the request for a moment, and then, finally, she nodded. "All right, but I will only allow it if you promise that if you have the slightest chance to fear that man in the barn, you will run to Lyla and Jonah's place and stay there until the boys and I return."

Ellis opened her mouth to respond, but Mama waved away the words. Instead she cupped her fists and let out a long breath.

"If I did not love Texas so much, I would be cursing this new land of ours for all the trouble it has caused my family." Her mother shrugged. "But who am I to complain when my husband and son have sacrificed so much to see to her protection?"

"They'll be home soon, Mama," Ellis said as she swiped at a rare tear that traced a path down her mother's cheek. "I know they will."

"As do I," she said. "And in the meantime, we will carry on. So, are you ready to promise you will do as I asked?"

"I will," she said. "I have no interest in sacrificing anything for Texas."

"Oh honey," Mama said with the beginnings of a grin. "You've already sacrificed so much."

Ellis shook her head. "Please don't you go telling me what Grandfather Valmont already has. I know there could have been fancy balls and a big home in New Orleans and all of the comforts that I don't have here in Texas if we had stayed there."

Mama's expression took on a wistful look, and Ellis wondered if she was considering what might have been or what she still missed. "Yes, there could have been."

"Well, I am sorry, but that sounds just awful. Dressing up in corsets that pinch and being polite to fellows who only want to get to know me because I live in a big house and have good prospects? No thank you."

Mama chuckled. "Oh Ellis," she said. "I did not grow up a Valmont, but I heard all the stories from your grandmother. The way she used to speak of her mother-in-law, Maribel Cordoba Valmont, is exactly the way you are speaking now. I do believe the apple did not fall far from the tree. Now come, let's go and try to convince a stubborn man to do what we want."

"That should be no problem at all for you," she told her mother.

"You've been doing exactly that with Papa for as long as I can recall."

"With one exception, you are correct," Mama said as she climbed the steps to return to the porch.

That one exception was when Papa determined to join with the militia along with Thomas and go off to fight. Ellis let that reference fall silently between them without comment.

A short time later, Mama and Ellis served a noonday meal that spread just thin enough to allow for the preacher's generous portion. After the preacher gave the blessing, Mama set to work convincing Mr. Jim that she needed him to help her with an errand to Velasco immediately after the meal.

"But I saw plenty of work to do right here, Sophie," he protested. "I know your daddy means well, but if those rows aren't straightened now, the Lord only knows how we will plant there come spring."

Mama sat patiently as the older man offered a long list of reasons why an afternoon in Velasco just was not possible. Then, a few minutes later, she had him not only agreeing to go along to help her but making her promise not to dawdle with the cleanup because time was wasting.

"I'll do the cleaning up," Ellis offered. "You all get going."

With the pastor headed back to Columbia and the rest of the family now heading downriver to Velasco, Ellis took the dishes out to do the washing in the summer kitchen. She had just dunked the first dish in the bucket when she froze.

In all the excitement of Mr. Jim's return and then his coerced exit, she had forgotten all about the soldier. Dropping the tin plate into the bucket, she quickly dried her hands on her apron.

Keeping as quiet as possible, she hurried to the small barn. Her fingers trembled as she reached out to lift the bar. The door swung open on hinges that Mr. Jim would complain needed oiling.

The barn was quiet and cool, and the sun filtering through the high windows gave enough light to see that nothing had changed in her absence. She approached the bed, uncertain as to what she would find.

The Grey lay very still, so still that Ellis paused to watch for the slow rise and fall of his chest before she reached down to press her palm against his forehead. No fever.

She sighed. "You're doing better, it seems, whoever you are."

With the soldier so deeply asleep, Ellis turned him so she could examine the wound on the back of his head. The healing was nearly complete here, and there was no evidence of new bleeding for days. As quickly as she could manage without awakening him, Ellis removed the bandage and set it aside.

He stirred as she rested his head back where it had been, but then he once again settled into slumber. "Who are you?" she repeated as she looked down at him. "How did you get here, and for whom do you work, soldier?"

The same question she had asked more than once. The same question he had yet to answer.

"Who are you?" came the whispered reply as his eyes opened.

"Oh no," she said. "I'm asking the questions today. And I asked first."

His eyes opened slowly, and he seemed to have trouble focusing. Finally he gave her a half smile. "Green eyes."

She sighed. "Ellis," she corrected. "Now. Who are you?"

He moved his head from side to side and then winced before returning his attention to her. "Your captive," he answered.

"What is your name?" she asked, ignoring the reference to the ropes binding him.

"I. . .I. . .I don't. . ." His voice fell silent. "You said Clay."

"I did. But is that really who you are?" She would say no more than that until she could determine his real name.

He nodded and then added, "Gentry?"

Same as the name on the papers in his boot. Either he was feeling better and remembering the false identity he'd taken on or this was the truth. Ellis kept a neutral expression.

Clay jerked his hands and then looked up at Ellis. "Why am I bound?"

"Safety." The truth. For if he made any attempt to harm her, even in his weakened state, he would be very sorry. "What are you doing in Texas, Clay Gentry?"

His eyes widened then closed. "Don't know," he said on an exhale of breath.

"Are you a soldier?" she asked.

He shook his head. "Don't know."

Something about the sound of his voice gave her pause. Unless Clay Gentry was very good at pretending, he had just convinced her that he spoke the truth. Mama was right in warning that the injuries he sustained could cause loss of memory.

"Hungry," he said again. "And thirsty."

She made quick work of offering him water by once again dripping water onto his tongue. This time he did not choke.

"More," he pleaded.

"Slowly," Ellis said as she repeated the process until she felt he'd had enough.

"Thank you," he whispered through cracked lips.

"Still hungry?" she asked.

At his nod, she glanced around to find the breakfast plate still sitting on the table. Asking to eat was always a good sign for a recovering patient. But to feed him, she would somehow have to get him into a seated position. Dare she try?

"Clay," she said as she moved closer. "If I feed you, I have to sit you up. Do you feel ready to do that?"

For a moment, he remained still and quiet. Then he nodded. "Yes."

"All right. Let me do the work. You just do as I say, and if you cannot or if it hurts too much, tell me."

She settled onto the side of the bed and wrapped her arm behind his neck. "When I lift your head, move up."

He tried but failed more than once. The reason was simple. He had no use of his hands.

Ellis sighed as she returned his head to the pillow. She had to either release him from his bonds or ignore the pleas of a hungry patient.

CHAPTER 11

"Clay, I am going to remove the bindings on one of your hands so you can sit up, but your legs and the other hand will remain tied."

His eyes watched Ellis as he nodded. Since his left shoulder had sustained the injury, Ellis decided to release his right hand. Her fingers fumbled with the ties, finally loosening the knot she'd made this morning.

As the ropes fell free, she scooted away from him. He flexed his fingers as if trying to get feeling in them but otherwise remained still.

"I will lift your head," she told him as she moved back into position. "Use your hand to help yourself sit up."

Ellis slid her hand under his neck. This time, he turned his head to look up at her. "Thank you," he whispered. "Green eyes."

He said the words in English, his first use of that language since he'd arrived on their property. What that meant, she would have to ponder later. For now, she had a job to do, and that job involved repositioning a very handsome but very mysterious wounded soldier.

"Ellis," she corrected as lightly as she could manage at this close distance. For up close his eyes were deep and soft and his weak smile would make the heart of any woman who had more than an interest in his health beat faster.

But she only held an interest in healing this Grey's wounded body and allowing him to return to the cause of freedom for Texas. If she was wrong and he was a foe, then she would still have a clean conscience knowing she had treated one of God's beloved children even if that child was an enemy to a cause Ellis held dear.

"Ellis," he repeated.

"Just as we tried before, only we will move slowly," she said as she lifted his head. "Are you ready?"

"I am."

Though the soldier groaned as if he was in agony, he refused to allow her to lay him back down. After a few minutes of the two of them working together, he managed to sit up.

Ellis grabbed two extra quilts and rolled them, then added his pillow to support his back and neck as she settled him into a semi-reclining position. Now, though he could sleep this way, he could also eat.

Unfortunately, the effort must have exhausted him, for Clay fell into a deep sleep as if he had forgotten all about his hunger. Ellis took the opportunity to remove the plate and return it to the kitchen, making sure to bar the barn door when she left.

Dumping out the old food for the dogs to devour, she made quick work of cooking another plate of eggs. She also pulled a tin mug down from the shelf. If the soldier could manage food, then he could also manage a mug.

She crossed the yard to return to the barn but paused to look up at the sky before she released the latch. Ominous black clouds floated toward her, the high-hat type that were known to come up off the Gulf on warm summer afternoons.

But this was October.

Still, the weather had remained temperate as it sometimes did here in this part of Texas. As long as the storm did not prevent Mama and the boys from returning, then a decent soaking of rain was always welcome.

Rain. He always loved the rain, didn't he? It rained where he was from, didn't it? Yes, he thought it did. Or maybe that was only the place where he visited?

Maybe all of this was just another thought the green-eyed woman had given him. Like the name that did not seem to fit or the accusation that he would somehow do her harm or escape if he were to be released from these ropes.

He was weak as a kitten and had no desire to do anything but sleep. *Not true,* he decided as he slid his eyes open just enough to catch sight of the woman reading by lamplight.

Had he the ability to focus well and to remain awake, he would want to look into those green eyes and manage to say something. Anything. Why did they render him mute?

But they did not, did they? For he had answered questions. That was her who asked, wasn't it?

Though everything that happened before the moment he saw those green eyes looking down at him was wrapped in a fog he could not yet penetrate, he knew this was not the first time he had seen her.

This woman held some meaning, but what? Was she only here to tell him things? To offer him water and change his dressings?

Was she real at all?

He exhaled a long breath. He was not so far gone that he did not recall the feel of her hand at the back of his neck. Of her encouraging words whispered against his ear and the warning look she gave him when she freed his hand.

Flexing his fingers, he glanced over at his left hand. A rope still held him to the bed, but even without that binding, the pain in his shoulder likely would have discouraged movement.

What had happened to him? Hadn't she asked him that? Had he answered?

She caught him staring and lowered the book she had been reading. "Hello again," she said to him. "You had a long rest."

A flash of lightning sizzled between them and then thunder shook the room. She had lit a lamp, but there were shadows all around.

He avoided the shadows, this much he remembered. Shadows held danger.

"Are you hungry?" she asked, diverting his attention from the search of the corners of the room. At his nod, she came toward him, a plate now in her hand. She offered a fork, but his hand shook when he tried to take it.

"Let me help," she said as she loaded the fork with something on the plate and offered it to him. His mouth opened, but he kept his attention on those green eyes.

On Ellis.

Yes, he must remember that name. Ellis.

"Slowly," she said again as his attention shifted to her mouth. Her lips were pursed into a pout. As soon as he took a bite of whatever she had put on the fork, those same lips curved into the beginnings of a smile.

After a few bites, she paused. "Slowly," she repeated as she set the plate aside. "Give yourself time."

Everything in him wanted to protest. To explain that although he did not currently recall with any accuracy his name or anything else about himself relating to where he was or how he got there, he was still a man who was not used to being fed or taking orders.

He gave the orders.

Or at least he hoped that was a memory and not just another thing Ellis had said to him.

No, he decided as he tried to force his feeble brain to focus. He had given an order once. An order he regretted.

But what was it?

After a moment, he let that thought go and watched it disappear like a wisp of smoke on a dark night. She was feeding him again. He accepted the sustenance, allowed her to care for him. He would do that until he was well enough for the balance of power to be restored.

For he was not a man to be ruled and run by a woman. He'd not been raised to lie abed without doing hard work, had he? The answer of no felt correct, so he hoped that was the case.

Outside, the thunder rolled on. The lamplight shook with each peal, and the patter on the roof continued. The combination was a symphony that lulled him to sleep once again, this time with his belly full.

Then something jarred him awake. Questions. Yes. She was speaking to him, the green-eyed woman who had tied him here. Something about his plans for a date in November.

November 18.

Recognition jolted deep inside him. *Focus.* What was important about that date?

Think.

He knew this. Knew why it was important. Something more important than anything else in his life.

He closed his eyes and then opened them again. Ellis had stopped talking and was looking at him as if expecting an answer.

Was he being interrogated? Yes, that was it. She knew something and thought he knew more. That was why he'd been trussed up like a Christmas turkey and relegated to some dark room in a place he could not name.

She walked over to the table and placed the book she'd been reading next to his lamp and a pair of oddly familiar Wellington boots. Then she offered more eggs, and he shook his head.

Still those green eyes kept watching him. Beneath the quilt, he pulled against the ropes holding his left hand and paid for the effort with a jolt of pain in his shoulder. Was she the one who caused him to be in this position, or had she merely followed the orders of someone else?

November 18.

He had no idea how long in the future that was. Or perhaps the day was already past and this had been the result.

In either case, what would she do next? Was she his healer or his prison guard? Rain continued to pound the roof and thunder shook the walls as he considered these questions with as much care as his feeble mind could manage.

Then he knew. It did not matter what she would do next, for he must strike first. If the green-eyed woman was a threat to his mission, he must neutralize the threat.

With his free hand, he motioned for her to move closer. Though he thought he detected reluctance in those green eyes, she did as he asked.

Quick as a snake, his hand wrapped around hers. "Who are you, and why are you holding a man who represents the president of the United States?"

The words were out, but he had no idea where they came from or what they meant.

Ellis willed herself not to panic. Though her heart raced and her fingers trembled, she kept her expression neutral. "Release me," she told him.

He ignored her.

She could hit him where it would hurt the most—namely his shoulder—but as a healer she would take that action only as a last resort. "Clay," she said gently, "I am the person who has kept you alive."

He blinked hard as if trying to understand the statement.

"You were bound for safety," she added.

His eyes narrowed. "Yours or mine?"

A flash of lightning split the sky outside the high window. This time there was no thunder, only a deafening crack and a flash of white light inside the small barn. Out of the corner of her eye, Ellis saw a slim thread of something bluish-purple race down the wall. Then came the unmistakable scent of something burning.

"Fire!"

With the soldier distracted, Ellis yanked her hand free. The wall had begun to glow with fire, though thankfully, the rain appeared to be keeping the old wood from igniting.

At least so far.

"Remove the ropes," the soldier commanded, reverting back to Acadian French as he fumbled with the bindings that still held his left hand to the bed.

Despite the rain that poured down on the roof, flames had begun to take possession of the wood on the opposite side of the small barn. Soon the fire would reach the table beside the door. There it would consume the lamp that held enough flammable oil to cause an explosion.

They would then be trapped.

Ellis hurried to the end of the bed and lifted the quilt just enough to tug at the ropes binding the soldier's feet together. Behind her she could feel the heat of the flames growing.

With her hands trembling, the knots refused to budge. She looked up from her work and their gazes connected.

"We will live," Clay told her as he jerked at the bindings on his left hand. "Keep trying."

"Yes," she shouted over the rain and her fear. "We will."

Ellis tarried only a moment as she tried to latch onto the claim. Then she went back to her work with the same result.

"There shall no evil befall thee, neither shall any plague come nigh thy dwelling. For he shall give his angels charge over thee, to keep thee in all thy ways. They shall bear thee up in their hands, lest thou dash thy foot against a stone."

The words of the psalm she had only just been reading moments ago. Psalm 91.

Her fingers stilled.

Though the flames grew and her heart raced, calm settled inside her. The next attempt to untie the ropes was successful. The soldier's feet were free.

Unfortunately, Clay had not yet managed to accomplish the same feat. He now lay back against the quilts, exhausted and seemingly unable to move.

"Go," he told her when their eyes met. "Save yourself."

CHAPTER 12

N o," Ellis shouted as she moved around to where Clay's left hand was tethered to the bed frame. "We will both live."

The knot had been pulled tight, likely by the soldier's futile work to release himself. The only remedy was to cut him free, but how?

Despite it all, she smiled. Of course. She had removed her rebozo and left it on the porch when she had been washing dishes after lunch.

"I will be back," she told him as she ducked her head to run beneath the cloud of smoke now settling on them.

"Save yourself," came his weak cry.

The first step into the pounding rain shocked her into stumbling, and she landed in a puddle on the ground. Rising, she swiped at her face and then raced toward the porch, more by memory than sight, for she was nearly blinded by the deluge.

There she found the rebozo made of colorful fabric her grandmother had purchased at the market in Matamoros. Grandfather Valmont said it looked almost exactly like the scrap that his mother, Maribel, had kept among her treasured possessions.

She snatched up the cloth and ran back into the rain, fumbling for the knife resting in the secret pocket. From this vantage point, she could see the extent of the flames. There was little time to spare before the roof would fall in or the lamp would seal their exit.

With the knife in one hand, she tucked the scarf around her and opened the door. Smoke billowed out, but she ducked beneath it and crawled on her hands and knees until she reached the spot where the soldier lay.

Clay's attempt at saving himself resulted in him lying in a puddle of quilts with his left hand still tethered to the bed. "Clay," she said against his ear. "Can you manage to walk?"

He looked up at her, dark eyes seemingly unable to focus. Then an expression of clarity. "I will," he told her, and she had no doubt he would.

The sharp knife made short work of the ropes. Now to get him to his feet.

Clay Gentry was easily head and shoulders taller than her, if not more, and having been lying abed for more than a week, he could offer little help in rising to his feet.

Ellis squared her shoulders and gave him an even look, banking on what she knew to be true about the hearts of men who served. A soldier left no one behind. If Clay was a soldier, then now was the time for him to prove it.

With this in mind, she managed to get him situated in a seated position on the mattress and then nodded toward the door. "The exit is there and we are here. I will not save myself if I cannot save you. What will you do with that information, soldier?"

Clay appeared dazed. Then he looked up at her. Something in his expression seemed to shift. She offered her hand and he took it, rising on unstable legs.

Instantly he fell into a fit of coughing that landed him back on the mattress. She helped move him back into a seated position.

"The smoke is too thick. We must stay down." She helped him slide onto the floor. "Can you crawl?" At his nod, she yanked a quilt from the bed and spread it over his head and shoulders, then poured the last of the water over it so that the flames would be repelled. She then used her rebozo, already wet from the rain, to do the same for herself.

"Keep your head low and follow me."

Crawling proved difficult, but the rebozo kept out the worst of the smoke. She got as far as the door before she looked back to see if Clay had followed.

She found him sprawled on the floor just a few feet from her, the quilt partially covering him from flames that were now reaching the legs of the table where the lamp stood. His eyes were closed, and she could see fresh blood on the shoulder of his nightshirt. If he remained where he was, Clay Gentry would die.

"Wake up, soldier," she shouted to him. "You will not die today."

His head lifted but then fell again. Clay Gentry appeared to be done.

"Well, I am not," she snapped as she closed the distance between them to grasp the man's wrists.

By giving his arms a tug, she was able to move Clay a few inches toward the door. Another jerk and she moved him closer. The pace was excruciatingly slow, and the smoke poured over them like a thick and poisonous blanket, but she never slowed her pace. Jerking and tugging, yanking the quilt and then moving it back over his head so he could breathe. In this way, she moved inch by inch until finally she gave one mighty pull and they both tumbled into the rain and the mud.

His feet still inside the barn, Clay rolled over onto his back and gasped. The fresh air and rain swirled around him, though the smoke also rolled past.

"Safe," he managed through a fit of coughing and then choking.

"Not until you are clear of the building," she told him. "There's a dry bed in the house, but I cannot pull you all that way."

He looked at her and then lifted up on one elbow, appearing to survey the distance between where he was and where he needed to be. "The bed will wait," he told her. "I think I can get to the porch."

He moved into a crawling position and remained there for what seemed like an eternity. Then he reached for Ellis, who offered her hand to raise him to his knees.

"I can go for help," she told him, knowing the nearest neighbor was miles away and the help the neighbor could offer would not arrive for hours, if at all.

"No," he said through a clenched jaw. "I will do this."

Ellis once again offered her hand, but he declined. Instead he groaned and then cried out in a mighty roar as he rose to his full height. The rain pelted down and lightning zigzagged across the sky toward the river, but Clay Gentry was on his own two feet.

He began to laugh, and despite the gravity of the situation, Ellis joined him. Then he swayed, and she caught him.

"I vote that we defer the celebration until we reach the porch," she told him as she urged him forward toward the house.

As with their trek across the barn, the going was slow and the distance seemed far more than expected. Twice they stumbled, but each time, Ellis caught him. Finally they reached the porch, where Clay sagged down on the topmost step and leaned against the side of the house.

Ellis tucked the quilt around him. "You're out of the rain here and will be safe until we can get you moved inside."

She looked back at the barn. It was almost completely engulfed in flames. The only side yet to erupt was the side where the lamp sat on the table.

Beside the soldier's boots.

The boots with the documents hidden inside.

Bolting away from the house, she raced across the lawn to reach the burning barn. The table was near to the door and yet just far enough away to be obscured by the smoke and flames. Arranging the wet rebozo over her head, Ellis ducked down and felt her way toward it. She snatched the boots, and something else hit her on the forehead.

Her book of psalms.

Ellis might have laughed if the flames hadn't taken over the lamp at just that moment. She threw the boots outside into the rain, tucked the book into her bodice, and then leaped toward the open door just as the lamp shattered behind her.

Her skirt caught on the hinge, and Ellis turned to snatch the fabric loose. Another explosion lit the darkness. She fell backward and then the world tilted and upended.

She fought the rebozo, now tangled in her hair and covering her face, to try to see what was happening. Rain pelted her and thunder continued to rumble overhead, but a deeper rumble sounded against her ear.

"Be still," it said. "I will keep you safe."

The scarf slid away from her face, and she looked up into familiar eyes. "Clay?"

A moment later, she landed in a soggy heap on the porch steps. Clay settled slowly beside her with a groan.

"How. . ." She shook her head. "But you couldn't possibly—"

A fit of coughing rendered her unable to complete the thought. When she could finally gasp for breath, she muttered a whispered "Thank you."

Eyes closed, she rested her head on her knees and allowed her breathing to return to normal. When she sat up again, she realized Clay had not responded.

He sat very quietly next to her, his breathing labored and his gaze fixed on the burning ruin of the barn. Ellis reached behind him to slide the quilt over his shoulders.

The gesture seemed to draw Clay from his trance. He returned his attention to her and used the corner of the quilt to swipe at her face.

They sat in silence as the fire fought the rain to claim the small barn. "How did you do that?" she finally asked.

"I'm not sure I did," he said.

The next time she looked over at Clay, he had fallen asleep. Though tempted to leave him there, Ellis knew she had to get him inside.

Clay opened his eyes to a slice of evening sunlight that blinded him. He shifted position and then groaned. The smell of smoke permeated the room, so much so that he lifted up on his elbows to look around and be certain the fire had not spread to the place where he lay.

Shaking the cobwebs out of his brain, he tried to recall just what happened that led him here, then sat up and put his feet on the floor. A wave of dizziness came over him, but he ignored it.

His last reliable memory was of waking up to a pair of green eyes looking down at him. There were things he knew to be true, like the fact that he had been shot more than once. Then there were the things he was uncertain about, things that could have been memories or merely suggestions given by his captor.

The captor who saved his life.

Clay let out a long breath, thinking on that for a moment. Each of the things he could hold against the green-eyed woman had been wiped away the moment she insisted she would not leave the barn without him.

Ellis opened the door and stepped inside, then froze. "Oh. I thought. . ." Then she appeared to collect herself. "May I check your bandages?"

He smiled. "I don't recall being asked that question before."

"You were sleeping." She set a basket of what looked like herbs and strips of fabric down on the floor at her feet. "Would you lie down so I can look at your shoulder, please?"

Though he considered lodging a protest, Clay complied with her request. "Might it be true that I was asleep thanks to something you gave me?"

She looked up but said nothing. Clay winced as she went back to her work. When she was done, she stepped back to regard him evenly. "To manage the pain," she told him. "You were shot. One went through, but the other did not. We had to remove it."

"We?" He sat up slowly, declining Ellis's help. "I only remember seeing you."

"My mother, Sophie, is the healer. I learned from her." She picked up the basket and hurried to the door but then paused at the doorframe. "What you did, saving me, I mean. Thank you."

He shrugged then winced when the movement caused a jab of pain. "We exchanged thanks already. No need to repeat them."

A nod. "I wasn't sure you would remember." She moved away and then returned to the door. "You're speaking in Acadian French. Why is that?"

"My grandparents were from Louisiana," he told her, though he had no idea how he knew this or even if it was true.

"Sometimes you speak English," she said in a tone that sounded as if she was accusing him of something.

"I do?" He had no recollection of that. But then, when he tried hard to think, he had very little recollection of anything.

"You do. And when you speak in English, sometimes you say things that are. . ."

"That are what?"

He moved to put his feet back on the floor, keeping the quilt around him. The time for lying in bed was over. He was no healer, but he knew he would never fully recover until he was back to doing the normal things he had done before he was shot.

Whatever those things were.

When he realized Ellis had not yet responded, Clay looked over in her direction and repeated the question.

She shook her head. "Never mind. I'll bring some food. It's cold, but that's what happens when you sleep away the day." She paused to offer a wry smile. "And that was without any sleeping medication, Clay."

With that, she closed the door behind her. A moment later, he heard the unmistakable sound of a key turning in the lock.

CHAPTER 13

Ellis sat on the porch and stared past the still-smoldering remains of the barn toward the place where the Brazos River rolled past. Mama and the boys were late. The sun had set an hour ago, and Ellis had begun to prepare herself that they might not return tonight.

Mama likely would expect her to have gone down the road to Lyla and Jonah's home by now. She'd certainly had her chance to do just that. Jonah arrived as soon as he spied the smoke, but there had been nothing he could do.

She'd already secured the soldier in Mama and Papa's bedroom behind a locked door, so she easily could have accepted Jonah's offer to stay with them until Mama returned. She'd been too tired to consider walking that far, even though the distance was only a few miles.

Ellis stifled a yawn. The boots she rescued sat beside her. Covered in soot and still stained with Clay's blood, they had been drenched in the downpour.

She picked them up and walked through the middle of the dogtrot, then paused at the locked door. The soldier was quiet, either sleeping or lying awake in the dark. She moved on to enter the front door and settle at the kitchen table.

Had they just gathered for lunch here this afternoon? So much had happened since then that it seemed like days ago rather than hours. She thought of Mr. Jim then and offered a prayer that the Lord would spare him, a prayer she had been praying each time he came to mind during the day. Tonight, she added more, a few lines from Psalm 91:

"Surely he shall deliver thee from the snare of the fowler, and from the noisome pestilence. He shall cover thee with his feathers, and under his wings shalt thou trust."

"Please, Lord," she said aloud, "deliver him." She paused and swiped at a tear. "Deliver us all."

The papers that were hidden inside the boot were a soggy mess, and the ink used to draw the map and complete the certificate was hopelessly smeared. The book of psalms had fared better, and she now held it in her lap.

Closing her eyes, she tried to remember each detail of the map that had been ruined. First she drew the Brazos and then the tree that split. Not recalling the exact number of steps, she skipped that part and moved on. After a few more minutes, she had a fairly accurate depiction of the ruined map, at least as best as she could recall.

She set the book aside. On nights like this when everything was quiet and she was home alone, Ellis loved to dig into the trunk beside Mama's bed and pull out one of Maribel's books. That would not happen tonight.

Though she was exhausted, she knew sleep would not come easily. Too much had happened today.

Still, she walked outside into the crisp night air and crossed over to the structure where her soft bed awaited. As she walked down the hall, she heard Clay call her name.

"Yes," she said. "It is me. Do you need something?"

"To talk," he said in Acadian French.

Her fingers touched the cool metal of the carved silver doorknob Mama had brought over from New Orleans, but she did not turn the key. "Then talk," she told him. "I can hear you just fine."

Silence fell between them, and Ellis felt certain Clay would not respond. After a moment, she turned away to go into her own bedchamber.

"I have questions," he said. "I don't know how I got here. Have you already told me the story?"

"In bits and pieces I suppose I have. I guess you do not recollect any of it?"

"Not much."

His voice sounded far too close for him to be abed, but she had heard no footsteps. "You should not be out of bed, Clay."

"Bed is for sleeping. Either tell me about how I got here or tell me why you keep me a prisoner. Or are each of these things part of one story?"

She let out a long breath. "The boys found you in a pirogue washed up into some reeds just off the edge of our property."

"In the river?" he asked as she heard the floorboards groan softly near the door.

"Yes. What are you doing in there?"

"Sitting down," he told her. "Please continue."

"All right. We managed to get you onto the shore and up under the pecan tree where my mother could assess your wounds. There were three, but you've probably already discovered that. And one was worse than the others. She and I cleaned it out—actually Mama did and I watched mostly—and then we dressed the wound. The pirogue turned out to be one that was stolen from a neighbor's home before you arrived in Velasco, so I know you are not the thief, although you may have purchased it from him."

"How do you know when I arrived in Velasco?"

"I was in Velasco that day," she told him. "I saw you get off the boat. The next morning is when the boys found you."

Silence fell between them. Then she heard him shift positions again. This time he stifled a groan.

"Are you all right?"

"I will be," he said. "Why can't I remember things?"

"You had a head wound, likely from falling backward onto the wood when you were shot. Mama says those can cause memory loss."

"Is it temporary?"

"It can be." She thought of Mr. Jim. "There are other complications, but you've survived for more than a week, so it is doubtful there will be anything more."

"A week?" His voice, even through the door, held a tone of surprise. "I thought I'd been abed a day or perhaps two. There is somewhere else I should be, isn't there?"

She laughed. "Unless you had set out to end up on our property in our neighbor's canoe, then yes, I would say so."

"November 18th."

Ellis froze. "What about it?" she said, noticing he had switched to English.

"I am supposed to meet someone on that day. Do you know who that is?"

"You told outlandish stories," she said slowly. "They made no sense. So, with any assuredness that it is true, I would say I do not."

The truth, even though the story told in the back of her book certainly was an interesting one. Still, there was no proof other than his fevered ramblings and a now-ruined map.

"Who are you?" he asked, surprising her.

"What do you mean? Have you forgotten my name?"

There was a moment of silence and then Clay said, "Are you the green-eyed woman?"

What an odd question. "I am Ellis, and I do have green eyes."

"But are you the green-eyed woman?" His tone was more insistent. "The one who came to me in my sleep and told me things about myself. That green-eyed woman."

"How could I know things about you that you do not know

about yourself?" she managed.

Again the floor creaked. "Because all I know about myself is what I have been told by the green-eyed woman. Either you are she or she is a dream."

"I don't know, Clay." She sank down to the floor and leaned against the locked door. "You had fevers, and there were the medications given to you to help ease pain and cause sleep."

"What did I say to make you afraid of me?"

She decided to tell the truth and see what he made of it. "You are working for someone important. Do you remember who that is?"

"I am not sure," he said.

"And that is why I am afraid of you."

"Because I might harm you?"

Her laughter held no humor. "No, Clay. You proved today that you would not harm me. But this person you work for, can you prove to me that he has not sent you on a mission to harm someone else?"

When he said nothing, she rose and walked away.

"Lightning strike, sir."

Clay faced the man, standing tall and trying not to sway. Through sheer will, he convinced the room to cease spinning so he could look Jean Paul Valmont in the eye.

"So my granddaughter said." He nodded to the two wooden chairs flanking the fireplace and indicated they should sit. "She is also convinced that while she is certain that she knows who you are, you do not. At least not completely."

"I have some recollections, although I am not certain which are authentic and which are not."

The well-dressed man gave Clay a sweeping glance and then shrugged. "You were quite ill. I saw this myself. Sophie and Ellis took good care of you, or you would not have lasted the first day."

So he had nearly died more than once this week. Sobering news, although given what happened yesterday during the fire, his life must still hold some purpose. If only he knew what that purpose might be.

"You saved Ellis's life."

The simple statement might have come from the man seated beside him, but perhaps that was the answer to his question of purpose. "I did what was necessary," Clay said.

Mr. Valmont seemed to consider the statement for a moment, and then he nodded. "Whatever else you know or do not know about yourself, you have the heart and mind of a hero. There is a concern here, though, regarding your allegiance. I don't suppose you recall with any certainty just which side of our current conflict with Mexico you're on?"

Clay knew he could lie, but he would not. "With any certainty, no."

His companion leaned forward and rested his elbows on his knees. "And therein lies the trouble."

"And the reason your granddaughter fears me."

"Yes." Dark eyes narrowed. "So it appears we are at an impasse. You do not know what you do not know." He paused. "Do you recognize Claiborne Gentry as the name you were given by your parents at birth?"

"I do," he said. "Though I did not at first. Now I have a recollection of signing that name to documents that were important. Unfortunately, I have no idea what those documents were."

"So your memories are returning, then."

"Possibly, though I did first hear the name when your granddaughter informed me of it." Clay paused to search for a way to adequately describe what happened. "The name didn't seem to fit then. Now I know it is my name."

"Good. Well, that is progress. Perhaps the mind is healing as the body heals." He sat back. "Would it surprise you to know that you're a military man?"

"Nothing surprises me right now," Clay said.

"A Grey newly arrived from New Orleans as of the day before you were found on my son's property in his neighbor's pirogue. I doubt you can explain anything of how you got from a cot at the fort to that pirogue, but that is apparently what happened. Ellis knows you to be a Grey because she watched you sign the roster and the certificate of Texas citizenship herself."

Clay turned over the statements in his mind and came up with a question. "What is a Grey?"

"New Orleans Greys, son," Mr. Valmont said. "First Company of Texian Volunteers from New Orleans. Here to fight for the side of the Texian army."

"And I am one of them?" Clay let this news settle in. "So my allegiance is to Texas."

Valmont nodded. "Based on what you signed at Velasco, it is."

"Then that is answer enough for me." He shifted position and winced. "And you're certain my wounds were not received in battle?"

"Anything is possible in these uncertain times. But there was no battle on the day you were injured. An ambush, perhaps, but on the night you were shot, your comrades were back at the fort awaiting transport to Columbia the next day."

"I see." He thought on this a moment. "Because I had no reason to be out, there are questions as to my reasons for leaving my post."

"There are." He shrugged. "A mystery that I hope you'll be able to solve very soon. Now, just one more thing. Do you speak English?"

Clay frowned. "I thought I was."

Valmont shook his head. "Son, every word that's come out of your mouth this morning has been in the Acadian language. I've just said that to you in Acadian French, but now I am speaking English. Can you tell the difference?"

"No," Clay managed.

Valmont gave him an even look. "Ellis says you speak both. The man she fears, however, he speaks English."

"I don't see how that's possible," Clay said. "I just talk and. . ." He scrubbed at his face and then groaned at the jolt of pain the action caused. "I cannot account for any of this. However, you have my word that your granddaughter has nothing to fear from me."

"I don't think she does either."

"Your family has been more than kind to me. Under the circumstances, I think it would be best if I went back to my company, but you have my word that I will send payment for whatever it has cost to care for me."

Valmont chuckled. "First off, I doubt you'll catch them with that shoulder still needing care. And if you could catch them, they'd likely send you home as unfit for battle, don't you think?" He paused as if to let that statement sink in. "And where exactly is home?"

"I have no idea."

"Exactly—so you do see the dilemma."

"I do. Perhaps I could work off my care, then? I am not the man I was before I was shot, but I am still strong and willing to work."

"I believe you're willing to work, but your strength is something you'll need to regain." He let out a long breath. "However, my son left women, children, and an old man in charge of the chores when he and his eldest son went off to war. If they can find work they're able to do here, then you can too."

"I would appreciate the chance to try," Clay said.

"Ellis won't be happy with me for giving you the chance," he said. "And I doubt Sophie will appreciate that the man who was abed for a week is suddenly up and around and being given chores." Valmont gave him a sideways look. "Did she happen to give you any of her sleeping medication?"

"I think that was mentioned," he said. "Why?"

"Because she keeps trying to ply it off on me to help me rest. I tried it once. Slept all night and half the next day. No wonder you're having trouble recalling things."

Clay chuckled. "I do feel more alert than I have in a while."

"Well, just don't let Ellis convince you to take any more of the vile concoction. It is excellent for keeping a man still when he is healing but terrible for allowing a man to get up and walk around or be of any use at all."

The perpetual fog that had surrounded him for all those days in the barn made sense now. "Duly noted. I am a soldier." Clay paused. "I should also make plans for my return."

And for November 18. Whatever significance that date held, he felt strongly it was tied to his service as a Grey.

"Word was sent when you were first found," Valmont said. "These things take time to reach the proper authorities. I expect a response soon."

Clay nodded. "I may not remember much, but I do recall that I had a purpose in joining the Greys."

Valmont gave him a sharp look. "And what was that purpose?"

Searching his mind, Clay finally shook his head. "I don't know."

"Right." He looked around the bedchamber and then back at Clay. "So the only question that remains is how fit are you, and when do you want to start working around here?"

"I think the only way to know how fit I am is to give me a chore and see if I can master it. As to when, I think now is a good time."

"Very well." Mr. Valmont rose, and Clay did the same. "I will speak to Ellis and let her know I am satisfied that she has no cause to fear you or your motives. Just one warning: at the first hint that I am wrong about you or that you are not a man whose intentions in this war are in agreement with mine, I will see that you are stopped, and that will be without regard to your life."

"I understand," he said.

"Good. Then we are in agreement."

Clay stuck out his hand, and Valmont shook it. "We are."

A moment later, Clay swayed. Valmont caught him. "Perhaps tomorrow is a better day to begin those chores."

He smiled. "Yes, perhaps."

"Stay here and make yourself at home," he said. "There are books in the trunk if you find yourself bored. Just try and stay away from Ellis as best you can today."

"Thank you. I will."

CHAPTER 14

Ellis stepped back from the door just in time to avoid being slammed by it. She held a dustrag in her hand, affecting the task of dusting the doorframe.

"Come," Grandfather Valmont told her. "You've heard all of it, so that will keep me from having to repeat."

"Not all," she protested.

He lifted one dark brow. "Dare I ask how much you missed?"

She laughed. "How can I even answer that?"

Her grandfather shook his head. "Well, child, the price of eavesdropping is that I will assume whatever you did not hear is something that was not meant for your ears in the first place. However, I will tell you that starting tomorrow, Mr. Gentry will be taking on some of the chores here."

She looked up sharply but said nothing. He had already heard all her protests on that subject.

"You're wondering why I would allow him this freedom with only women and children here?"

"I was, actually." Ellis paused to consider how best to air her doubts without disrespecting her grandfather. "I understand you've made your decision, but don't you think Mama should have some say in the matter?" she finally asked.

"Your mother is not here," he said in that matter-of-fact manner he took when a decision was final. "I have forbidden her to return for the time being. She is exhausted and needs a rest. What? You look surprised."

"That she is exhausted? No. That is obvious. I'm just surprised she actually obeyed your order."

"She saw the logic in my argument," he told her. "As will you."

Ellis shook her head. "Me? What do you mean?"

"Come with me."

Grandfather Valmont linked arms with Ellis and led her outside onto the porch between the buildings. The air was a bit cooler this morning, and the once-welcome breeze that drifted through in early August was less welcome in late October.

Ellis shrugged into her rebozo, shivering as much from the chill of the air as from the scent of burned wood that it contained. The same scent that permeated her scarf and her best dress.

Her grandfather moved toward the edge of the porch to the place where Papa liked to stand to survey his land. *"Land is the only thing worth dying for"*—that was what Papa used to say. *"When a man owns land, especially a piece of this wild Texas land, then he owns something worth keeping."*

Worth fighting for.

Grandfather motioned for Ellis to join him. "It is good news about Mr. Jim, yes? Sophie said that bump on the head might have been fatal."

"It is very good news," Ellis said. "I hope he is well enough to return to work soon. Is that selfish? I've missed him, and I know Mama has too."

When Grandfather did not immediately respond, Ellis looked up to see an expression on his face that gave her cause for concern. "What is it? Is there more to Mr. Jim's injury than you're telling me? He isn't coming back, is he?"

"Oh, he will come back," Grandfather Valmont said. "Of this I am certain. In fact, I believe he has negotiated a pay increase and has convinced one of his grandsons to join him here for the winter."

"Well, that is good news." Ellis relaxed her worries. "An extra set of hands will be most welcome."

"Speaking of that, I don't think we finished our discussion on Mr. Gentry. I will be supervising any chores he is given. Trusting the man and allowing him to be alone with my granddaughter are two very different things. He will work as he can manage it here until he can return to the Greys. That is the offer I have made to him just now, and he is in agreement."

"Thank you," she said. "But aren't you needed at the shipyard?"

"Yes, but I have more important work here."

Ellis snuggled into his embrace. "Again, thank you."

"You may not thank me when you hear what I have done," he told her.

Ellis gave him a questioning look. "What do you mean?"

"I have sent your mother and the boys to New Orleans. They left this morning."

"I don't believe you," Ellis said with a gasp as she nearly stumbled backward into the porch railing. "That is. . ." Words failed. Finally she managed, "Impossible," on an exhale of breath.

Grandfather Valmont caught her and chuckled. "No, I didn't suppose you would, but it is true. You see, Sophie confided something in me that I am now going to share with you. It is the substance of the conversation we had last week when I came to see the injured soldier for myself. Do you remember when we left to converse alone over coffee?"

"Vaguely," Ellis said. What could possibly have convinced Mama to leave Texas? Not now. Not with Papa and Thomas not yet returned from the skirmish at Goliad. "Is this some secret I am supposed to keep?"

"Hardly," he said, "though I suppose it has been a secret your mother kept until she admitted it to me. You see, there is to be a new addition to the Valmont family in the spring."

The breath went out of her. "Oh."

Then came the realization of what he said. Of what he meant. Of why

Mama sent her over to attend the birth of Lyla and Jonah's child.

She wanted to give her experience in case she was called on to attend Mama's birth. Ellis shook her head. "Mama is going to have a baby?"

His smile was broad and quick. "She is."

Then another thought occurred. "Does Papa know? That is, did he know before he left?"

"He did not, nor did your mother realize her condition then," Grandfather Valmont said. "Else I doubt very much that he would have gone off and left Sophie here to take care of you children and the farm alone, even for the cause of his beloved Texas."

That did make sense. Mama leaving Texas did as well. Life had not been easy since Papa and Thomas left, and war was a constant worry.

Still, Ellis found it hard to believe, especially at Mama's age. And Papa was surely close to forty by now, wasn't he?

When she told her grandfather that, he chuckled. "Take my advice and do not mention her advanced age when you next speak to your mama. A simple word of congratulations will do nicely."

Ellis leaned against the porch railing and looked out on the property that unfolded before her. "I still don't see how you got Mama to go so easily and so quickly."

"She's known for a while that I have been determined to get my family out of Texas to safety in New Orleans until this war is over. We've fought right here in Velasco just a few years ago, and I think we will soon be fighting here again, so when Sophie confided in me about the baby, I knew this was God's way of giving an old man an answer to his prayers."

Ellis shook her head. "How did you manage it, though? Mama can be a bit. . ." She shrugged. "Well, stubborn."

"I'm a shipbuilder, child. I know every vessel that goes in and out of here, what kind they are and where they're going. When Sophie and the little ones arrived at my home with Mr. Jim, I figured this was my chance, so I booked passage for her before she ever knew what was happening.

Then I told her about it and dared her to tell me that my son wouldn't have done the same thing."

"And she couldn't deny it."

"She certainly could not, but your mother drove a hard bargain. There were conditions to her getting on that steamboat this morning."

"Oh, I am sure there were," Ellis said as she tried to take hold of the idea that Mama and the boys were gone from Texas.

"She wants the trunk with Maribel's books in it, as well as a list of other things." He looked down at her and patted his jacket pocket. "I have the list here, and together we can gather everything up. Her most important condition, however, is that I make certain you also relocate to New Orleans until your father and brother return. I assured her that Mr. Jim's daughter had already agreed to act as chaperone for your trip. You remember Rosalie, don't you?"

"Yes, she is a very nice lady, but I assumed I would. . ." She shook her head. "Actually I hadn't thought what I would do if Mama wasn't here, because I cannot imagine what that is even like. This is my home, but I wouldn't mind coming to stay with you until Papa and Thomas come home."

"Let your aunts spoil you in New Orleans, child. You'll be the belle of every ball and you'll very much enjoy it. Mr. Jim and I will see to things here in Texas for now."

Ellis swiped at a tear shimmering in the corner of her eye. "I don't want to be spoiled. I just want my family back together right here in our home." She paused to lean against her grandfather's broad shoulder once more. "I hate war."

"As do I, child," he said softly. "But you forget that war or not, your mother needs you."

Ellis returned a few hours later to change Clay's bandages and add the familiar foul-smelling poultice to his wounds. She was quiet, unnaturally so, and an air of sadness surrounded her.

Something had happened since he last saw her.

When she finished her work and stepped away, Clay decided to try to coax a smile from her. "You're just making me stink so you won't want to be around me so much."

Her brows rose and then she shook her head. So much for that feeble attempt at humor. As he watched her meticulously return her herbs and bandages to her basket, he decided to try again, this time without using humor.

"Something has happened," he said, causing her busy hands to pause. "Do you want to talk about it?"

She whirled around to face him. "Why would I want to do that?" Then she spied his choice of reading material, a book about pirates he found in the trunk beside the bed. "Put that back where you found it. That is not yours to read."

"I am sorry," he said gently as he lifted the lid and settled the book carefully back inside. "Your grandfather told me to make myself at home, so I just assumed that I, well. . .again, I am sorry."

When Mr. Valmont requested he stay away from Ellis today, perhaps it was because he expected she might be in a foul mood. "Did you get bad news from your grandfather?"

Crimson flooded her face. Ellis appeared unable to speak for a moment. "Please do not tell me that my grandfather confided in you before he told me."

"Maybe he thought I would forget?"

"Oh! You are impossible." She snatched up the basket, upsetting her work and causing the bandages and some of the herbs to scatter.

"It was a joke."

"It wasn't funny," she snapped.

He bent down to grab a bandage as it rolled to a stop against the trunk. The effort cost him in a pain that took his breath away, but Clay refused to allow it to show.

"I have few memories, so why would he think I would be able to re-member anything. . ." He paused as Ellis knelt down to scoop the herbs into the basket. "Never mind. I'm not much for telling jokes."

"You're terrible at it, actually."

"Am I?" he said, feigning innocence while he waited for his shoulder to cease its throbbing. "I don't recall."

Ellis looked up and met his gaze. And then she laughed.

He tossed a roll of bandages at her and then winced. Unfortunately, the expression did not escape Ellis's green eyes.

"You're still in pain." She rose and picked up the basket. "You shouldn't have done what you did yesterday. I fear you've harmed yourself."

"Don't you think that fire would have harmed you worse than any-thing I could have done in making sure you escaped it?"

He hadn't intended to snap at her. The damage he did likely was out of his own stupidity. He could have just helped her to her feet. Could have somehow released her tangled dress from the burning hinges.

Instead he had to play the hero and carry her out of there.

Clay closed his eyes and allowed the memory to return. Though he had few enough memories, this was one he knew would have stood out even if he'd had a lifetime of recollections left in his brain.

The green-eyed woman in his arms, her head against his chest as he saved her life. . . Yes. That was a memory he would never lose.

When he opened his eyes, she was standing just inches away. Her fingers were probing the bandage she had just replaced. "Tell me if this hurts."

He leaned forward just enough to smell the scent of fire still lingering in her hair. She'd changed into a dress that hadn't been streaked with soot or torn, but it was of a similar style and color.

"Why do you dress like the Mexican women?"

Her fingers stilled. "My clothing is practical for the climate and easily obtained at the market." She went back to her work as if he hadn't spoken.

"That scarf of yours was handy."

Again her fingers stilled. "Rebozo," she corrected. "And yes, it has many uses."

"And pockets, apparently," he commented.

"Which also have many uses." She stopped her examination and looked down at him. "Have you felt anything that hurt?"

He had, but he'd ignored it. "Not bad enough to complain," he said. "Why?"

Ellis shook her head. "I'm worried that you're undoing what my mother and I have done in repairing your shoulder wound. The leg and head wounds are healing nicely, but that one concerns me. I have to wonder if I have allowed you to skip the sleeping medication too soon. If you were less active, there would be less use of that shoulder."

He wanted to tell her right then and there that he would never take another one of those herbs she gave him to make him sleep. Ever.

Instead he offered a change of topic as she stepped back and indicated that he should cover his shoulder once more. "Why would it bother you that your grandfather might have confided in me?"

It was an idiotic thing to say given the way she reacted earlier, but the comment did the trick. Her frown had returned, but at least the topic had been successfully changed.

"Why indeed?" she said in that tone women used when they were at a loss to describe the level of disdain they held for whatever they'd just been told.

Clay leaned back against the pillows and let out a long breath. The change of positions did ease his shoulder pain some. He should have let her fuss her way right out the door so he could get some rest.

Oh, but she was so pretty—with that color in her cheeks and that expression that spoke fire—that he didn't want her to leave just yet. So he said the first stupid thing that occurred to him.

"He's a nice man, your grandfather. We got along fine."

That did it.

"I suppose he told you everything, then." At Clay's casual shrug, she continued. "About New Orleans, and my mama, and the baby too?"

"Baby?" His attention shifted to her midsection and then back up to her face.

"Not mine," she snapped.

"Oh."

"What are you smiling at?"

"Nothing. I. . ." He shrugged. "So, as long as we're talking about what we know, I would like to know what I said to you while I was under the influence of your sleeping potions."

"That was a medication, not a potion," she said with more than a little defensiveness in her voice. "And it was used only for the purpose of—"

"Rendering me quiet and unconscious so you could hold me prisoner," he interjected.

"Keeping you still so you could heal," she finished. "Keeping you quiet was merely an additional benefit."

"And yet I still said things, didn't I?" Her expression let him know it was true. "You know things I have forgotten."

She let out a long breath. "You said things that made no sense, Clay. You were in pain and suffering from fevers. There is nothing in all of your ramblings that I can say for certain I believe is true."

"But you know that the date of November 18th is important."

She gathered up her basket and walked to the door without a backward glance. In Ellis Valmont's lack of an answer, Clay had his answer.

CHAPTER 15

Supper that evening was made up of the last of the vegetables Mama had put away and a mess of fish that Grandfather Valmont caught that afternoon. Ellis had just set the table for two when the door opened and Clay Gentry stepped inside.

Clay was taller than she remembered, taller and leaner but with a breadth of shoulder that hadn't been evident until now. He wore one of Thomas's buckskin shirts with a pair of patched and mended trousers that had to have belonged to Papa.

It took a moment to realize those trousers were tucked into a pair of bloodstained boots that could only have been the ones Clay was wearing when he was found. Now they were shined and polished, a feat that must have taken him most of the afternoon.

His dark hair appeared damp as if he'd just come from a bath. No one would believe this man had been at death's door a week ago. Only the slight paleness to his complexion gave any indication that he had been unwell.

She glanced down at the hat in his hand and recognized it as the hat the soldier had been wearing when he arrived. Likely it needed a good cleaning, unless he'd seen to that too.

Their gazes met and locked. "My apologies. I don't mean to interrupt."

"Come in and join us, Clay," Grandfather said. "You are welcome in this home until such time as you give me reason to say otherwise. I made that clear, didn't I?"

"I couldn't, sir." He tore his attention away from Ellis to focus on Grandfather Valmont, his hands now worrying that hat. "I would be obliged if I could get a fresh cup of coffee. I smelled it brewing in the summer kitchen but didn't want to take any without asking."

"Nonsense." Grandfather nodded to Ellis and then the cupboard. "Child, get this man a plate and a mug. And fetch that coffee off the stove too, please. He's got to be starved given what he's been through."

Clay winced, and Ellis wondered if it was from pain or from what her grandfather just said. "Thank you, sir, but I generally work for my supper."

Grandfather Valmont chuckled. "I reckon you respect your elders too, don't you, son?"

"I try to," he said, "at least best as I can recall."

"Well then," her grandfather said, "whether you used to or not, you can get started on it right now. You can respect your elder by taking a seat down there by my granddaughter at the end of the table and helping yourself to some supper. You might even pretend you're hungry and get seconds if you really want to make a good impression. Tomorrow you can earn your keep by starting on a list of chores long as my arm."

Clay looked reluctant. Knowing her grandfather, the soldier would be convinced, so Ellis slipped out the back door to head toward the summer kitchen. The air held the promise of a chill, though the wind had died down. Summer was well behind them, and the fall would soon turn to winter in this part of Texas.

Removing the coffee from the place in the chimney where it had been warming, she returned to the house to find Clay sitting at the table just as she expected. She poured coffee into three mugs and brought two to the table.

"So, Clay," her grandfather said, "I figure we'll start with our field hand Mack's jobs, and then once you can get those tasks mastered, I'll add more. There's a fellow we like a lot named Lucas who just took off on a trip with family. He and Mack are going to be hard to replace, but I am going to let you try." He spared Ellis a covert wink and then returned his attention to Clay. "How does that sound?"

Ellis stifled a grin as she handed her grandfather his mug.

Clay nodded, though he did look a little concerned. "I'd say that's fair," was his quick response. "Like I said, I earn my keep."

"Good man," Grandfather Valmont said. "If you're intent on earning, I'll certainly put you to work."

The poor man thought he was about to get a lengthy list of difficult jobs instead of taking over for an absent six-year-old. Ellis almost took pity on him. Instead she set the mug down on the table in front of him and then returned to the cupboard for her own.

Because Grandfather Valmont insisted Clay be seated at the other end of the table, the two men spent the evening talking across her. Had Ellis intended to join in the conversation, which she decidedly did not, then she would have had to turn her head back and forth just to speak with both of them.

Thus, she ignored the men's conversation of weather and cleaning leather and such to think about the verse she was attempting to memorize from the Psalms. Though that was her intention, she couldn't help but occasionally slip a glance out of the corner of her eye at their guest.

Had she seen him walking down the street, she might have noticed him. Indeed, of all the men she saw sign the roster that morning, his was the only face she could recollect. Never in a million years would she have expected that the handsome New Orleans Grey who signed on as a brand-new citizen of the Republic of Texas would end up sitting at her mama's table chatting away with Grandfather Valmont.

And to think she had actually entertained the thought that Clay Gentry was mute. Of course, that was long before she heard his fevered ramblings and began wondering if he was friend or a foe.

She still wasn't certain which it was. But then, Clay probably didn't know either, not unless his memories had returned and he just hadn't bothered to tell her.

Ellis considered the possibility. Yes, Mama had said the lack of recall could be temporary. She glanced over at Clay and found him staring at her.

"Ellis," Grandfather Valmont said, "did you hear me?"

She shifted her attention to her grandfather as heat rose in her cheeks. "No, I'm sorry. I had my mind on something else."

"So I see."

The heat rose higher. She refused to allow even a glance at their guest. All she could do was hope he hadn't noticed. "What were you saying?"

"I was telling Clay to be watchful while walking around the property. I saw fresh bobcat tracks down by the river this morning, and I wouldn't be surprised if there's more than one of them. Best keep a weapon on you if you're going out to gather herbs tomorrow."

She shook her head. "How did you know I was going to do that?"

He shrugged. "Your mama always did her gathering on Wednesdays. I figure you're doing the same since you're taking over for her."

She smiled. True, she had planned on filling the emptying stores of herbs before cold weather took them all, but that had nothing to do with the day of the week. Rather, it got her out of the house and away from the men for the day, a much-needed respite given the events of the last week.

"Yes, of course," she said.

Then a thought occurred. So it was Wednesday already. How had that happened? The days had all run together since the soldier landed on the riverbank. She hadn't given a thought to anything related to a day of the week since then.

Which meant she'd missed Sunday services too.

Mama had been kind not to mention it. Or perhaps she'd done what they sometimes did and held church right there in the parlor with Mama playing the out-of-tune piano that she insisted be hauled here from their home in New Orleans.

Either way, Ellis realized she was due for some time with the Lord. All the better to go out tomorrow looking for herbs. She would bring her book of psalms and hold a little church service of her own right out there.

She returned to her meal and ate in silence. When the men were done, they took their coffee out on the porch while Ellis washed the dishes and then slipped upstairs. With Clay occupying her parents' bedchamber, Grandfather Valmont had insisted Ellis move into a room upstairs at the far end of the house for propriety's sake. He would take her bedchamber so that he could keep watch over the soldier.

Or at least that was the reason he gave Ellis. She figured it was more likely that Grandfather wanted to keep watch over her and know when she came and went from the upstairs of the house.

She settled into a bed nearest the window at the front of the house, tucking the quilts up to her chin. For the first night in more than a week, her eyes fell shut before she'd completed her prayers. After rousing herself enough to finish her lengthy prayer list, and adding a prayer for safe travels for Mama and the little ones and a thank-you to the Lord for her new baby brother or sister, Ellis finally settled onto the pillow.

Outside her window, the murmur of male voices drifted up like woodsmoke on a winter evening, lulling her to sleep.

Apparently Mack the farmhand had a list of chores that even a man with a limp and a hole in his shoulder could complete. Gathering eggs had almost been his undoing on his third consecutive day of completing the list, however. Clay stepped into the chicken coop only to be confronted with a chicken snake set on finding its breakfast.

The snake dispatched, he had finished the job and delivered the eggs to the summer kitchen. There he spied Jean Paul Valmont surveying the ruins of the small barn and went over to join him.

"Looks like it went up pretty quick," he said when Clay stopped beside him. "I'd say it's God's own miracle that you and my granddaughter weren't harmed."

"I wish I remembered more of the details clearly, but I was still trying to get over whatever the ladies had given me for sleep."

"I do understand," he said. "But maybe you'll remember more than you think once you get to talking about it."

"All right," he said slowly. "What I do recall is that there was a lot of lightning and thunder. And a hard rain. Beating on the roof until you could hardly hear yourself think. Might even have been hail at some point."

"We had hail down in Velasco. I was afraid we'd get boats damaged. The Lord was kind and that didn't happen." He paused. "Go on. What else do you remember?"

"Then there was a flash of light that looked almost blue that went down the wall opposite where they were keeping me. Next thing I know the place is on fire and we're trying to save ourselves."

Valmont glanced at him. "Ellis told me her dress caught on the hinge. Said she was stuck with the fire coming right at her."

"I reckon she was," he said.

"Said you hauled her from right here"—he gestured to the pile of rubble then turned toward the house—"to over there. How do you figure that happened, because I'm trying to sort it out and cannot."

"I picked her up and carried her," he said. "It wasn't far."

He gave Clay a sweeping glance and then shook his head. "Son, you were like as dead a week ago and couldn't stand up straight without falling over after a few minutes just yesterday. How do you figure you just 'picked her up and carried her'?"

Clay looked into the old man's eyes and gave him the only answer he knew to be true. "Because I was supposed to."

Valmont nodded and then looked away. His eyes seemed misty, though he said nothing.

After a moment, Clay cleared his throat. "I got Mack's chores done and killed a chicken snake in the process."

"Good man. I've been after that snake. Mack won't go in if there's a snake inside, so I'm glad it was you who went in there this morning."

"Sorry, sir, but it would have been hard to miss," he said, wondering just why a man like Mack was still in their employ when he didn't have much in the way of responsibilities. He couldn't even kill a snake?

"Need a rest yet?"

"No, sir," he said, though he probably did.

"Ellis left without her breakfast this morning. Why don't you go find her and see if she's hungry? Bring her a few of those boiled eggs I saved on the sideboard."

He nodded and then paused. "Sir, I have noticed that you're the one who does the cooking around here. First the fish and then the eggs. It is probably none of my business, but doesn't your granddaughter know how to cook?"

The old man chuckled. "Of course she does, but I enjoy it more than she does. Why? Are you worried she'll starve her husband when she marries?"

It was his turn to smile. "I doubt a man who marries her will be worried about whether she will starve him. He'd have much bigger problems than an empty belly if he were to take that lady on as a wife."

Chapter 16

As soon as the words were out, Clay cringed. "I'm sorry. That's not what I meant. It's just that she's. . ." He shook his head. "I can't even define it, but I can say that Ellis Valmont is someone I will never forget, and that's coming from a man who can't remember most of his life."

Valmont patted Clay's shoulder. "Trust me," he said. "I know what you mean. You should have met her great-grandmother." He paused. "And yet my father survived, as will whatever man is privileged enough to be allowed close enough to Ellis Valmont to wed her."

"I'm sure she's got plenty of choices."

"To be certain," he said. "But that girl is stubborn and knows what she wants. So far it hasn't been any of several dozen suitors. And counting." He looked at Clay as if sizing him up. "I wouldn't get my sights set on her if I were you. She's not hunting for a husband, so if you're aiming to think that direction, you ought to think again."

"What?" Clay shook his head. "Me? No. That's not at all what I was thinking. Look, I am just going to go get those boiled eggs and see if I can find her. Any suggestions on where she might be about now?"

"Try north of the smokehouse up in the thicket. Her mama has a little patch of herbs that she keeps up there behind a fence. Says the deer stay out of them up there. If she's not there, then I'd head east from that point. She helped a lady named Lyla give birth last week, so she will probably go see her and Jonah while she's out and see how things are going there. Take a walking stick with you, though. I'll fetch one."

"North of the smokehouse or east to Lyla and Jonah's home," he repeated as he slung a rifle over his shoulder and accepted the walking stick, then bid the older man goodbye. His speed was excruciatingly slow compared to the swift pace he would have preferred as he set off on his mission to feed the herbalist.

Or was she a healer? Yes, that's what he'd heard her call herself, although where he was from she would have merely been called a doctor.

Clay froze. Where he was from? And exactly where was that? An image tried to rise in his mind, something with trees and a mountain ridge off in the distance.

Definitely not New Orleans.

And yet Ellis had told him he was Claiborne William Andre Gentry from New Orleans, and she was certain of it. She had declared she'd seen him sign the roster herself, hadn't she? That much he thought he remembered.

The image of the hills, however, felt very real. What else could he recall? Clay stood very still under the pecan tree and begged another memory to rise.

Nothing.

He tried again and failed, so he set off down the path, leaning heavily on his walking stick and stopping frequently. Finally he heard what sounded like *snip, snip, snip.*

Clay followed the sound until he found Ellis halfway up a tree balancing a basket on her elbow and reaching for something hidden in the branches.

"I hope you've got a plan for how you'll be getting down from there," he called. "I doubt I can repeat the adventure from the other day and carry you home again."

Her laughter carried across the distance between them and made him smile. A moment later, she scurried down the tree and landed on the ground with ease.

"You've done that before," he said as he paused to catch his breath.

"Since I was a child," she told him. "I've been teaching Mack and Lucas in anticipation of the day I no longer want to be the one climbing, but so far only Lucas has taken to it. Mack gets a little distracted."

"About this Mack fellow," he said. "I know that many of the men have gone off to fight, so that would limit the ones who are available to work. However, I hope you don't pay Mack much."

Ellis covered her smile as she walked toward him. "We don't pay him at all, actually."

He nodded. "That explains why you keep him employed here. Took me longer the first couple of days, but today I completed all of his chores in less than an hour. Did you know that according to your grandfather, when Mack goes into the henhouse, he leaves the snake if there's one in there? What kind of farmhand is that?"

She reached him and allowed her smile to show. "The kind of farmhand who just had his sixth birthday."

"Wait." Clay shook his head. "Mack is a child?"

She laughed as she pressed past him to walk down the path. "Mack is my youngest brother. He loves to gather the eggs, but we don't trust him with the snakes yet."

"I'd say not." Clay turned to follow and then had to stop to catch his breath. "So this Lucas fellow?"

"Also my brother," she called over her shoulder. "He's eight, going on nine he would tell you, and is missing his front teeth, but he does everything I tell him to do without question."

"This is beginning to make sense now."

She paused and turned around. "What do you mean?"

Clay began walking toward her, leaning heavily on the walking stick.

"Your grandfather doesn't think I'm well enough to do actual chores around here so he's giving me child's work."

"I might argue with you, but you look terrible right now," she told him. "Put your bag and rifle down and let's rest."

The bag. He'd forgotten all about the reason for following Ellis. When she'd settled on a grassy spot beside the path, he eased himself down and prayed he could stand back up again when the time came.

"Your breakfast," he said as he handed her the bag. "Your grandfather said you left without eating."

"I suppose I did." She opened the bag and retrieved the tin to remove a boiled egg. "Have some," she told him.

Eggs were not his favorite, but Clay picked one up to be polite. "How many did he think you would eat?" he asked as he counted at least ten eggs remaining.

"Grandfather always cooks for a crowd. Too many years of living in New Orleans where any number of family members could drop by at a moment's notice, I suppose."

Clay found himself at a loss for words. He had no idea if he had a similar story or if his family was smaller. Perhaps even nonexistent.

There was just a blank where that memory should have been.

He turned his attention to Ellis. She wore a more traditional day dress today, made of pale green cotton and sprigged with yellow flowers. Her hair had been captured into a thick braid that hung down her back.

"Something wrong?" she asked him.

He swiveled to face her, rolling the boiled egg around in his palm. "During the time I had fevers, did I ever talk about my family?"

She looked at a spot off in the distance and then returned her attention to him as a warm breeze blew past. "I don't think so. Why? Did you remember something?"

Clay toyed with a blade of grass and then tossed it away. "Possibly. I have this memory—at least I think it is a memory—of green hills and trees with a house down in a valley and. . ." He shrugged. "Well, that's about it. I don't know where it is, but I feel certain it isn't New Orleans."

"No," she said with a chuckle. "There are none of those things in New Orleans. Well, there are houses, of course, but that's where the similarity ends." Ellis paused. "Do you truly think this image you've seen in your mind could be your home?"

"I do," he said. "Although I cannot tell you why I would think so. It makes no sense, and yet it feels like it's supposed to be my home."

Ellis pressed an errant strand of hair away from her face. "Maybe your memories are returning."

"That is possible." He let out a long breath. "It is frustrating not to know what I don't know. If that makes sense."

"It does." Ellis appeared ready to say something more, but then she shook her head.

"I would like to earn your trust," he told her.

Her gaze jolted toward him. "Why?"

He affected an innocent look. "Because I like you. I mean, now that you aren't forcing that sleeping potion down my throat, that is."

"Sleeping medication," she corrected, though he thought he noticed the slightest twinkle in those green eyes.

"Whatever you call it, I think that foul-tasting medication either helped me remember or caused me to forget." He plucked another blade of grass and glanced at her. "What do you think? Did I happen to say anything that might fill in where my memories are blank?"

Immediately he knew he had struck a nerve. Though they had danced all around the subject before, there was no doubt she had just answered in the affirmative.

Ellis had made much of the fact that she did not trust him. Was this just a way for her to deflect the fact that it was he who should not trust her? Whatever side he was on in this conflict—if indeed that was what brought him to Texas via the Greys—was it possible that the flame-haired beauty might be on the opposite side?

He would certainly never find out this way. With little time left before the day of his mysterious meeting, Clay decided to take a different approach.

"You know what?" he said as he stood and dusted himself off and then offered his hand to help her up. "I think you and I have just about exhausted this topic. If I said anything or if I didn't, neither of those things matter right this minute."

As he expected, Ellis looked confused. She picked up her basket and then returned her attention to Clay. "No?"

"No," he said as casually as he could manage while he retrieved his rifle and slung it back over his shoulder. "If the Lord wants me to remember so that I can be where He wants me to be, then He will make that happen. In the meantime, I have work to do here." Clay paused to offer a smile. "Apparently I am about to graduate to doing the chores of a seven-year-old."

"Eight," she corrected with a grin.

"Yes, that's right. Eight. So I might need to get in a few more days of healing before I can manage that."

Her expression went serious. "Are you having any more pain?"

He was, but he wouldn't admit to it. Nor would Clay tell her that he felt weak as a kitten after walking just from the farmhouse out here to find her.

He'd had enough of being treated like a sick man to last a lifetime. And although he did have an ulterior motive for changing his tune and ceasing the conversation about his missing memories, he was also ready to think of himself as whole again and not in need of being cared for by a woman.

"I'm fine," he told her.

"And you've been changing the bandage on your shoulder and leg?"

"Every night after I wash up."

Finally he'd had enough. "Ellis," he said firmly, "change the subject. I am healing in my body and am tired of talking about whether I'm going to be healing in my mind or not."

Her expression told him he'd spoken too harshly. "Sore subject," he said gently. "Pardon the pun. So why don't you tell me what was so important that you were climbing a tree and risking your pretty little neck to cut it?"

Had Clay Gentry just called her pretty?

As she fell into step beside Clay, Ellis launched into an explanation of the supplejack vine and its usefulness in taming coughs and strengthening the blood. As she spoke, she was aware that Clay appeared less attentive to her words and more concerned about something behind her.

His hand traveled slowly to the stock of his rifle and remained there. Far from a casual gesture, it appeared he had gone on the defensive. But against what?

"Is something out there?" she said as she glanced behind her to see nothing other than foliage that crowded the path through the woods.

"Ellis," he said slowly, his voice even. "Come stand behind me, please."

"Why are you speaking like that? What is—"

He hauled her behind him in one swift, firm move and then drew his rifle.

"Is it the bobcat?" she whispered.

Rather than respond, he touched his index finger to his lips to silence her. "Stay behind me."

"Come out," he shouted. When nothing happened, Clay made the demand again.

"Clay," she finally said, "if you saw someone out there and they don't speak Acadian French, they aren't going to know what you're saying."

"I'm not speaking French," he snapped.

"You are," she whispered again. "Say this: Come out."

He repeated her words. This time the command came out in perfect English. At her nod, he smiled.

A rustling in the brush not far from where they had just been sitting caught her attention. Clay backed up until they were hidden in the brush.

"Be very still," he said softly.

"You're still speaking English," she said with a grin.

Then a shot rang out, shattering the bark of a sweet gum tree just behind her. Ellis dove to the ground and stifled a scream.

"Take cover over there," he told her as he nodded toward the depths of the thicket. "Stay down low. Do you have a pistol?"

Heart racing, Ellis retrieved the pistol from her skirt pocket and showed it to Clay. "In case I had to shoot the bobcat."

He glanced around then returned his attention to Ellis. "It's not a bobcat this time. Be ready to shoot anyone who isn't me or your grandfather."

She nodded even as she prayed she would not have to do as he asked. Time seemed to stand still, and every noise in the forest became amplified. Something crawled across her leg, but she crouched down stock-still and refused to move.

A hawk screeched overhead, and Ellis gasped. " 'With long life will I satisfy him,' " she whispered as she quoted the last line of Psalm 91. "Let me have a long life, please, Lord. I promise I won't waste it."

The crack of a rifle rang out, echoing across the forest. A man shouted something she couldn't quite understand. Then silence.

How long she crouched there with no idea whether Clay was alive or dead, Ellis had no idea. Finally she heard footsteps. With her pistol in hand, she lifted up just enough to see Clay hurrying toward her on the path.

She stood and shook the leaves off her dress with her free hand. Clay grasped her by the elbow.

"Come on," he demanded.

Ellis leaned down to reach for her basket but he pulled her back. "No time," he said. "Let's go."

She followed him through the woods, along the path that skirted the northernmost part of the Valmont property. They were almost home when she realized he had taken the long way.

There was only one reason a man in a hurry would do such a thing. "You're avoiding the clearing, aren't you?"

Ignoring her, Clay kept walking. He had slowed his pace to match hers, this much Ellis knew, and so she hurried as best she could. Still, she was winded by the time the house came into view—remarkable considering Clay's recent brush with death. Who was out there who would cause pain and weariness to fade for speed's sake?

For her sake too. Like once before. . .

At the edge of the clearing, Clay grasped her elbow. "Walk normally. I don't want anyone who might be watching to know you're aware of them. However, here's the path I want you to take."

He described a trek that involved going from the forest to the pecan tree and then around the large barn and chicken coop to reach the summer kitchen. "I will be right behind you, but don't look back. Just know I will be there. From the kitchen, we will walk into the house together."

"Kitchen!" Ellis shook her head. "We forgot the eggs."

Clay sighed. "That is the least of our concerns."

"Why? Who did you shoot?" she demanded.

"Not now," he said. "Wait until I give the signal and then go." She frowned but did as he told her. "And remember I am right behind you."

She nodded and then smiled. "Oh, and Clay?"

"Yes?" he said as he checked the ammunition in his rifle.

"You may not realize this, but everything you've said since you yelled in the woods has been in English."

"Good to know," he responded as he glanced around and then

returned his attention to her. "But can we discuss this later?"

She smiled. "Count on it."

With Clay right behind her, Ellis hurried forward to pause at each place along the route to the house. As soon as he gave the nod, she walked as casually as she could to the next agreed meeting place. Finally they arrived at the summer kitchen.

There Clay held his finger to his lips and then pressed past her to look out the door. After a few minutes he turned to face her.

"Who shot at me?"

She shook her head. "I have no idea. I was crouching down and couldn't see a thing."

His gaze darkened. "Not today, Ellis," he said as he gestured to his shoulder. "Who did this to me?"

Chapter 17

A gain," Ellis said, "I have no idea. You were already shot when we found you."

"But did I say anything that would indicate who did it?" His eyes narrowed. "And now is not the time to debate whether I am friend or foe. Both our lives as well as your grandfather's could depend on your answer."

"I do not know," she told him. "You said a lot of things, but I don't remember anything you said about the person who shot you. Although. . ."

She paused to decide whether to continue. For to continue would be to confide in him that she had taken notes on his fevered ramblings.

Something on the perimeter of the property caught his attention. After a moment, he returned his attention to Ellis. "Although what?"

"That you out there, Clay?" Grandfather Valmont called from somewhere inside the house. "You'd better have my granddaughter with you."

"Yes, sir, it's me. And yes, sir, I do."

"All right, then," he said. "Come on in. I'll cover you."

"Arm in arm this time," Clay told her. "I don't want to take any chances."

Ellis hurried inside with Clay practically attached to her at the hip. Once they reached the door, it flew open and Grandfather Valmont stepped back, his rifle at the ready.

"Did you get a look at them?" Clay asked him.

"Saw two of them," he said. "Not certain, but from what little I heard of them talking, I believe they were Mexican. Couldn't tell whether they were army or just men up to no good. However, the night you got shot, I followed a pair of men who sounded a whole lot like these two—speaking Spanish the same as they did and calling each other the same thing. I lost them when I had a coughing fit. Guess they heard me coming and scattered."

"If you'd taken the medications I left for you, you wouldn't have had that cough," Ellis told him.

"And if I had taken that awful sleeping stuff, I could have been shot in my bed."

"That isn't funny," she said.

"Didn't mean for it to be." He turned back to Clay. "So it's possible those two ran from me and right into you that night. That may be what got you shot, and it may be why they're back. Could be you they want."

"It's possible," Clay told him as Grandfather Valmont bolted the door. "I think I got one of them. He took off running, but I was more concerned about getting Ellis back here in one piece than I was going to look for him."

Her grandfather smiled at Clay. "Good man," he told him. "You made the right choice."

Clay responded with a curt nod. "If they come back, we'll be ready for them. In the meantime, I don't think Ellis ought to be out gathering plants."

"I agree. Or out any more than she needs to be, at least until we know what they're after, if anything."

"Hold on a minute," she told them both. "I am right here. Please do not speak about me like I am absent from the room."

Clay caught her gaze. "You're right, Ellis," he said. "We should absolutely consult you first. Would you like to take the chance of going back out there alone and being shot? It'll be completely up to you."

"Very funny. Of course I don't. I just wanted to be consulted, so thank you for that." She turned her attention to her grandfather. "Ever since he's started speaking English again, he's become insufferable."

Grandfather Valmont chuckled. "I did notice the Acadian French was gone. Does that mean your memories are returning?"

"Just the one," he said. "Something about a home in the woods. I don't know where it is, but I know it isn't New Orleans." He shook his head. "That's not completely true. When you mentioned the men speaking Spanish, that did remind me that I thought maybe I heard Spanish too while I was recuperating."

"Not a chance," Ellis said. "None of us speak it well enough to converse with one another."

He shrugged. "Then before? Maybe the men you heard, Jean Paul?"

"Could be," he said. "Unless someone got close enough to that barn for you to hear them, which meant they got close enough to my family to cause harm." He shook his head. "I don't want to think that's possible, but I must concede that with my son and grandson away, it could happen."

"No," Ellis said. "Mama and I would have seen them. I think he's remembering what happened when he was shot, not while he was recuperating."

Grandfather Valmont shook his head. "No matter."

But it mattered to Clay. This much was obvious by his expression as he moved to the other end of the room to take up watch over the south side of the property.

After a while, she joined him there. "Clay, I don't know the answer to whether you heard Spanish before or after you were shot. Nor do I know who shot you." He turned to look into her eyes. "If I did, I would tell you."

Silence fell between them. Finally he nodded and went back to keeping watch. "I believe you."

Ellis allowed her gaze to follow Clay's, searching the property lines for signs of anyone who might be hiding there. She saw nothing out of the ordinary, and certainly no people.

"What is happening November 18th?"

She looked at him from the corner of her eye as she considered how to respond. "You claimed that you have a meeting," she told him.

"With whom?"

Ellis rose and got halfway across the room before thinking better of making a swift exit. She returned to his side and touched his shoulder. "I can tell you where," she offered.

He looked up at her. "All right," was his simple reply.

"Mission San Jose."

Clay searched her face as if looking for clues and then returned to his watch. "Thank you," he said as she turned to go. "I'm supposed to bring something with me, aren't I?"

She paused in her steps and glanced back at him. Then, without another word, she walked away.

CHAPTER 18

Ellis found Clay the next morning at dawn standing at the bank of the Brazos River. How long he'd been standing there, she couldn't tell, but he was not so wrapped up in thought that he didn't turn to watch her approach.

"End or beginning of the watch?" she asked him as she handed him the cup of coffee she'd brought.

Clay accepted the coffee with thanks and took a sip. "The watch never ends when you are a soldier."

For lack of a better response, she nodded. The always-brown water glowed a deep gold under the rising sun. Out of habit, she searched for snakes but found no evidence of them.

"We found you over there," she said as she indicated the reeds where the pirogue had been located. "You were lying in the boat unconscious."

"What happened to the boat?"

Ellis met his stare. "It was your resting place for the first two days. We feared moving you would do more harm than good, so my mother padded the space around you with quilts in hopes it wouldn't be too uncomfortable."

He offered a wry smile. "I do not remember any discomfort associated with my bed."

She matched his grin. "Yes, I would imagine you had other concerns. After we were sure we could move you, we brought in a bed and returned the pirogue to the neighbors."

"The neighbors?" Clay shook his head. "I don't understand."

"I thought I told you." She caught herself. "I'm sorry. You likely don't remember that I explained the pirogue had been stolen a few days before you arrived at Velasco with the Greys. I knew you couldn't have stolen it because I saw you leave the ship from New Orleans and knew exactly when you reached Texas soil. Thus, you could not be the thief."

"And yet you found me in a stolen boat." He took another sip of coffee and let that statement settle between them. "Just one of the mysteries."

A cool breeze off the river drifted past, and Ellis tucked a strand of hair behind her ear. The air was crisp this morning, a warning of the winter to come.

Much as she disliked the heat of summer, she hated the chill of winter.

"I need to speak to your neighbor," he said. "He might have an idea of who took his pirogue."

"You could do that," she said. "His house is down the main road to the south. But he will tell you he saw nothing and only noticed the pirogue was gone well after it was stolen."

"How could he tell that?"

Ellis shrugged. "I don't know. But that is what he told Mama and me when we returned the pirogue."

"And you didn't question him?"

She gave the soldier a pointed look. "My mother and I had just delivered a pirogue several miles downriver with two fidgety boys. The last thing we were thinking of at that point was interrogating Mr. Vaughn as to why his boat was stolen."

"Your point is taken," he said. "I just find it strange that the owner would realize a boat was gone and then somehow know it had been gone awhile before he noticed it."

"Clay," she said wearily, "are you certain you're not missing a memory of having been an investigator before your accident?"

His expression sobered. "I'm certain of nothing."

"Oh," she said quickly. "I didn't mean to be so insensitive. You just seem very good at seeing the details."

Clay took another sip of coffee. "Except the details in my past."

"But you saw something yesterday. That house, mountains, trees. . ." She paused. "And you were able to concentrate and switch from Acadian French to English. You haven't gone back to French, just in case you weren't sure."

"I wasn't," he said. "Though I hadn't thought about it."

"Well," Ellis said slowly, "maybe the key to getting back the important memories is to concentrate on trying to recall them."

"I have been doing that," he snapped. "It doesn't help when you won't answer my direct questions."

"Like what?" she asked.

"You know what I am supposed to bring with me to that meeting at Mission San Jose. Why won't you just tell me?"

He'd allowed his frustration to cause trouble again. Though he couldn't remember most of what happened up until the day he awakened in the barn, he had an innate sense that his temper had always been his downfall.

Clay turned to face the beautiful lady who had saved his life and offered his most penitent expression. "I'm sorry," he told her. "I don't know much about myself, but I do know that I don't take well to having missing pieces of what is an important puzzle." He paused. "I also don't like getting shot at."

"Nor do I," she agreed. "But that is part of what it means to live in a land at war."

The truth of her statement hit him hard. Here was this family—wife and children—who had made a choice to remain on their land despite the fact that they were living in dangerous times.

"Dare I ask what you're thinking?" she said. "Other than why I won't answer your question regarding what you need to bring with you to Mission San Jose?"

"Won't or can't?" he asked.

"The result is the same," she said evenly, obviously refusing to rise to his level of irritation.

And it was. Something in him settled then. The hard jolt of anger softened, and his hands unclenched.

He looked at her then, really looked beyond the beauty of her face to the strength of her spirit. "I am thinking that you are much braver than I ever was."

Ellis laughed. "I doubt that. I am regularly terrified. It was all I could do to remain cowering in the brush while you went out and challenged whoever it was who had followed us. You are the brave one."

His fingers wrapped around the coffee mug, but they would have preferred to wrap around the auburn curls that escaped from Ellis's braid. He would leave soon, heading toward Mission San Jose, though he did not yet know what awaited him there.

He would miss her. Terribly.

And for a man whose mind was unreliable at best, he knew that standing here at the river's edge with a good cup of coffee and Ellis Valmont was a memory he would always have.

Clay shook off the thought and finished the coffee in silence. After walking Ellis to the house, he set off to have a conversation with the neighbor. He found the man standing at the edge of his property looking down the road.

The man was younger than he expected with dark hair and a suspicious look on his tanned face. Clay studied him to try to make a determination of whether he might be Texian or from farther south of the border, but his features were of the sort that allowed a man to pass unnoticed among a number of cultures.

"You Mr. Vaughn?" he asked.

After introducing himself, Clay added, "I wonder if I could speak to you about that pirogue you had stolen."

"No need to," he said. "My neighbors returned it. Said there was a man shot up in it, which is why it came back bloodstained. What interest is it of yours?"

"It was my blood staining that pirogue. I'd say that gives me a strong interest." He allowed that to sink in, then added, "I'd be much obliged if I could look at it."

Vaughn seemed to consider the request, and then he nodded. "Come on, then."

They walked together toward the river where the pirogue was leaning against an outbuilding that appeared to be a smokehouse. "Miss Valmont says you didn't see who took it."

"She'd be correct," he said, displaying enough of an accent to identify the man as possibly being Acadian from south Louisiana. "But it isn't the first one I've lost. Didn't think I'd get this one back."

Clay turned to look over at the man. "Don't you find it odd that you keep getting boats stolen?"

He removed his hat to run his hand through thick black curls, then replaced his hat on his head. "I find it more odd that I actually got one back." He paused. "Mr. Gentry, we are a country at war. There was a battle fought just down the river at Velasco not four years ago, and we will have battles come to this river again. You watch. So during times of war, things happen. Boats disappear."

Clay nodded. "That's a fair assessment. Do you figure the thief was friend or foe?"

"I figure it doesn't matter. Result was the same. Until war came here, we all lived together in relative peace. Whether you were of Mexican descent—we prefer the term Tejano—or had come here from other places and call yourself a Texian, we were all one people, you know? Then came talk of freedom from Mexico and suddenly no one knew which side your friends and neighbors were on."

Clay couldn't disagree, so he decided to turn the conversation in a different direction. "Have you seen any strangers around here lately?"

Vaughn chuckled. "I'm looking at one right now."

"Fair enough," Clay said. "But I'm thinking in specific about one, maybe two men who I caught shadowing Miss Valmont over on their property. He aimed a rifle at me but it misfired." He paused. "Mine didn't misfire."

"You think you hit him?"

"I know I did." He shrugged. "I didn't go after him because I was with Miss Valmont at the time. I felt it more important to see her safely home rather than hunt down the intruder and take the chance that he was not alone."

"I would have done the same." He shook his head. "Sad news about Boyd and Thomas. I promised him I would look in over at his place while he was away, but I've been remiss in my duties. I will do better."

"What sad news?" Clay asked.

He shook his head. "Didn't they tell you? Father and son went off together to defend the cannons at Gonzales back in September. Any man not returned or accounted for is considered now to be lost."

"Lost?" He shook his head. "Are you saying Ellis's father and brother are dead?"

"I am saying that's common knowledge here."

He shifted his stance. "So everyone around here knows that this family has no men in residence?"

"I suppose. Why?"

Because now that he knew this, Clay also knew he could never leave

Ellis and her family there alone and unprotected. "No reason," he said instead.

Later that evening as he and Jean Paul held their nightly chat on the porch after Ellis had gone up to bed, he broached the topic of Boyd Valmont. "I'd been thinking of checking into the fellow next door's story about his missing pirogue, the one I drifted up on."

"Is that right?" Jean Paul asked.

"It is," he said. "So I spoke with him today. He didn't have much to add. Just that it had come up missing and then Ellis and her mama had returned it."

"That they did," he said.

"Kind of dangerous, what with who knows who is out there, don't you think?" he said.

Jean Paul swiveled to face him. "What do you mean? Has there been another threat to my family?"

"Nothing specific, but you said yourself that war is coming." He paused. "It might already be here."

"It might," he said. "Though I am not convinced that one shot in the woods the other day scared off the entire Mexican army. More likely a couple of renegades or some deserters looking for a place to hide and food for their bellies."

"They were shadowing Ellis. I saw them." He shook his head. "I saw him. Just the one. But I saw evidence of what looked to be more than one."

The old man's frown was evident even by moonlight. "How many more?"

"Hard to say, but probably just one more." He sat quietly in hopes that Mr. Valmont might say something else. When he did not, Clay continued. "I'm worried about the women being out here without men. I know you mentioned that Ellis's mother is away right now with the little ones. Might she have gone with them?"

"She might have," he said. "Had there not been a need to take care of you. I certainly couldn't have done it. And you were in no shape to do it yourself."

Guilt slammed him nearly backward. "Ellis is here and in danger because of me."

A statement, not a question. Also a situation he could remedy.

"Didn't say that."

Clay frowned. "Yes. You did."

The older man rose and stretched out his back, a sure sign the conversation was done and he intended to head for bed. Then he turned back to Clay, his face now in shadows and his expression unreadable.

"When Boyd came to me with this wild idea of taking up arms to defend the cause of Texas freedom, I told him he had plumb lost his mind. He had a wife and children here to take care of. He had a home he'd built by hand and a farm that he'd put everything he had into. Know what he said?"

"What?"

"He said, 'Pa, if I don't go do this, how will I live with the fact I could have given them not just a better house or a better farm, but a better life?' " Mr. Valmont shook his head. "My son went off to give his family a life where they could be here and be free. His eldest went with him for the same reason, and oh, if you knew Thomas, you'd know he was as stubborn as his father."

And his sister, Clay thought.

"So away they went, but not before they offered the chance to talk them out of it. See, all I had to do was tell them I didn't intend to look after Sophie and the children, and neither of them would have set foot off the property." He let out a long breath. "It was an impossible choice, but I made it."

He left Clay with those words, trudging off at a pace that was far slower than on previous nights.

"Sir," Clay called over his shoulder before the man disappeared inside. "You made the right choice."

The door hinges squeaked, and he figured he would get no answer. Silence fell. Then he heard the old man clear his throat. Finally the hinges creaked again as the door closed behind him, leaving Clay alone in the dark.

As was his habit, Clay moved from the porch to the stairs and settled there beneath the stars. Could he have made a choice like that? A decision to give up someone he loved for the greater good?

Somehow he knew this was a decision he had never faced. It was more than a thought. It was knowledge. He did as Ellis suggested and thought harder. Tried to form in his mind the missing information that would offer more than just an idea of how things were.

Of what had happened.

Of whose side he must be on.

He leaned forward and rested his elbows on his knees. Gradually he became aware that he was being watched. His hand went to the pistol at his side.

Then he heard the footsteps and knew the only threat was to his heart. "Ellis?" he said without turning around.

"How did you know?" she said as she settled beside him on the steps.

He shrugged. "I'm sure I would have an answer if I could remember one. What are you doing out here?"

She was still fully dressed as if she hadn't been upstairs asleep, and she wore a quilt around her shoulders for warmth. "I was waiting for Grandfather Valmont to go to bed. I wanted to speak with you alone."

He gave her a sideways look and tried not to notice how beautiful she looked by moonlight. "How did you know I would be out here?"

Ellis ignored the question to look past him out toward the river. He followed her gaze but said nothing more.

Of course. She was as watchful of what happened here as he was.

A companionable silence fell between them. Finally Clay spoke. "I haven't remembered, but I know which side I am on."

She seemed to understand his cryptic comment, for she merely nodded. After a moment, she added, "You don't have to tell me."

"I am on your side," he told her. "I owe you the debt of my life. I will not betray that. So tell me what I have to do and I will do it."

CHAPTER 19

Ellis did not know what to say, so she said nothing for what seemed like a very long time. There was only one thing she could ever ask of anyone who presented her with such an offer.

She looked over at Clay and thought of how very different things were now. He had quite literally floated into her life needing to be saved from certain death. Now he was returned to health—at least as far as he would allow her to know, for he had continued to forbid her to treat his wounds—and apparently had settled in his mind what would come next.

"Your grandfather means to take you to New Orleans next week."

Her breath caught. "No. I will not go."

"I know."

"How could you know?" she said.

"Because you are making your impossible choice."

She felt Clay shift positions beside her, but she dared not look at him. "What do you mean?"

"Your safety or something greater. I think I made mine when I joined the Greys and came here to Texas."

"Yes," she said on a whisper of breath. "My impossible choice. But it only looks that way, you know."

"No," he said softly. "I don't."

She toyed with the edge of the quilt. "The right choice is always the one that brings you home."

"So you're staying here," he said. "Your grandfather will see that doesn't happen. He's adamant that you go to safety."

"Of course he is," she said. "But he cannot make my choice for me. Not permanently."

"Are you saying if he forces you to go, you'll find a way to come back here?" Her silence must have been answer enough for Clay, for he added, "Why?"

"Texas is my home," she said with a shrug. "And my father and brother will come home again. I won't be alone once they've returned. And when she can, Mama will come back with the little ones."

"Ellis, are you out there?"

Grandfather Valmont. She turned in his direction. "I am. Is something wrong?"

"No," he said with unmistakable happiness in his voice. "Something is very right. Come inside. I have something to show you."

Ellis climbed to her feet, tucking the quilt around her as she followed her grandfather inside. He was at the dining table lighting the lamp. In front of him a folded piece of paper waited on the tabletop.

"When I was in Velasco this morning to check on the shipyard, my assistant gave me a pouch of documents to review. I thought perhaps they were contracts, so I saved them for this evening." He looked over at Clay. "I love building boats. I do not love reading page after page of agreements written by lawyers. Give me a man's handshake any day, even if he is a man who works for the United States government."

"Grandfather," Ellis said gently. "You were going to tell us why you called us in here?"

"Yes," he said with a chuckle. "Well, imagine my surprise when I sifted through that pile of contracts to find a letter." His chuckle turned into a laugh. "From Boyd."

"Papa?" Ellis cried. "You got a letter from Papa?"

"I did," he said. "But I haven't opened it yet. I thought to wait until we could read it together. However, my son is ever the practical one. You will notice what he wrote beneath his name?"

Ellis peered down at the letter. " 'Boyd Valmont,' " she read. " 'And yes, I am alive and well.' " Tears of relief began to fall as she flung herself into Clay's arms. "Clay, isn't that the best news?" she said.

Clay's eyes drifted shut as he held Ellis against him. He winced but not from the pain of her pressing against his injuries. Rather, in the moment after she grasped his shoulders with laughter in her voice and called his name, he had felt something he couldn't recall ever feeling before.

And he had no idea whether he truly had never felt it or whether he just could not recall. He wrapped his arms around her and felt certain that lost memories had nothing to do with the feelings swirling inside him.

Ellis went on about her father, her tears staining his shirt, but her words fell on deaf ears. Instead he inhaled the delicate scent of whatever herb or flower she used in her hair.

Felt the warmth of her arms around him.

And in that moment, though he knew so little about her, or for that matter about himself, he knew that Ellis Valmont felt very right in his arms. Anything she asked at this moment would be granted to her, of this Clay was certain.

If she asked him to be more than just the man whose life she saved. . . What would his future look like then? Would his missing past not matter? And what of the mission he had come to Texas to complete?

He tightened his grip on her and ignored the inconvenient questions. In this moment, there was nothing else outside the four walls of this home.

Outside the embrace of this woman.

"Read the letter," Ellis said, bringing him back to reality.

Clay released her along with the breath he had not realized he was holding. Ellis Valmont was a dangerous woman. If he wished to control his own destiny, he would stay away from her.

And that just might be his own impossible decision.

He turned his attention to her now, her head together with her grandfather's as they read the letter. Slowly her grandfather placed his arm around her. Then she leaned against his shoulder.

"What is it?" Clay asked, for obviously the letter from Boyd Valmont had not continued with all good news.

"My brother," she said softly as she handed the letter to Clay. "Papa says he has been taken prisoner."

Clay's eyes scanned the letter, landing on the sentence that read: *Fallen into a company of prisoners of Santa Anna's army marching toward the Alamo where he will likely be held.*

He offered the letter back to Ellis, his mind made up. "I will need my Greys uniform," he told her.

She pressed the letter against her heart. "Why?"

"Tomorrow I ride for San Antonio de Béxar. I cannot save your brother in his borrowed clothes." He paused. "That is, if I might trouble you to loan me a horse, Mr. Valmont. I assure you I am good for the payment."

"Clay," she said with a gasp. "You cannot go alone. The Mexican army is too much for one man. I will go with you."

He laughed then, at himself, at her, at the situation. "I will not be alone. My guess is here in Texas the Mexican army has a common enemy. Although I am sure when they hear I've got you with me. . ."

"Stop teasing me. I know what my brother looks like and you do not."

Jean Paul nodded. "I will go with you. I can certainly point out my grandson in a crowd, even at my age."

"And leave her here?" Clay said. "You know she will follow."

The older man looked over at his granddaughter and then back at

Clay. "Yes, you are right. But let me send some of my men with you. It is a simple matter of going down to Velasco and bringing them back here, and it will delay you a few days at most. I will also see that there are people assigned to keeping Ellis out of trouble. She does tend to find a way to—"

"You're doing it again," she snapped. "I am right here in this room, and neither of you are bothering to recognize the fact that I am a grown woman who not only can make her own choices but also just might have something worthwhile to contribute to the conversation."

"Ellis," her grandfather said sharply.

"No, Grandfather Valmont," she responded quickly. "I will be heard. And please understand I mean no disrespect to you. But Thomas must be found. Papa cannot leave his men to go and search, so that responsibility falls to us."

"It falls to the men in our family," Jean Paul said.

"I would be honored to take that responsibility from you," Clay said to Jean Paul. "Ellis can be emotional, but this time she is right. Someone must go and find Thomas. With your permission, that will be me."

"In a few days, yes. But not tomorrow or the next. You cannot go unprepared. Do I have your word?"

"You do, but reluctantly."

"That will suffice, and understand I would go if I did not have a reason to stay." Jean Paul studied him for a moment and then nodded. "There is not a man alive who would be able to keep my granddaughter where she does not wish to be. Perhaps if she knows you are doing this, then she will wait patiently here with enough guards to keep her safe."

"But Grandfather Valmont, truly I would be no trouble if I went along just to help and—"

"Ellis Valmont, do not mistake me." He shook his finger at her. "I am only allowing you to remain here because I know if I deliver you to New Orleans as your mother has requested, you will only leave again and be back in Velasco on the next steamer going west."

"I cannot deny this," she said softly.

"And in doing so, do you not realize how much worry you will cause an old man?" He shook his head. "Truly you do not understand how much trouble a willful woman can be."

At Clay's laugh, both Valmonts swung their gazes in his direction. "No," he said, quickly sobering. "I am certain she does not, or she wouldn't do it, would you, Ellis?"

Put on the spot, she had to agree with him. With the victory, Clay said his good nights and hurried back to his bedchamber. He awakened the next morning to find the coffee on and Ellis seated at the dining table with a basket of mending.

Ignoring his cheerful good-morning greeting, she continued to work on something that looked suspiciously like his uniform. Seating himself at the far end of the table, he slathered butter on bread and dined in silence.

After a few minutes, she tossed the garment toward him. Clay caught it, narrowly missing upending his chair and taking his breakfast plate and coffee with him onto the floor.

"One of the buttons won't match the others, but otherwise that part of your uniform is restored and ready for use. I will have the trousers done soon. The bullet hole on the leg is proving stubborn to close."

"I am glad that is only the issue with my trousers and not with my actual leg. It has healed nicely," he added when she appeared not to have understood the meaning of his jest.

Without a word, she went back to her work, and Clay went back to his breakfast. Finally he'd had enough.

"Look, Ellis. Not speaking to me is childish."

"No," she said as she yanked the thread through his trouser leg and then looked up at him with a pointed expression. "Not speaking to you is a good way to keep myself from saying something I will wish later that I had not said."

He set down his mug and then rested his newly mended jacket on the back of the chair beside him. "Go ahead and say it. There's no one but you and me here. If you're lucky, I will forget all about it."

Though he was being sarcastic, Ellis took his words for a joke. At least that was what he assumed was the cause of her smile.

"All right," she finally said. "I do not appreciate the fact that you took my grandfather's side against me last night. Your comment was completely uncalled for. I should be going with you to find Thomas. And I won't even begin to tell you what we Valmonts think about luck. We don't believe in it, by the way."

He met her steely gaze with a smile. "Ellis, my comment was completely true, and I am on your grandfather's side. I understand your impossible choice is to remain here for all the good reasons you indicated last night. However, knowing who you are and why you are doing it does not make it easy on those of us who care for you. In fact," he said as he warmed to the topic, "you are a difficult woman to care for. Do you know why?"

She shook her head.

"Because you are stubborn and bullheaded and you do all the wrong things for all the right reasons."

"I see," she said softly. "Do elaborate, and please, speak freely. Since, as you said, it is just the two of us here." She jabbed the needle back into his pants leg, and Clay winced. "I cannot wait to hear your explanation," was added as she drew the needle through and then looked at him with an expression of pure anger.

"Last night we talked about making the impossible choice," he said. "What if you were someone's impossible choice?"

He let that thought settle between them. A movement outside the window behind her caught Clay's attention. "Ellis, where is your grandfather?"

"He went out."

"Out the front or the back?"

She dropped the trousers into the mending basket. "I don't remember. Why?"

He nodded toward the back of the house. "I see two men, maybe three. None of them look like your grandfather."

Ellis crept over to where he was now standing and then nodded. "I see them too. And they're wearing uniforms of some kind."

"Get down so it appears no one is home," he told her as he moved toward the window to see if he could hear the language they spoke.

Unfortunately, from this distance their words were lost. Only the sound of voices, at least a half dozen now, could be heard.

Because crossing the open dogtrot would alert the intruders to his presence, Clay postponed a trip over to his bedchamber to retrieve the extra weapons stored there. Instead he kept watch over the men as they gathered near the burned-down barn.

Each was dressed the same as the other with trousers of pale brown and jackets dyed blue. Several wore a white cord across the front of their uniform, while the remainder did not. All of them appeared to be on foot.

"The horses," he said. "That's what they're after." He nodded at Ellis. "Bar the doors and windows and watch for your grandfather. If he hears a disturbance in the back of the property, he may not realize what he is walking into."

"Where are you going?"

He gave her an even look. "To prove to you which side I am on."

CHAPTER 20

Ellis spied Grandfather Valmont and Jonah walking up the path toward the house just as Clay slipped out the back door. Hurrying onto the porch, she waved them down and motioned that they should be quiet.

Both men hurried toward her and then slipped inside. "Soldiers," she told them. "A half dozen at least, all on foot."

"Where is Clay?" Grandfather Valmont asked.

"He slipped out the back door. He believes they are after the horses."

"I agree," Jonah told her. "I've seen a few soldiers come through, and not a one of them has a horse. I figured them for deserters and just chased them off with a few warning shots, but if you've got more than a couple of them, I'd say that's trouble. What do you think, Jean Paul?"

Grandfather Valmont went to the window and looked out as carefully as he could manage. "I see six, maybe seven, all standing there trying to figure out what happened to the small barn. It'll just be a matter of time before they head for the house or the other barn."

Jonah leaned past her grandfather and then returned to his spot. "Yep, those are Santa Anna's boys. I heard tell he was concentrating on towns south of here, but you can't never tell anymore."

"Are they armed?" Ellis asked, mindful that Clay was out there with the soldiers while the rest of them were safe inside.

"Can't tell," her grandfather said. "Wait, I see one with a rifle over his shoulder. So at least one is."

She spied Clay moving between the summer kitchen and the chicken coop, taking the same route they had traveled when she was forced to leave her basket in the woods. If he continued on that path, he would soon end up behind the soldiers.

"I think I know what he is doing," she told them. "Look over there past the chicken coop. He is headed for the thicket. I think he will pin them between the river and the house."

Jonah smiled. "Good plan. If we show our force here, maybe they'll take off down to the river."

"And then what?" Grandfather Valmont said. "Swim away?" He shook his head. "I doubt that."

"They may have a boat," he offered.

"Or they've seen ours," Ellis said.

Jonah nodded. "Likely that's it. So what do we do?"

"We can't let them take our boat," she told her grandfather. "Isn't there something we can do to stop them?"

"Better the boat than our horses," he told her. "I do know where we can get another boat," he said with a gleam in his eye.

A moment later, Ellis spied Clay again. This time he was headed back toward the house.

"Go to the door," Grandfather Valmont told her. "Open it when I give you the signal."

She hurried to unbolt the door and then waited for the signal that would let her know to allow Clay inside. At her grandfather's command, she yanked the doorknob to pull the door open. Clay rolled inside, moving out of the way just in time for Ellis to close the door.

"There are seven men," he told them. "One is on a litter that is being pulled by the others. My guess is he is the man I shot in the woods."

"So we've got six with weapons," Jonah said.

"We've got six. I didn't see weapons on all of them. Just on two or three."

Clay went back to the window and looked out. "These men might be Mexican Republic soldiers, but they're not acting like it."

Ellis came to stand beside him. The men appeared to be deep in conversation. It was as if they never saw Clay at all.

He pressed past her, pausing for just a moment to look down into her eyes. "I said I was going to prove what side I am on. I still will, but I don't think these men mean us harm. We talked about your stubbornness. Understand if you don't remain here where I can know where you are, you will be risking my life."

She looked up into his eyes and considered what he said. "Yes," she managed.

"Then here is how I will show you what side I am on. I am about to walk out there and speak to those men. If I cannot control the situation by knowing you will not come running out with your rifle or making a fuss, then the few who have weapons will likely shoot me." He paused. "So I trust you."

Ellis managed a smile. "I will stay put," she told him. "Besides, you've reached your limit of shotgun holes a body can tolerate, haven't you? I've certainly reached my limit of treating them."

His lips turned up in the beginnings of a smile. Then he leaned down to kiss her forehead. "Then I will be careful to return without more shotgun holes in me."

"That's right," she said, fear rising. "I still have plenty of the sleeping medication. I don't want to have to use it."

"Keep your potions to yourself, woman," he said as he reached for the doorknob. "I plan to stay wide awake around you from now on." He turned his attention to Grandfather Valmont and Jonah. "I don't mind having backup, but I'd be much obliged if neither of you looked as if you were about to shoot. Best you stay out of sight until I give my signal."

"And what signal is that?" Jonah asked.

"I'll raise my right hand if I need you to come out with your weapons down," he told them.

"And if you want us to shoot?"

Grandfather Valmont grasped Jonah's shoulder. "I believe that signal will be when the other side shoots first."

"That works for me. Or I can just yell for you to shoot," he said as he went to the door. At Clay's nod, Jonah opened the door, and Clay stepped outside.

Ellis raced to the window to watch as Clay shouted something to the men. Was he speaking Spanish?

Several pulled their weapons while the rest gathered in close formation. An answer was yelled from one of the men in the group, but Ellis could not understand what he said.

Clay continued moving toward the men at a slow but steady pace, his rifle drawn. When he was within a few yards of the group, he paused.

Now they were too far away for Ellis to hear the conversation, but she could tell from Clay's stance that he was definitely the one in charge. He gestured back toward the house, using his left hand, then returned to speaking with the men. After a moment, Ellis heard her name being called.

"Come to the door," he told her.

Grandfather stepped into her path. "Don't do this," he told her.

"I have to," she said.

When she appeared in the open door, the men began to murmur. All but one put their weapons away.

"Where is your basket of herbs and bandages?" he asked her. "A man is hurt."

"I'll get it." Ellis hurried to retrieve the basket that had been retrieved from the woods and then returned to the door.

"You ought not go out there," Jonah said from behind her.

She turned to look at the two men. "I trust Clay."

And with those words she stepped out onto the porch and then, at his bidding, crossed the lawn to stand beside him. She reached his side and clasped her hand to his.

Clay looked down with a smile and then returned his attention to the man with the weapon still drawn. He said something in Spanish that caused the man to put away his weapon.

"Ellis," he said gently. "Please see to the man over there. I have explained that you are a healer. They understand we do not mean them harm as long as they promise they are of the same mind." Clay turned his attention to the man in charge. "And that they will move along without returning to harm us once you are finished with your work."

Apparently the man spoke enough English to understand. He nodded and then looked over at Ellis. "Thank you, *doctora*."

At Clay's nod, Ellis moved over to where the man was lying very still on a blanket tied to two sticks. As Clay had assumed, the man was being carried this way due to his condition. When she spoke to him, his eyes remained closed, but his breathing was steady.

After a cursory examination, Ellis turned her attention back to Clay. "Please tell them that the patient may complain of pain as I treat him. The bullet has gone straight through, but I will need to be certain there is nothing in the wound that will cause infection. This process can be painful."

Clay translated and the men murmured among themselves. One said something to the leader, who nodded.

"He has offered assistance."

Ellis managed a smile. "*Gracias*. Please tell him I gratefully accept his help."

Under the watchful eyes of the soldier's companions, Ellis examined the wound. As expected, the patient objected loudly and with so much strength that two more of the soldiers were pressed into service to keep him still.

Finally she completed her work and tied the last knot on the bandage. Nodding a thanks to her assistants, she rose and dusted off her skirt.

"He will live?" the man in charge asked.

"I believe he will," she said. "Someone must clean the wound and administer the herbs to keep the infection away. If that is done, he should make a full recovery."

Clay translated and the men all nodded. Ellis handed a roll of cotton cloth and a leather pouch of herbs to the man who first volunteered to help. With Clay providing the proper words, Ellis explained to him what to do and what to watch for.

The helper repeated the words back to Clay, who nodded. Then the man said something else. Clay looked over at Ellis but said nothing.

"What did he say?" she asked, but still he remained silent.

The man in charge smiled. "He asked why he had not made the doctora his wife yet."

Ellis grinned. "Tell him the doctora is perfectly happy without being his wife."

When he translated to his men, they all fell into gales of laughter. Only Clay remained stoic. Finally he shrugged and joined in.

A thought occurred, and Ellis spoke up before she could convince herself not to. "Are you hungry?"

The men fell silent. Apparently the word *hungry* needed no translation.

She looked up at Clay and then over at their leader. "I will bring you what we have." Then she walked away with the full knowledge that every man there was watching her leave.

As she stepped into the house, Grandfather Valmont grasped her arm. "What happened out there?"

She told him as she gathered what provisions she could find into a wooden trunk and then went out to the summer kitchen, followed by the two men. There she added enough salted meat and other dry goods to a bag to feed the men for a week or two.

Long enough to get them home to their families, she hoped.

With Grandfather Valmont and Jonah trailing behind, Ellis stepped back out onto the porch. At the sight of the armed men flanking Ellis, the company of soldiers scrambled together.

Clay must have said something, for the men set their weapons aside. Grandfather Valmont stepped forward.

"The doctora's *abuelo*," he told them.

One by one, the men lined up to shake the older man's hand and to offer appreciation. Ellis remained behind, happy to have someone else be the center of attention.

"I pledge a promise to you," their leader said once the greetings and words of thanks were finished. "We will leave you and your neighbors in peace and tell our comrades of your kindness."

"Thank you," Grandfather Valmont said. "And we will tell our neighbors that you have left us in peace."

"There is just one thing." The soldier moved around Grandfather Valmont to stand in front of Ellis. Instinctively, Clay blocked his path.

He looked up at Clay. "I wish to offer her a gift of gratitude and nothing more."

With a curt nod, Clay stepped aside. Still, he remained at Ellis's elbow.

From around his neck, he removed a wooden cross on a length of leather and placed it in her hand. "Doctora, with deepest gratitude for saving my brother's life."

"He is your brother?"

The soldier nodded.

Smiling, Ellis clasped the necklace in her palm. "I will cherish this," she said as she placed the necklace around her neck.

One by one the Mexican soldiers filed past to offer their thanks. Finally the leader pressed something into Clay's palm. He attempted to argue, but the man would hear nothing of it. Then they packed their cask of food onto the pallet along with the wounded soldier and disappeared into the woods.

Ellis tucked the cross into the bodice of her dress and then picked up her basket to follow Grandfather Valmont and Jonah to the house.

Clay moved into her path to turn and offer a smile. "Great work, doctora."

"About that," she said, looking up at Clay. "I had no idea you spoke Spanish."

Clay shook his head. "I don't."

Ellis laughed. "Yes," she said. "You did. How do you think those men understood what you were saying?"

He seemed to consider her statement for a minute. "He told me he shot me," Clay finally said. "I stole their boat, the boat they took from your neighbor, and so he shot me."

She froze. "You mean the man who tried to kill you is the brother of the man we just saved?"

Clay let out a long breath. "You had to save him because I shot him." He paused. "So whatever language I was speaking, I think we all understood that we are all very much alike."

CHAPTER 21

The next day, there was no more talk of Ellis being returned to New Orleans to join her family. Unfortunately, neither her grandfather nor Clay would discuss the possibility of her making the trip to San Antonio de Béxar.

The day after, when a rainstorm kept them inside and away from chores, Grandfather Valmont announced he was returning to Velasco tomorrow to make arrangements for Clay's search, and his granddaughter would be joining him.

"But that was not the plan," Ellis protested.

"The more I think of what could have happened with the Mexican soldiers, the more convinced I am that we cannot help Thomas until we help ourselves. And that means we move to a more secure location first," he said in that offhanded way he had of making a declaration sound like something far less than final.

Ellis remained quiet, knowing that the argument she wished to have would not give her the result she wanted. The days were passing quickly and the eighteenth of November was coming soon. With that deadline looming, where would the search for Thomas fit in?

"I think that is wise," Clay said. "With your permission I'll ride on toward the Alamo tomorrow morning at first light."

"If you're still willing to do this for our family, I would be much obliged, Clay," her grandfather said. "I will write you a letter of introduction that ought to help should anyone question why you're looking for Thomas." He paused. "And why a Grey isn't with his fellow soldiers."

"Thank you, sir," he said. "I hadn't thought of that. With my papers ruined by the fire, I would appreciate any help you might give me so that I can return."

Ellis's eyes narrowed. "So you would go alone? Even knowing how I feel about that?"

He gave her a pointed look. "Yes," she heard him murmur as he walked out the door into the rain.

She whirled around to see her grandfather watching. "Why tomorrow?" she asked. "Why not a few days ago?"

"I have given you enough time to get used to the idea. That is my compromise. I have also given you enough time to realize New Orleans is where you should stay until the war ends. That is your compromise, and I do hope you are mature enough to accept this."

"Mature enough?" She bit back the remainder of the reply she wished to give voice to. "Surely you see the wisdom of having someone here to keep the farm in good order until Papa can return."

"I can and I have," he said. "Which is why I have arranged with Jonah to have him take over the duties here. Vaughn has also agreed to look in on the place. Between the two, I'd say things should be fine until your father returns." He paused. "Oh, and as thanks for Clay's work he has done here, I will be sending him off with one of the horses."

He returned to his book, a distinct warning that the conversation was over.

"I suppose you've thought of everything," she said as she made her way upstairs. "Except for asking my opinion on the matter. You know if he leaves alone, he may just forget altogether that he is looking for Thomas. Have you considered that?"

"He will not, though I did consider that you're most upset about this because you do not get to go with him. I do not believe for a moment that you want to stay here for any reason other than to get on a horse and follow that man to San Antonio de Béxar. I know you love your brother, but you must see reason."

"Why must I if you do not?" she called.

With each step up the stairs she felt a little more foolish. Her grandfather meant well. She knew this. He was keeping a promise to Mama and doing what he thought was best for the family.

But he didn't know. . .

Oh. He didn't know.

An idea occurred, and it was brilliant. Absolutely brilliant.

She had information that Clay wanted. Information that she could trade for something worth more to her than anything else she might want.

Ellis retrieved her book of psalms from the bedside table and bided her time until she heard the door slam downstairs. Grandfather would be going to bed for the night, leaving her time to slip out and find Clay.

Because they had plans to make for tomorrow.

Tucking the book and a quilt under her arm, Ellis moved quietly down the stairs, bypassing the step that squeaked. Though her grandfather's sleeping chamber was on the other side of the dogtrot with ample space in between, his hearing was such that he just might awaken.

Ellis tucked the book into the pocket of her rebozo and stepped out onto the porch, then went through the dogtrot to look out into the back of the property. Clay was not in his customary place on the porch steps, nor was he anywhere within sight.

Rather than wait for him, she ducked under the quilt, picked up her skirts, and sloshed through the rain to the barn. The soft nickering of the horses drew her inside, where she settled in a warm corner on clean straw to wait for first light.

Knowing he would never be able to say goodbye if he left at the time he said he would, Clay stepped into his trousers and put on the uniform of the New Orleans Greys. It should not have seemed odd that the uniform fit so well, and yet it had been made for a man whom Clay might never recall.

He had no other possessions, so he left the bedchamber in the same clothes he had arrived here wearing. He had tried more than once to remove the bloodstains from his boots but had not yet managed the feat. The boots that bore the mark of snake fangs that never touched his skin deserved better.

When he got where he was going and completed whatever mission he was supposed to complete, then he would see to that unfinished business. After he brought Thomas Valmont home too.

The rain had slowed to a drizzle as Clay stepped out onto the porch. Stars peered out between raindrops, brightening the sky with pinpoints of light. He followed the familiar path to the barn, where he would leave a note of thanks and apology for Ellis and her grandfather, but stopped short when he saw the door was slightly ajar.

He retrieved his pistol and then pushed the door open just enough to step inside. The horses were fidgeting, their nervous whinnying out of character for the docile creatures.

"Took you long enough," Ellis said.

And then he heard the low, menacing growl.

"Ellis?"

"I am here in the corner," she said softly. "But the bobcat is in the rafters above you. Trust me and shoot directly up, then move out of the way. Quickly," came out as a whispered plea.

He moved slowly, aiming the pistol up into the black depths of the rafters.

"He shall cover thee with his feathers, and under his wings shalt thou trust."

The words came from a place so deep, so hidden, that Clay knew they were a truth he had long held close. "Yes, amen," he whispered.

Another growl from overhead, and Clay moved slightly to the left to center himself under it. Then he pulled the trigger and jumped out of the way.

The big cat howled and then landed with a thud. A moment later, it raced out the door. A second shot fired and then silence.

Ellis scrambled out of her corner and launched herself into his arms just as the elder Valmont stepped into the barn. Clay held her upright as she began to shake. "I was so afraid," she whispered in his ear. "That thing came in and I never heard it until it growled. Then I saw it was overhead and I didn't know what to do."

"You did the right thing," he whispered against her ear as he held her tight.

Jean Paul walked over to the lamp and lit it. Firelight blazed, temporarily blinding Clay until his eyes adjusted.

In a moment of clarity, Clay realized how things might look to Ellis's grandfather. A darkened barn, a quilt in the corner, and the last night they would be in close proximity? He was preparing his defense when Jean Paul spoke first.

"So you fired the first shot," he said to Clay.

"And you fired the second," was the best he could manage at the moment with Ellis still clinging to him.

"I did." Jean Paul turned his attention from Clay to Ellis. "I suppose you have good reasons for being here in the barn at this hour."

"Very good reasons," Ellis said. "I am going to San Antonio de Béxar with Clay."

Both men's objections were swift and vocal. Finally Ellis had had enough.

"Please," she said, holding up her hands to indicate she was done listening. "I am going because without me Clay cannot do what needs to be done."

"Child," her grandfather said in his most exasperated tone, "I have already written a letter of introduction. That is all he needs to find your brother. Anyone who reads that letter will understand and offer assistance to find my grandson."

"Yes, I'm sure, Grandfather Valmont," she told him as patiently as she could manage, "but I am the only one who can tell Clay where the treasure is."

At this, Clay's eyes widened. She watched his face carefully as he caught her gaze.

"Clay?" her grandfather said. "What is she talking about?"

He stood as if transfixed. Then slowly he moved his attention to her grandfather. "My grandfather's treasure," he said softly.

"What in the blazes?" Grandfather Valmont exclaimed. "Talk of treasure is nonsense and has nothing to do with finding Thomas. You'll not need funds to get him. Just bravery and good timing. Go in and snatch him, Clay. That's how it is done."

He shook his head. "Not for that mission," he said. "For the other one."

"The one you can't remember?" her grandfather snapped. "Blast it all, Ellis, what is he talking about?"

"Clay?" she said.

His expression was unreadable. Then he turned his attention to the older man. "I'll take her with me."

"Just like that, without any discussion on the matter and against my wishes?"

Clay appeared to be considering his response. Then he squared his shoulders. "For the good of Texas, I would do that, sir."

"The good of Texas, is it?" Grandfather Valmont's attention moved to

Ellis. "Do me the courtesy of explaining if he will not."

"I will, sir," Clay offered. "If you insist. But the less you know about this, the better, should you be required to answer for it later."

"Now I truly have no idea what either of you are talking about."

Ellis closed the distance between them and took his hand. "Clay came to Texas on a mission that involved more than just being a Grey. He doesn't fully recall what that mission is, but I do."

"How could you possibly know?" her grandfather demanded. "Before he arrived at the riverbank, did you know this man?"

"I did not."

He divided his attention between them and then looked down at Ellis. "Then I do not understand."

"During his early time with us, he said things. A lot of things. Because they seemed so outlandish, I began to write them down. I soon realized he was telling me about his mission."

"And?" he said. "What about it?"

"Please trust me when I say that those who sent him to Texas have our republic's best interests at heart."

Grandfather Valmont looked as if he might argue. Then he frowned at Clay. "If one hair on her head is harmed, just one hair, then you will have to fear for your life the remainder of your days." He turned back to Ellis. "You need an escort. I will find someone. Jonah perhaps."

"Jonah has a wife and baby to take care of. I will be fine," she told him. "There will be allies to our cause everywhere we go."

"And enemies to it as well," he said.

"Which is why it is important that Clay be allowed to complete the work he was sent here to do." She offered a smile. "If it is my reputation that gives you concern, remember you told me we are sometimes called to do out-of-the-ordinary things during times of war. I am only doing what I must."

"Take care you remember this when your mother hears of it. I will write her, but it would be much better if you were the one telling her."

Ellis shook her head. "Why tell her?"

"Child, you forget I promised I would send you to her within the week. It has been well past that. My fear is she will return and come looking for you."

Ellis grinned. "Yes, that is something my mother might do. I believe the only remedy may be to go to New Orleans yourself."

His laughter held no humor. "Have you forgotten I have a shipbuilding enterprise to supervise? I'm terrified what has happened in my absence, and I have only been gone a short time. Do you expect I can run that business from New Orleans?"

"No," she said slowly, "but I expect you might recruit a few of my cousins to come back with you to help. Once you have soothed my mother's concerns, that is."

He thought on the suggestion a moment and then shrugged. "I will take it all under advisement. I am certainly getting too old for all of this. I do still wonder about the propriety of you riding across Texas alone with this man."

Ellis grinned, secure in the knowledge that she had won this skirmish. "Don't worry, Grandfather Valmont. Clay Gentry is the last man on earth I would have any romantic interest in. Now if you'll excuse me, I need to finish packing."

She walked out of the barn with a broad smile, but she dared not let the two men she left behind see it. Instead she kept her back straight and her pace slow until she reached the stairs.

A few minutes later she returned to the barn ready to leave. Unfortunately, both Grandfather Valmont and Clay were gone.

CHAPTER 22

Clay returned from disposing of the bobcat in the woods to find Ellis gone. "What has that woman done this time?" he asked Jean Paul.

"Likely set off without you thinking you'd left her." He nodded to the empty stall where her horse had been earlier. "Best you catch up to her."

He nodded. With his meager supplies, it did not take but a moment to toss a saddlebag over the borrowed horse. "I will see to her safety above my own," he told her grandfather.

"I have no doubt you will," he said. "I would be much obliged if you would return safely so I do not have to explain to her family why I allowed her to go with you."

Clay chuckled. "No doubt her family will understand you had no choice, given it is Ellis we are talking about."

"She is a willful creature." His expression sobered. "But I value her above any treasure, even the land beneath my feet. Bring her home safely. And if you bring her brother home too, even better. But he can care for himself. My granddaughter may believe she can, but she is prone to impetuousness. She is your first priority."

"Sir," he said slowly, "Texas is my first priority. Ellis is next."

Jean Paul Valmont took a step back and studied him for a moment. Then he nodded. "Go with God, young man. Return with Ellis, though."

"I will."

Reaching down from the saddle, he shook the old man's hand and then set off. He'd gone less than a mile when he spied what had to be Ellis riding up ahead at full speed down the trail that led along the river. Stifling the words he longed to say, Clay urged his mount forward until he was within shouting distance.

"Ellis," he called. "Stop."

No response.

After closing the distance between them slightly, he tried again. This time the rider slowed and the horse turned. Indeed it was the feisty female.

"Where were you?" she demanded when they met on the trail.

Her skirt was speckled in mud, and her hair had escaped the impractical straw hat she had chosen for the trip. The brightly colored scarf she wore tied around her waist would have served as much better protection, but he would give her that advice later. After she stopped scowling at him.

"There was a dead bobcat to get rid of," he told her. "Did you think your grandfather should have to take care of that alone?"

Her haughty expression fell. "Oh," she managed. "I thought you had. . ."

"Left without you?" he supplied. "Yes, I see that. Did you know where you were going?"

"Not specifically, but this was the direction Papa and his men went, so I assumed it was the right way." She turned her horse around and nodded toward the narrow trail. "Go ahead."

He lifted one dark brow. "You're certain?"

"Do not be unbearable," she told him. "Just go."

He did, but not before fixing a broad smile on his face. "Yes, ma'am," trailed him as they set off.

After a few hours, Clay stopped to water the horses. He had given Ellis the courtesy of silence and of not continually turning back to check on her. However, he had also maintained a good idea of where she was based on how far away her horse's hooves sounded.

Landing on the ground, he grasped the reins and led the horse to the river before turning back toward Ellis. He grasped her by the waist and set her on her feet, then held her still when she wobbled.

"Slow down," he told her. "We've got a few more days of this."

"How many?" She winced as she took a few steps away from Clay.

"If we make good time, we should be in San Antonio de Béxar in five days," he said as he led the horse over to drink. "Taking the coastal route would be faster, but there is too much danger of attack coming from that direction."

"Five days?" she said. "I had no idea."

"Didn't you?" he said as he knelt down to drink. He lifted his head to find her watching him, a coffee mug in her hand. "What?"

"Nothing." She dunked the mug into the river and then took a sip of water.

Clay took the opportunity to scout around the area, leaving Ellis to watch the horses. When he returned, he found her sitting beside the river with her head resting in her hands.

"Regrets already?" he asked.

"None," she said. "Shall we go?"

"We shall," he said in his most formal voice.

Ellis declined his help as she climbed into the saddle. After a few minutes, they were well down the trail again, stopping only when they arrived at the steamboat landing. Though the trail was a better means of travel for a man on a horse, the steamboats were faster.

"And you'll take the horses?" he asked the fellow in charge of the vessel.

"If you'll warrant they aren't skittish enough to jump, then I'll take 'em," the young man said.

"I cannot warrant that, but if you give me a space to tie them in place,

I can promise they will not get away."

After inspecting the space offered, Clay struck a deal. He handed the fellow one of the four silver coins the Mexican leader had pressed into his palm—the same coins that Jean Paul refused to take when Clay offered them—and then headed back to Ellis.

"I thought we were going by horseback," Ellis said when he returned.

"We are," he told her, "but this fellow is going as far as Washington. From there we can take the La Bahia Road."

Though she said very little on the daylong journey, Clay had to admire the fact that she did not complain when informed that her sleeping accommodations for the night included bunking next to her horse. The next morning he awakened before the sunrise and found Ellis cuddled down into her bedroll with a wild spray of red curls covering her face.

His fingers itched to press away the errant strands so he could see her beauty. For as much as she was an irritating woman at times, Ellis Valmont was a true beauty.

Not one of those belle-of-the-ball types he knew from New Orleans, this one. Rather, she was just as lovely with hay in her hair as she was. . .

Clay froze as he realized he'd had a memory return. How else could he compare this beauty to others he had known in New Orleans? To a dark-haired woman who scandalized society by demanding he dance every dance with her. But where had they been?

Then he knew. The governor's ball. New Orleans. She had been the intended of another and he did not care. That night caused it all to happen.

But what was *it*?

Before he could turn away, her eyes opened and she caught him. "What?" she said as she scrambled into a sitting position. "Is something wrong?"

"No, just something I remembered," he said.

"About your mission?" she asked in a sleepy voice.

He shook his head. "Something else. About me and who I was."

Ellis found the steamboat trip upriver to be completely different from the voyages the family used to take between Velasco or Quintana and New Orleans. While those trips hugged the coastline but remained in open and unobstructed waters, this voyage by steamboat was vastly more complicated.

Men were employed to do all sorts of moving of obstacles in the river, often to the point of removing an entire felled tree blocking the way. The captain of the vessel not only had to steer around obstacles that could not be moved but also was required to avoid sandbars and areas too shallow for the vessel to pass.

At some points in the trip the going was so slow that Ellis was wishing for the trail and her horse. Most of the time, however, she reveled in the voyage upstream.

From a brief stop to take on supplies to the occasional stop along the way to pick up or deliver items, Ellis found it all fascinating. When their trip ended at the town of Washington late the next day, she was almost disappointed.

Almost but not quite, for when her feet touched dry land, she found she very much had missed walking where the ground beneath her was not rolling. Removing the horses from the steamboat was much more difficult than getting them on, so Ellis left the taming of them to Clay while she stood back and watched.

He brought them to her one at a time, and then together they led them up the embankment to the town of Washington. It was a tiny town, though one she could easily learn to like.

While Clay made their purchases for the remainder of the trip, Ellis waited with the horses. Two ladies in fine hats and dresses strolled past her as if she weren't there. With pieces of hay likely still hiding in her curls and the mud from two days of being on the road decorating her skirt, who could blame anyone for thinking the worst of her?

Ellis moved around to the other side of the horses and spied a sign advertising an inn. Closing her eyes, she imagined an actual bed with no straw or horses and a bath in a tub with real soap. She opened them to see Clay standing there.

"I have some news," he told her.

"Please tell me it involves real soap and a bed with no straw."

He shook his head as he untied his horse. "I have no idea what you're talking about, but no. It does not involve either."

"Then enlighten me, because I cannot imagine that anything other than that would actually be good news."

"I made a trade," he said over his shoulder as he motioned for her to follow him. They plodded along down the muddy street until they arrived at the livery. He indicated for Ellis to wait and then went inside.

He came out with a young man who nodded enthusiastically. Clay's horse was led away. Then Clay came back for Ellis.

"We'll be making the rest of the trip in a wagon," he told her.

"A wagon?" She shook her head. "I don't understand. Why?"

"I traded my horse for one. A wagon will let us travel in more comfort, and after we find Thomas it will allow for more room to bring him home. Two on a horse would mean for much slower going than three in a wagon."

"Oh," she said, feeling like a fool. "I hadn't thought about that."

The wagon in question was nothing spectacular. Indeed, she had seen finer quality work on the rag wagon back home in New Orleans. But the wheels looked sturdy, and there was a seat that spanned the front that had to be more comfortable than a horse's saddle.

Ellis nodded her approval even as she went back to wishing for that bed and bar of soap. Clay supervised the moving of the packs into the wagon and then hitched the horse himself. When all of that was done, he helped Ellis up onto the seat and then stepped around to the other side to join her.

They set off down Washington's main road, falling in behind a wagon of similar style and condition. "The talk here is that the convention will be held over at Noah Byers's place. It'll be spring before the delegates can all arrive, but the men in the store were adamant that there will be a declaration of Texas independence signed then."

Ellis smiled. "How exciting," she said. "I would love to see it."

"You'll have to take that up with your family," he said. "You'll be home with them well before then."

"I should hope so," she said as she shifted position.

"Comfortable?" he asked as he negotiated a turn in the road.

"Yes," she said. "Much better than on horseback."

He glanced at her and nodded. They fell into a companionable silence as they left the city of Washington behind and rolled onto La Bahia Road. Built for the royal use of the Spaniards, the road was surprisingly smooth and wide. The roll of the wagon wheels lulled her into an almost sleeplike state.

Ellis jolted. The wagon had stopped in a shaded spot with a view of rolling hills dotted with cattle. A brook bubbled beside them. She blinked and then realized her head rested on Clay's shoulder.

"Oh," she said as she felt the heat rise in her cheeks. "I'm sorry, I—"

"Get out and walk some while I water the horse," he told her, chuckling.

She walked off her embarrassment, stretching her legs by venturing downstream to a spot away from Clay's view. There she knelt down to cup water in her palms. Though it was icy cold, she splashed her face with it and felt the dust of the miles slip away.

Had it not been November, Ellis might have been tempted to jump in, clothes and all. For surely her dress would be improved by a quick dunking in clean water. Still, she did have a quilt in her bedroll that would keep her warm until her garments dried.

Was it better to be warm or clean?

"Ellis?" Clay called, ending any opportunity to decide.

She rose and shook the water off her hands then dried her face with her sleeve.

Clay eyed her curiously but said nothing as his hands grasped her waist to help her up onto the wagon seat.

That night they camped at a place that looked very much like the Valmont land in Quintana. Clay made a fire and brought back something he'd shot for their evening meal. When he offered to also clean and cook it, Ellis readily agreed.

"I'm not much of a frontier cook," she told him later after the food had been cooked. "But I do know my way around a kitchen. This is delicious, by the way."

"Thank you. If only we had a kitchen nearby," he said with a grin.

Clay offered her seconds, which she quickly accepted. "My grandfather loves to cook. Until now I have never met another man who did."

"Well," he said slowly, "I wish I knew who to credit for the skill, but I don't."

"No," she said as she set her tin plate aside. "I don't suppose you would remember, and yet the actual skill of cooking is something you did not forget."

He shrugged. "I can also tie bootlaces, hitch a horse to a buggy, and do any number of other things. My mind may be filled with more holes than swiss cheese, but at least I can remember the things I need to survive."

When it came time to prepare for bed, Ellis moved their supplies to the center of the wagon and then settled her bedroll down on one side, leaving room for Clay on the other. If he had any complaints about her system, she never knew about it, for she was sound asleep before he finished hobbling the horse.

Chapter 23

Ellis awakened in the morning to the smell of coffee for the first time since she left Quintana. Stretching, she sat up on her elbows and looked over the pile of supplies to where a dark head was visible in the vicinity of the fire.

Clay must have heard her moving around, because he stood to regard her from his vantage point on the other side of the wagon. He had removed his Greys jacket, and through the white fabric of his shirt, she could just see the outline of the bandages on his shoulder.

Until just then she had forgotten about the nature of his injuries, of how he nearly died. Instead she had allowed him to do most of the work of getting them this far. And truly, the fact that they were going after Thomas at all was also her fault.

"Were you expecting coffee in bed, ma'am?" he said in an affectation of a British butler's accent.

"No," she said as she hurried to scoot out of the wagon and shake the wrinkles out of her dress. "In fact, I was just thinking that I ought to be doing more. You've done all the difficult things and you are barely recovered."

He shook his head. "Will you forever be my nursemaid?" he said. "Please just trust that you and your mother did a fine job of plugging the holes that someone put in me and setting me back to rights." He paused to let out a long-suffering sigh. "I am fine."

"And would you tell me if you weren't?" she asked as she walked around the wagon to join him by the fire.

"No," he said as he quietly sipped his coffee. Then he gave her a sideways look that made her laugh. "But I am fine."

"Of course you are," she said.

A tripod of iron had already been set up on the fire, and Clay had an iron skillet warming atop it. Ellis rose to look through the supplies until she found eggs, a side of bacon, and a crock of butter and then set about making a proper breakfast. When she was done, she handed Clay a plate overflowing with food.

"See," she said as she reached for the other plate to fill her own. "I told you I can cook if I must."

He nodded, his mouth already filled with bacon. When he said nothing further, Ellis began to wonder if something was wrong with the food she'd given him. Then he took another bite, and another, and after a few minutes his plate was empty.

"I see you liked it," she said without looking over at him.

"That is one possibility," he said as he scooped more eggs onto his plate and then added two slices of bacon atop them. "Or perhaps I am just too polite to tell you that the eggs need more salt and the bacon wasn't crisp enough."

He held her gaze for just long enough to allow Ellis to see the twinkle in his eye. Then he took another bite. And another. This time when his plate was empty, he set it aside.

Ellis looked down at the empty plate and then back up at Clay. "Your mother taught you to be very polite."

"She did, actually." His smile froze. "She did," he repeated. "We cleaned our plates and never forgot to thank the cook. She required both."

He looked over at her, his eyes wide. Though he appeared to want to speak, he seemed incapable of it.

"You're welcome," she said to fill the silence.

"No, yes. I'm sorry. It's just that I can see her. See them. Well, not literally, but I remember them. She is where I get my dark hair. Her name is. . ." He shook his head. "I don't know."

Ellis smiled and then gently touched his sleeve. "Your memories are coming back. That is a good sign. Let them come as they come."

"I suppose," he said.

She took the plates and utensils and stood, then paused. "You know, I was thinking of something you said yesterday, and I meant to talk to you about it last night. Unfortunately, I fell asleep before I could say anything further. You said that you were fortunate to remember the things you need to survive."

"Yes, I did say that."

Ellis gave him a pensive look. "Then maybe that is the key to getting your memories to return. If your mind believes you need a skill or a memory to survive, then maybe it will deliver that skill or memory at the time you need it." She shrugged. "It is something to consider."

While Clay put out the campfire, Ellis went down to the stream to wash the plates and mugs. She returned to the sound of men's voices.

Another wagon had stopped beside theirs, and Clay and the driver were exchanging pleasantries. A young woman sat on the seat cradling an infant.

Clay spied her and waved her over to make the introductions. "These are the Cochrans. They're heading east from San Antonio de Béxar."

"Oh?" she said after she'd greeted them properly. "How did you find things?"

Mr. Cochran shook his head. "It's no place for women and children, even at the missions. General Cos has the Alamo locked up tight, but our boys are giving him a fit, so we're hopeful that there will be a surrender soon." He nodded toward his wife. "In the meantime I'm taking Leah and the little one to her mama in Opelousas, then I'm going back to fight."

The woman looked away, giving Ellis the idea that while Mr. Cochran was anxious to take on the enemy and win, Mrs. Cochran was not in agreement.

"Have you heard whether Cos has prisoners of war there?" Clay asked him.

"I wouldn't doubt he does," he said. "We saw a passel of 'em being marched that direction on our way here. I hid the wagon and let 'em pass. If it'd been just me, I would've taken 'em, but I didn't want to risk any harm to the wife and child."

Ellis kept a neutral look even as she seriously doubted the man's boast. "So you're saying all of the Mexican prisoners of war are being taken to the Alamo?"

He looked past Clay to Ellis. "I'm saying it looked that way to me. Can't see as there is any other place that'd keep them, what with the other missions being solid in Texian hands far as we know."

She nodded. If this man was right, it was likely they would find Thomas at the Alamo.

The men chatted for a few more minutes and then the Cochrans went on their way. Ellis climbed up onto the wagon seat and took her place beside Clay.

"It appears we're going in the right direction," he told her. "Unfortunately, it sounds as if we will be heading directly into a battle unless it is won before we arrive."

Ellis opened her mouth to speak and then thought better of it. According to Clay, there were still three more days of travel left before they reached San Antonio de Béxar. If they were not delayed any further, that left two full days to search for Thomas before making the trek to meet Houston.

Was he trying to justify going to Mission San Jose first?

She decided to offer a response that was neutral and yet let Clay know she would hold him to his promise. "Given that we're in a time of war, that could be the case no matter where we go, couldn't it?"

He nodded. "It could."

Clay slapped the reins and set the wagon in motion. An uncomfortable silence fell between them.

Finally Ellis decided to speak. "Do you know what *Ventana de Rosa* is?"

He glanced her way. "Are you testing me to see if I can speak Spanish?"

"You can," she told him. "So I am not testing. I just. . ." She paused, searching for the right way to continue without giving away her reason for asking. "Never mind," she finally said.

"Well, there are no such words in Spanish, just for the record."

Ellis might have laughed that his pride had proved her point. However, she elected to keep her smile to herself.

They fell into silence again, and this time Ellis was determined not to speak first. What was it about this man that made her continue to question his motives even as she proclaimed she trusted him?

It had to be the fact that at any moment he could remember something that would change everything. That might even change his loyalties.

Ellis let out a long breath. It was indeed a conundrum. Finally she decided she'd had enough of the uncertainty.

"Clay," she told him. "I need you to see something."

"Not now, Ellis," he told her as he eased the wagon around a muddy spot on the road. "We need to keep going. Anything else can wait."

"Even if I want to show you what you forgot?"

He met her gaze. "What do you mean?"

"I told you I had written it all down." She paused. "I brought the book with me where it is all there in my notes. I'm tired of guessing when you're going to remember something that will change your loyalties. I would rather show you now and let you decide if you're going to continue to honor your promise to find my brother."

Clay pulled up the reins to stop the horse. Then he swiveled in his seat. "Is that what has been bothering you?"

"Since the beginning," she said. "I wanted to trust you, and I mostly did, but there is so much you don't know. And even beyond that, so much I don't know. So how can I not think that you may just remember something that changes everything?"

Clay let out a long breath and chose his words carefully. As much as he had forgotten, he still remembered that women could be exasperating.

"I wish I had something to say to make you feel like I am trustworthy. I don't know what I don't know, but I do know that whatever you have written in that book will not change anything between us." He paused. "Unless I confessed I have a wife and children somewhere that I need to get home to. If that is the case, that would make a significant difference."

Her laughter was most welcome. "No," she told him. "You confessed no such thing, although that doesn't mean they don't exist." She shrugged. "Do you see my dilemma?"

"No," he said. "Not unless you're falling in love with me. Then it would be extremely problematic for me to have a wife and children. I don't, though."

"How do you know?" she said.

Because if I did, I wouldn't feel this way about you, he wanted to say. Instead he offered a smile. "Don't you think that a vow like that and a love that produces a family would be something that would never leave a man? Even if he cannot remember the specifics, he would remember they exist."

He looked over at her. "You look doubtful."

"That is because I have been doubting you ever since you floated up on Valmont land full of shotgun holes and trying to die on me. I have doubted who you are, doubted what you were doing there, and doubted where your allegiance lies. Clay Gentry, I am extremely tired of doubting."

"Sounds exhausting."

Her green eyes narrowed. "Are you making a joke?"

He was, but Clay had the distinct impression that his timing was not the best. So he improvised. "No, it does sound, well. . .exhausting." He shook his head. "Yes, I was trying, but I failed. Look, Ellis, I am bad at this. I'm willing to read your notes now or wait until we make camp for the evening. You decide."

She looked away and then returned her attention to him. "Now."

"All right." He steered the wagon to a shady spot where he could water the horse.

Ellis climbed into the back of the wagon and pulled a book out of her bag. She turned around to pass it to him but kept her hand on it.

"Have you changed your mind?"

Shaking her head, she tightened her grip. "Understand that I wrote down things in no particular order. At first I wasn't keeping track of what you were saying because you were so ill. And we didn't think you would survive." She shrugged. "When I realized you were saying things that could be important—if they were true, that is—I did not write them down so that you could read them later."

"No?"

"No." She paused and released the book. "I wrote them down because I thought you might be some kind of spy and I would need to tell someone about you. If you lived, that is. And then I thought maybe there were others like you out there and someone ought to be told and then. . ." Ellis took a breath. "Oh, never mind. Just turn all the way to the back of the book and start there."

Clay turned the book over in his hand and then took note of the title. "You wrote the things I said in the back of your book of psalms?"

"It was all I had. I've been memorizing Psalm 91, or trying anyway, so when it was my turn to sit with you in the barn, I brought this book. I like making notes to help me memorize, so that is why I was able to do all of that writing when you were saying those things."

"Those things?" he repeated as he turned to the back of the book. "Were they so peculiar that you didn't believe they were true?"

"Not exactly peculiar." Ellis nodded toward the book of psalms. "Just see for yourself."

CHAPTER 24

Ellis sat very still as Clay read her notes. A few times he asked what a word was, but otherwise he sat still and read in silence.

When he was done, he closed the book and handed it back to her. Then he picked up the reins and set the wagon in motion again.

"Don't you have anything to say?" she demanded when she realized his intention to remain silent.

"No." He kept his eyes on the road and a tight hold on the reins, not sparing her a glance.

"No?" She shook her head. "Did you read it all?"

"I did," he said calmly.

"All right." She waited a moment and then tried again. "You have an important job, Clay, and I have kept that from you. The meeting you have in a few days could mean the difference in winning the war."

Clay shook his head. "First, I doubt that. Yes, I believed I had to be at Mission San Jose on November 18th. That is true." He spared her a glance. "But how much of that came from something else that got mixed up in my mind? I don't know if you've ever taken any of those herbs you use to make people sleep, but they are powerful. Isn't it possible that what I said—all of those claims I made—were caused by what I had taken?"

"Anything is possible with a head injury, but—"

"But now that I have read all of that, I am more convinced than ever that there never was any secret mission. I'm just a man who believed in a cause and joined up with the Greys in order to put some action into that belief."

Stunned, Ellis sat back against the seat. "I suppose I shouldn't have been worried about losing you to the mission, then. We can forget going to Mission San Jose and proceed to San Antonio de Béxar to find Thomas."

"Exactly," he said.

They rode in silence until it was time to stop again. While Clay watered the horse, Ellis took a walk. Somehow she had gone from disbelief to doubt to worry and now this. It was all too much.

The longer she walked, the less sense any of this made. Did Clay truly believe all of that was the ranting of a mind influenced by her sleeping medication? Surely he did not.

She stopped short.

No. Of course not. Ellis smiled. All of that was correct, and he was just trying to keep her from seeing the truth.

She picked up her pace as the knots in his story unraveled. If a man came to Texas as a soldier and had a secret mission to complete, he certainly would not want anyone to know about that mission. If he happened to be wounded before he could finish what he had come to do, then how would he handle that?

"He would keep the mission secret until the time came for him to complete it, even if that meant pretending to have forgotten everything."

"That's very clever, but you're completely wrong."

Ellis stopped short and then whirled around to see Clay walking toward her. Until now she hadn't taken the time to notice how very handsome he looked in his uniform.

How very much like a soldier on a mission.

"Why are you following me?" she demanded. "Don't you have something to do back at the wagon?"

"I am following you because you've been gone the better part of half an hour and have walked a very long way away from the wagon and you are completely alone and without a weapon." He shook his head. "Are you aware that the enemy could be hiding anywhere in these hills?"

Ellis touched her rebozo. "I have a knife in here."

"Considering I was able to walk right up behind you without you noticing, how well do you think a knife hidden in your scarf would work on a man who meant to harm you?"

"You know what, Clay Gentry, any man who tried to harm me would be very sorry." With that, she walked around him and stormed back toward the wagon. Unfortunately, he easily caught up to her.

"I guess I did pretty good work on your injuries," she said when he fell into step beside her. "Between the hole in your leg and the bullet in your shoulder, you certainly couldn't move this fast a few weeks ago."

"Thank you for that." He stepped in front of her, causing Ellis to stop or slam into him. "Truly," he repeated. "Thank you."

She looked up into his eyes and saw sincerity there. "It is what I do," she said simply. "I am glad you lived."

"So am I." He grasped her gently by the shoulders and offered a smile. "About those things I said. . ."

"So you do believe you said them?" she asked.

"I do," he said. "But those were the words of the man I used to be. I don't know that man, at least not fully, but I know who I am today. And today I am a man who keeps his promise. We will find your brother. Then I will go to Mission San Jose."

"Oh."

The grip on her shoulders softened but his hands remained. "I keep my promises, Ellis." He stepped back with a grin. "Now if you are finished delaying our mission with your walk, I would like to get a few more miles down the road to San Antonio de Béxar before we make camp for the night."

She shook her head. "Our mission?"

"It is now," he said. "Come on. Your leisurely stroll is costing us valuable time."

Ellis gave him a sideways look and then picked up her pace. Of course, he matched it.

So she walked faster. So did Clay.

With the wagon in view, she picked up her skirts and raced toward it, arriving a split second before him. As Clay landed against the wagon, she raised her hands in victory.

He leaned against the rough wood with a half smile. "Oh sure, you enjoy that victory. You beat a man with holes in him."

Ellis quickly sobered. "Oh Clay, I'm so sorry. You seem so healthy and recovered that I forget I had to patch bullet holes in that uniform you're wearing. Are you hurting?"

"Only my pride," he said as he lifted her up onto the wagon seat. "I had no idea you could run that fast."

"I grew up with brothers," she said. "Three older and two younger. Of the older brothers, only Thomas survives."

He nodded. "All the more reason to bring him home."

The remainder of their trip to San Antonio de Béxar passed quickly, with Clay guiding the wagon within view of the city on a cool November afternoon just two days before he was due to make the trek to Mission San Jose. "Wait here," he told her, "and I will go and see how things are at San Antonio de Béxar."

She opened her mouth to protest and then thought better of it. A nod sufficed for an answer as Ellis watched Clay walk away in his Greys uniform with a rifle slung over his shoulder. Had she not known better, she would think he was marching off to war.

Clay walked into San Antonio de Béxar as if he was marching off to war. Searching the streets as he made his way along, he looked for men wearing his same uniform. Men who would have been arriving alongside him on that beach in Velasco.

He found the streets fortified and trees cut down. The sound of a cannon alerted him to dart to safety even as he continued his trek toward the mission. Men were racing about, some filling cannons and others bringing supplies or aiming weapons at the old church.

He stopped a man dressed in homespun clothes. "What is the situation?"

The man looked him up and down and then shook his head. "You're one of those Greys. You ought to know there's a meeting to be held up at Mission San Jose. Your fellows are joining up with the Texians there."

Clay shrugged to cover his astonishment. "How do you know this?"

"We've all been waiting for them," he said. "Old Cos, he's running scared. He knows we're about to make him surrender. He wants to be gone from here before the next wave of troops arrive."

"I wonder how the prisoners are faring."

"I'd say they're faring much better than the Mexican soldiers." The soldier shrugged. "The general wants to bargain his way out of here, and the only thing he's got to bargain with are those men he is holding. Only a fool would harm them. Like as not they're being fed and catered to well away from the cannon fire. Safer in there than out here as it were."

"I appreciate the information," Clay told him. "I'm looking for a fellow by the name of Thomas Valmont. The word we received is that he was taken prisoner at Goliad."

He nodded toward the church. "Then he's either escaped or is held in there. We're about to take the church, so you'll likely see him soon if he's in there."

Another volley of cannon fire prevented further discussion. Clay made his way back to Ellis to share what he was told.

"So we cannot get into the church to search for him?" she asked.

"Not unless you can figure out how to get behind enemy lines into a church that is under attack by our own forces." He paused. "The good news is if he is indeed in there, he will remain safe until the negotiations for General Cos to surrender are complete and then he will be released."

She sighed. "Then there is only one thing to do. We go to Mission San Jose and wait for word that the Alamo is back in Texian hands."

Clay nodded and turned the wagon in the direction of the mission. Just under seven miles away, the mission also sat along the banks of the San Antonio River. They rode in silence with the occasional sound of cannon fire echoing behind them. A few hours later, the spire of Mission San Jose came into view.

Clay drove the wagon up to the mission and under the archway that allowed access to the city-sized walled area of the mission. There he found an active community of citizens strolling about as if a war was not raging just down the river.

To his right were rows of small dwellings built right into the thick stone walls. To the left, barracks and other more utilitarian spaces had been situated. The church building loomed directly ahead, and in the immense space in the center of the plaza were men and women going about their daily work.

Behind the church were more buildings hidden by a wall decorated by an arched walkway. There he saw several groups of men in uniform, though none bearing the colors of the New Orleans Greys.

After situating the horse and wagon, Clay escorted Ellis toward the imposing edifice that constituted the main church building. "Who are we looking for?" Ellis asked as she stepped through the massive wooden doors.

"I have no idea," Clay admitted. "But someone here must know what's about to happen."

"You there," someone called from the plaza.

Clay turned around to see a man in the cloaks of a padre hurrying toward him. The man gestured for him to follow, and together they walked across the plaza to pause beneath the arched walkway.

"You are early," he told Clay as Ellis hurried to catch up to them. "And who is she?"

"She is under my protection," was all he was willing to say as he studied the old man's face. With skin darkened by the sun and a black beard heavily speckled with grey that hid most of his face, the man could indeed have been a padre.

The man thought a moment. "Then she is also under mine."

"Thank you." Clay motioned for Ellis to join them. "This is Miss Valmont. She is in search of her brother who has been rumored to be held prisoner by the Mexican army, possibly at the Alamo." He returned his attention to the priest. "And you are?"

"A friend." The older man smiled. "Miss Valmont, I will send a man to find your brother. What is his name?"

"Thomas Valmont," she said. "And thank you very much."

After a nod in response, he continued, "In the meantime, please be my guest here at the mission." He lifted his hand, and three of the soldiers hurried to his side. "Make Miss Valmont comfortable, and put out word that I am seeking news of a Thomas Valmont who may be held by the Mexicans at the Alamo."

Clay stepped in between Ellis and the soldiers. "Where do you propose to take her?"

"The women's quarters," the old man said. "She will be safe. But why don't you go along with them to assure yourself of that? I will wait here."

He ignored the man to look down at Ellis. "We do not have to stay here."

"That is true." She touched his sleeve. "But I trust you. Go and do what you think is right. I will be safe here. After all, it is a church."

He wanted to remind her that battles were just as often fought at churches as they were anywhere else in this war. Wanted to add that the Alamo was also a church.

Instead he nodded and then looked back at the padre. "I will go to see her settled in."

"And I will wait," was his response.

Clay grasped Ellis by the elbow as they followed the soldiers along the arched walkway and then turned to step out into a small courtyard lined with what appeared to be apartments. The soldiers led them up the stairs and then opened the door to a room that would equal any inn of quality.

When the soldiers stepped away to allow entry, Clay released Ellis and they both walked inside. "What do you want to do?" he asked her in a voice soft enough to prevent their escorts from hearing.

"I want to find my brother," she whispered. "And I want a bath, clean clothes, and a very long nap in an actual bed."

Clay laughed. "Well, it appears you will do fine here." He turned to instruct the soldiers where they could find Ellis's things and then requested they be delivered to her.

The men hurried away, leaving Clay alone with the green-eyed woman. "I cannot promise when I will return," he told her. "But I will return for you."

She smiled. "Goodness, Clay, we sound like an old married couple."

In that moment, he allowed the briefest thought of what it might be like to come home from war to a woman like Ellis Valmont. Life with her would be a trial and an adventure, both of which just might suit him well.

"That is not the worst thing you've said to me," he told her.

And then, defying all logic, he kissed her.

Ellis gasped, and he quickly released her. Before he could apologize for his clumsy and idiotic actions, she fell into his embrace again.

"I don't know what came over me," he told her. "I had no right to—"

"Don't you dare apologize or I will think you were taking advantage and not expressing something of what you were feeling."

He shook his head. "I would never take advantage of you, Ellis."

"Good," she said in that matter-of-fact way she had of putting difficult things into perspective. "Promise me you'll come back and kiss me again like that, and I will believe you," she told him.

"Still doubting me?" he asked lightly. "I am only going downstairs to speak to the padre. You act like I am not coming back."

"Clay," she said as she looked up at him with all humor now gone from her face, "you and I both know that is a distinct possibility. I want you to take this and wear it. I have no need of it here."

She lifted the cross from around her neck and handed it to him. Though he wished to protest, he knew it would be futile. So he slipped the necklace around his neck and tucked it under his shirt.

Then he shook his head and stepped back to trace the length of her jaw. In that moment, he saw the most amazing thing.

"Ellis," he told her as he reached to pull two small feathers from her curls, "look." He cupped the feathers in his hand and then gave one to her. " 'He shall cover thee with his feathers.' "

She smiled. " 'And under his wings shalt thou trust.' "

Despite his promise to deliver a kiss upon his return, Clay stole one more. Then he tucked the feather into his pocket and made his escape before he changed his mind and hauled Ellis back home away from danger.

He found the padre waiting where he left him. "Are Miss Valmont's accommodations sufficient?"

"They are," he said. "Now what is it I am to do?"

CHAPTER 25

Ellis lay awake on her soft mattress, a clean nightgown and a warm quilt covering her freshly washed body. Every ounce of her strength had gone toward staying awake until Clay returned. Only after she seemingly blinked twice and then opened her eyes to greet the early morning sun did she realize that she had fallen into a deep sleep.

A commotion outside drew her from her bed and into her clean dress. Draping her rebozo around her shoulders, Ellis hurried down the stairs and into the courtyard. There she found a group of women surrounding a younger woman in obvious distress.

Though Ellis spoke only a few words in Spanish, she knew enough to tell that the young woman was in the last hours of her first pregnancy and having difficulty delivering the child. Ellis stepped into the circle to regard the woman, now seated on a bench.

Immediately her mother's instructions came to mind, and Ellis knelt down to speak to the expectant mother. "How long have the pains been going on?" she asked.

The girl shook her head and then cried out. A woman of approximately the same age as Ellis pushed forward through the crowd and knelt beside Ellis.

"I am Rose," she said and then repeated something to the girl in Spanish.

"Two hours before sunset yesterday," she told Ellis. "And it is now almost eight o'clock."

Ellis peppered the girl—who she discovered was named Marianna—with questions, each one patiently translated by Rose. Finally she asked that the girl be lifted to her feet and brought to her bedchamber. She also requested the girl choose two or three women and then requested the others to wait in the courtyard.

An older woman grasped Ellis by the arm and complained loudly.

"Tell her I am a healer. I have done this before," Ellis said.

Rose's translation had the desired effect. The older woman stepped back and ushered them to a room just off the courtyard where the girl was settled onto a quilt. Ellis left instructions for Rose to translate her instructions to the women who were chosen and then left to return to her own apartment for her supplies.

By the time she returned, Rose had marshaled the team and the room was being prepared for the new arrival. She went to the woman's bedside and set to work.

The hours passed in a blur of activity, but before the sunset, Marianna was delivered of a beautiful baby girl. With a tired smile, she motioned Rose to her side to translate.

"She wants to know your name," Rose said. "The baby will be named for you as she owes you much for what you did for her today."

"Ellis," she said. "Although you owe me no thanks. I only did what I was taught to do."

Word of Ellis's abilities as a healer spread throughout the mission, and soon she had plenty of use for her time. From sprains and snakebites to men injured on the battlefield, her days began to run together. Soon it was December, and there was no sign of Clay.

Several times the padre visited her to say he had information that Thomas was safe under his protection but as yet not located. How he could know one but not the other was a question the priest was unwilling to answer.

Writing to Grandfather Valmont and Mama, she sent the letters with anyone willing to take them as far as Velasco or New Orleans. She told them of life inside Mission San Jose, of the women who had accepted her and had begun to teach her Spanish, and of the good news that Thomas was safe and under the protection of the padre. The letters painted a picture of hope that left out any mention of the cannons firing downriver and of the fact that she had not seen Clay in what felt like an eternity.

One afternoon in December, she was sitting in the courtyard writing a letter when Rose came to stand beside her. "Might I interrupt?"

"Please sit down." Ellis put away her letter and smiled. "You are a welcome interruption."

Rose took her place across from Ellis at the small table. She seemed to be uncharacteristically searching for the words to say as her attention drifted to the floor.

"Is something wrong?" Ellis asked.

"Marianna wishes to pay you back for your exceptional kindness."

"Payment is certainly not necessary."

"It is payment with information, not in coins." Rose looked up at her. "Your brother," she said slowly. "He has been found."

"That's wonderful news," Ellis exclaimed. "Where is he? I want to go to him now."

Rose reached across the table to clasp her hand atop Ellis's. "You cannot. He is being taken to Mexico."

"Mexico?" She shook her head. "How is that possible?"

As a pair of women entered the courtyard carrying laundry, Rose lifted her index finger to cover her lips. Once they passed by, she leaned forward. "Some of the prisoners were marched out of the Alamo in the uniforms of their captors. We believe your brother was among them."

"So he is marching with General Cos?" At Rose's nod, Ellis stood. "I cannot wait for Clay to return. I must go and find my brother."

"Ellis," Rose pleaded. "You cannot do that. They will not let anyone approach the army."

"Oh, I think an exception can be made for someone who is willing to buy back a prisoner, don't you?"

Rose shook her head. "You propose to buy your brother back? With what?"

Ellis leaned close, unwilling to spell out the fact that she was desperate enough to trade a freshly drawn treasure map for her family member. Let General Cos figure out where it was; she was confident she could convince him of the fact that there were riches to be found if only he looked.

"That is my concern. If Marianna knows of Thomas's whereabouts, then she can certainly get word that a ransom will be paid."

"You are asking for something that is dangerous at best," Rose warned her. "But I will convey the message."

The next morning, Rose slipped up next to her at the well. "I have an answer," she whispered. "I will take you to your brother. Only nod if you are still in agreement."

At Ellis's nod, Rose continued. "I will come for you at night. Which night, I cannot say. Be prepared to travel quickly."

Ellis smiled and went back to her work. Soon she would see Thomas. *Thank You, Lord.*

Three nights later as Ellis was about to undress for bed, she heard a soft knock at her door. Accustomed to such interruptions, she reached for her basket of herbs and then opened the door.

Clay pressed past her to step inside. Ellis hurried to close the door and then deposited her basket on the table and launched herself into his arms. "I am so glad you're safely returned."

He held her for a moment and then stepped out of her embrace. She allowed her gaze to travel the length of him, noting that he appeared not to look any worse for wear.

"Where have you been?"

"With the Greys," he told her. He nodded to the chairs flanking the small table in her apartment. "There was some trouble a few miles from here and our men were sent out to quell the disturbance. I had reason to travel to San Antonio de Béxar on behalf of my commander, and I used that opportunity to come here first. But now that I am rejoined with them, my time is no longer my own."

Ellis's brow furrowed. "Did you expect that? And how did you come to rejoin with them, now that I think of it?"

He seemed to be sorting through answers. Finally he settled on one. "The padre did lead me to the meeting place as expected. It did not matter that I was early. The man I was to meet was on the other side of a blockade and could not get through. It was decided the only way I could be found by him was to rejoin my men. He will come looking for a Grey when he can, and I will be the Grey he seeks."

"And is it Houston himself?"

Clay seemed reluctant to answer. "That is not clear."

"I see." She paused, suddenly ashamed of what she was about to ask. "And the treasure?"

He shook his head. "There has been no need to search for it, even if I knew where to start."

"But the map I drew, that should make it clear where to find it."

Clay shook his head. "I've had little time to search, but the starting point baffles me. You wrote, 'Ventane Rosa.' " He slapped his forehead. "Of course, *Ventana de Rosa.* The Rose Window."

"The window in the church?" Ellis's hopes rose even as her heart dropped. Now she could easily find the treasure, and she could certainly tempt the general with something of actual value.

And yet she was completely ashamed that she was reduced to being willing to take treasure that did not belong to her in order to redeem Thomas. Clay reached across the table to thread his fingers with hers.

"Something is wrong," Clay said. "Tell me."

"I have news," she managed. "Thomas has been found. He is marching as a prisoner with General Cos and heading toward the border."

He gave her a strange look. "Who told you that?"

"A reliable source," she said, although, as she thought of it, was that truly the case?

"Tell me how you came to have this information."

As she told Clay the story, he listened in silence. When Ellis was done, she waited for his reaction.

"You are going with me this night," he told her. "It is not safe here."

"What?" She shook her head. "But I have friends here, and I am needed as a healer. How could it possibly be unsafe?"

"They are not your friends," he told her. "Thomas is at the Alamo right now. I have seen him myself. That is why I came to see you."

"How can that be?" Again she shook her head, this time in surprise. "But oh, it is true, isn't it? That is good news."

He nodded. "Pack your things. I am taking you to him tonight."

"Yes, of course," she said as she rose and took a step toward her bag.

Clay caught her hand and turned her toward him. "You told me once that in times of war you must make difficult choices about who is friend and who is foe."

She nodded as he rose, her hand still in his. "These are times of war, Ellis. But we will not always be fighting. When that day comes, I would very much like to—"

A knock at the door interrupted him. Clay moved to a place behind the door, his pistol in hand, and then instructed her to open it. There she found a gap-toothed boy of no more than seven or eight. She thought of Lucas safely back in New Orleans and her heart twisted.

"My mama, she wishes you to help," the child said in broken English. "My papa has the snakebite on his foot."

"Tell her I will gather my herbs and come to her. But tell your papa to wrap a string around his ankle and then put his foot up on a pillow like this." She illustrated by lifting her foot to show how she wished to find him. Then she asked where he lived and sent the child on his way.

Stepping back inside, Ellis slammed into Clay. "What?" she said. "The child's father is in distress. It will take only a moment to offer comfort."

"A moment that might get you killed, Ellis," he told her.

She filled her bag as he continued to protest and then wrapped her quilt into a bedroll. When she was done, the apartment looked as it had when she first arrived.

"I am ready," she told him. "But I will see to this man's snakebite before I leave."

Clay let out an exasperated breath. "I know you well enough to know that arguing will get me nowhere. Go and do your good deed. I will be waiting in the wagon just outside the gate."

Clay tucked Ellis's bag up under the bedroll and strolled casually across the plaza. Though it was very late, fires still lit the vast expanse of space and men still laughed and talked around them.

He kept to the shadows as he walked briskly, something he knew he had done before although obviously not here at the mission. When he reached the livery where the wagon and horse had been kept, he was surprised to find the same boy who had come for Ellis.

"Why are you here?" he demanded.

The boy nodded toward the back of the barn. "My papa, he has been bit."

"And the healer has come to make him well again?" Clay offered.

At the boy's nod, he left the bags in the wagon and moved toward the soft sounds of voices. He stopped then and turned back to the little fellow.

"I have coins here that I will give you if you take this wagon out beyond the gate. Allow no one but me to take the reins from you. If you are successful. . ." He reached into his pocket and pulled out enough coin to make the boy's eyes widen. Still, he felt he should add, "This is for the healer, but please do not tell. You will do her a great favor if you do this for her."

His smile broadened. "The healer does many good things here. I will do this for her."

With the horse and wagon heading for the gate, Clay returned to follow the path to where Ellis was leaning over a man whose leg had indeed been elevated on pillows.

Though he could not hear everything she said, he could tell the man's wife was being given instructions on how to care for the wound. As he watched Ellis offer kindness to these strangers, his blood boiled that someone inside these walls wished to harm her.

The woman smiled and nodded, and the man reached up from his sickbed to shake her hand. "We must pay you," the wife protested.

Ellis shook her head and offered an embrace instead. And then she turned toward Clay. Whether she spied him there, he couldn't tell, but she was smiling.

He caught her hand as she stepped into the barn. "Follow me and do not make a sound," he whispered as soon as they were out of sight of the grateful wife.

She nodded and did as she was told. He kept to the shadows, this time with Ellis holding tight to his hand. An image appeared. Fog. A destination that was important. New Orleans. Magazine Street.

Thoughts slammed him, but he ignored them all. There would be time for memories later. For now, he had to remain solidly in the present.

He found the boy where he promised he would be. Slipping the coins into the boy's hand, he hurried him away and then helped Ellis up onto the wagon. A moment later, they were off down the river road headed to the Alamo where Ellis would be safe.

CHAPTER 26

Despite the fact that the sun had yet to rise on the new day, the Valmont family reunion was a noisy one. While Thomas Valmont whooped up quite a noise at the sight of his sister, Ellis did her part as well. It took a few minutes for the lanky soldier to notice that his sister had not arrived alone.

"And who are you?" he asked Clay.

"He is the man who made sure I found you. Clay Gentry, please meet my brother Thomas Valmont."

Clay shook hands with the man who stood eye-to-eye with him. Though Thomas grunted a sufficient greeting, it was plain he was not overjoyed at the thought of his sister arriving alone in the early hours of the morning with a New Orleans Grey.

"I thought you boys were out fighting nearer to Goliad," he said. "Heard there was some trouble out there."

"Nothing we couldn't handle," Clay said. "I am here on behalf of my commanding officer. Bringing your sister along was just a bit of good luck."

"We Valmonts don't believe in luck." He gave Clay another looking over. "The Lord takes care of us in His own way. If we manage to have something go our way, we figure it's because it is His way."

Clay smiled. "You sound very much like your grandfather. And yes, I do agree. My mention of luck was just a figure of speech."

Thomas gave him a doubtful look and then returned his attention to Ellis. "Now that Mr. Gentry is off to speak on behalf of his commanding officer, let's you and me go find a place to catch up."

Ellis looked back over her shoulder as her brother led her away. Her smile gave away her elation at the reunion, but it also made being summarily dismissed by her brother sting a little less.

Clay went off to impart his message to the post commander, James Neill, that the Greys did not intend to fall back to Gonzales for the winter. Rather, they wanted to fight and were willing to offer their help to the garrison here.

His message was well received, especially in light of the fact that a group of General Burleson's men, now under the command of General Johnson, planned to leave San Antonio to pursue an invasion of the Mexican city of Matamoros. Though Clay felt for the commander, he understood the ways of war and the idea that doing something—anything—was preferable to waiting.

Carrying a note of thanks for his commander, Clay stepped out onto the now-sunny plaza and looked around for Ellis and her brother. He found them huddled together near the officers' quarters laughing and telling stories.

"Remember when you beat us all racing to the riverbank?" Thomas said. "Mama sure was mad at us."

"Probably because I nearly died after getting bit by the snake that was waiting for me at the finish line." She spied Clay watching and smiled. "Come and join us. We were just catching up."

"So I heard." He shrugged. "And if it eases your pain any, she recently beat me at a race too."

The Valmont brother frowned, and in that moment Clay recognized two things. First, with his hair color and green eyes, he looked an awful lot like Ellis. And second, he was very protective of his only sister.

"Oh," Ellis said as she linked arms with Clay. "Thomas told me the best news. Papa is at Gonzales with General Houston. Apparently he has become an aide to the general. He is hoping to make a trip to the Alamo soon."

Though her tone was light, her meaning was clear.

"That is good news," Clay said. "I'm sure you will have much to discuss with him when you see him again. In the meantime, would you mind if I borrowed your sister, Valmont? I'm leaving soon and would like to have a word with her."

Ellis grinned and rose, but Thomas stood as well. "I'd like a word first," he told Clay. "In private."

They walked together to the other side of the garrison where Thomas stopped beneath a tree beside the north barracks wall. Though he had maintained decent humor toward Clay while in his sister's company, he now dispensed with the farce.

"I want to know who you are and why you think you can compromise my sister as you have," he demanded, his eyes narrowed and a flush of obvious anger rising up his cheeks.

"Compromised," Clay managed. "I've done nothing of the sort. What kind of stories has she been telling you about me?"

"It is what she hasn't told me that has me worried," he muttered through a clenched jaw. "You were alone with her for five days traveling to San Antonio de Béxar. Two nights sleeping together unmarried on a steamboat and three in the back of a wagon."

"Hold on now," Clay said. "Two nights on the deck of a steamboat with two horses separating us and dozens of passengers as our chaperones. And three nights with all our supplies stacked between us. I assure you nothing happened to compromise your sister, so stand down, soldier."

Clay thought he had defused the situation with his strong words. Then Ellis Valmont's brother punched him. Twice.

Before he could land a blow, Thomas's comrades had Clay in arms. To his credit, with Clay unable to defend himself, Thomas took a step backward.

"Hit him again, Valmont," one of them challenged. "He's a Grey. He ain't one of us. Whatever he did, he deserves a good thrashing."

It occurred to Clay that the problem of what to do about his feelings for Ellis Valmont could be solved right now. If he admitted to compromising her, then her brother would likely haul the two of them off to a padre and have them married before the lunch bells rang. On the other hand, if he argued the point, three members of the very same army the Greys were trying to help could very well beat him to a pulp.

He opted for the third option. "I said stand down, soldier."

Thomas looked at him as if he'd lost his mind. And then he started laughing.

"You heard the Grey," Thomas said. "Stand down."

The moment the men released him, Clay returned the favor and landed a blow to Thomas's midsection. "Never accuse me of impropriety with your sister," he told the man as he doubled over in pain and his friends once again grabbed hold of Clay's arms. "I love that woman and would never harm her reputation."

This time none of them stood down, but they did allow him to walk away with no more bruises than a man with his level of stupidity deserved. He had almost reached the corner of the garrison when Thomas caught up to him.

Stepping in front of him, Ellis's brother stuck out his hand in an offer to shake. "Welcome to the family, Grey."

Clay shook his head. "What are you talking about?"

"I've never met a man more suited to marrying my sister than you. I just hope you live long enough to smarten up and ask her."

Reaching out to accept the handshake, Clay laughed. "I hope so too."

Ellis came around the corner then and stopped short. She took in their disheveled appearance and likely what was a rising bruise under Clay's left eye.

"What in the world have you two been up to?" she demanded, her hands on her hips.

"Nothing," they said in unison as they both fell into a fit of laughter.

Thomas pressed past Ellis, pausing long enough to kiss her on the top of her head before moving along. When Clay reached her, she put her hand out to stop him.

"What happened to your eye? Did my brother do that?"

He grinned. "Not everyone is smart enough to land a punch where he doesn't have to give an explanation."

Now that she knew Thomas and her father were safe, a weight was lifted from Ellis's shoulders and the days went by quickly. Though Papa had written that he hoped to join them for Christmas, that did not happen. Ellis longed to tell him he was to be a papa again, but she would allow Mama that privilege. She wrote to her mother and to Grandfather Valmont and told them how her letters could reach Papa.

She also enjoyed her time with Thomas and the occasional visit she had with Clay. The two seemed fast friends now, which she found odd since they did not seem to get on so well at their first meeting.

Though there were few women and children at the Alamo, Ellis managed to befriend them all. She told the little ones stories and helped the women with the cooking and washing. When called upon, she also acted as healer.

Her first real friend there, Susanna Dickenson, introduced herself shortly after she arrived. The wife of Captain Almaron Dickenson, she was the mother of a delightful baby girl named Angelina. Ellis and Susanna spent many hours conversing over their chores. Her time with Susanna made the wait for Clay's return much easier.

Supplies were meager and morale was beginning to fall among the soldiers. Rumors abounded that General Santa Anna and his massive Mexican army were marching their way. With her supply of herbs dwindling, Ellis determined to go and find what she needed. Though Thomas had ordered her to stay inside the compound, there had been little in the way of a threat for what seemed like ages.

Besides, it was a beautiful afternoon and uncharacteristically warm. She alerted Susanna to her mission and asked if she would like to come along. Unfortunately, little Angelina was fussy, so she declined.

Ellis loaded her pistol and tucked it into her pocket and then took up her basket. Walking past the sentries, she promised them she wouldn't be long.

And she would not, for she'd had word that Clay would be coming in to deliver a message to the new commander. Now that Colonel Travis had assumed the post, the Greys were often seen at the garrison.

Perhaps this visit would be the one where Clay told her that his men would be coming to stay here. The herbs and medicinal plants that grew near San Antonio de Béxar were more difficult to find. Thus, it took Ellis much longer than she expected to fill her basket.

The sun was sinking as the garrison appeared in the distance. Tired, hungry, and more than a little frustrated that she hadn't paid more attention to the time, Ellis picked up her pace. Then she heard the cannon fire once. And then twice.

As she rounded the corner, she came face-to-face with a Mexican soldier who appeared barely old enough to be in uniform.

"Doctora," she said as she held up the basket filled with herbs.

He shot her anyway.

Chapter 27

C lay expected to hear the cannons in the distance. He did not expect to hear gunfire so close. Reining in his mount, he rounded the corner to see a young Mexican soldier standing over someone on the ground. In his hand was a basket of some sort. He seemed to be digging through it for something.

At the sight of Clay's approach, the soldier tossed the basket aside and drew his weapon. Clay quickly assessed the situation. It appeared the soldier was a scout sent out alone. Or perhaps his companion had fled at the sight of a Texian soldier.

In either case, the man had been caught in the middle of robbing a person already dead or had been the one who pulled the trigger. The second being the more likely scenario, Clay decided, when the soldier tossed the basket away and sighted his weapon.

"I will let you live if you walk away now," he told the soldier. "Just go."

His ability to speak Spanish had failed him this time, or the soldier had no care for Clay's warning. He continued to stand there as if his next act would be to dispatch Clay just as he had obviously done with this civilian.

"Go," Clay repeated.

The man set the sight against his eye, the barrel of the rifle now aimed directly at him. Then, from nowhere, a noise crackled through the air. The Mexican soldier crumpled.

Clay jumped off his horse and ran, closing the distance to remove the soldier's weapon. Then he turned to see if he could identify the civilian.

"Ellis."

Black rage mixed with fear flooded him as he gathered her into his arms. Blood stained his jacket, but still he held her against him.

"Clay," she whispered, and he nearly cried out with joy. She was alive. Ellis was alive. But there was so much blood.

"Ellis, I love you. Do not die," he said as he took off his jacket and held it against the source of the blood.

From somewhere behind him he heard footsteps. Heard yelling and words and names being shouted but there was nothing, there was no one, just him and Ellis and all the blood and the anger that flowed as red as that blood.

Then someone wrenched her from his arms. Clay came up swinging.

The world tilted and then Thomas Valmont stepped in front of the men who held his arms back. "Stand down, soldier," he told him. "We're taking her to Pollard at the hospital."

The rest of the night and following day was spent in a haze of white-hot fear and blood-red anger. Clay paced, he prayed, and then he paced some more. Finally in the middle of the next afternoon, Amos Pollard lifted the ban on visitors in his hospital and allowed Clay inside.

He stepped into the room where Ellis lay—not the sickroom where the soldiers were kept, but a smaller and more comfortable chamber that Clay had been told was the doctor's own quarters. The walls here were painted in the bright color that was common in Mexican homes, and the bedposts had been carved with flowers of all sorts.

Ellis lay still and quiet, white as the linen that wrapped her up to her chin with her flame-red hair spread out on her pillow. Clay froze.

Though he had determined he would neither cry nor allow Ellis to see how terrified he was at the prospect of losing her, Clay did both the moment he fell on his knees beside her bed. How long he knelt there, he had no idea. When a hand touched his shoulder, he jumped to his feet.

"I didn't mean to surprise you." The man stuck out his hand. "Name's Amos Pollard. I understand you found her."

Clay managed a nod. Anything further seemed impossible.

"She's lucky," he said. "Either the man who shot her had terrible aim or she surprised him."

"I don't believe in luck," he said, thinking back to Thomas Valmont's take on that subject. "The Lord takes care of us in His own way. If we manage to have something go our way, we figure it's because it is His way."

Pollard smiled. "Well then, I will rephrase my statement. The Lord has taken care of this young lady, and I believe with care she will be just fine."

"With care?"

He shrugged. "If she were my daughter—and I have one, you know—I wouldn't allow her to stay here. You see for yourself what is outside these gates. I don't think it will be long before they'll make a try for us."

"Then I will take her to safety."

"That is wise," he said, "though she won't be fit to travel far. I suggest you move her to the mission at San Jose. She should be safe there for now."

Thomas Valmont appeared in the doorway. "Consider it done."

"No," Clay snapped. "She will not be safe there."

Pollard shrugged. "You two decide. I've got somewhere else to be, but please do not tarry in making your choice. It won't be long before no one will come or go from this place."

When the surgeon was gone, Clay let out a long breath. "I cannot trust her safety at the mission because there are people there who mean her harm. A woman tried to lure her out of the mission with the promise of seeing you. She said you'd been taken by the Mexicans and were marching to the border but she could facilitate your escape. It was a lie, of course, because you were here all along."

Thomas laughed, and it was all Clay could do not to punch him. "Was her name Rose?"

"Maybe," Clay said slowly. "Why?"

He shook his head. "Because I'd been told that my sister was looking for me by one of the sentries."

"Yes," Clay said. "I did inquire about you when I first arrived here. When I saw the conditions, I knew I couldn't allow Ellis to stay, so I took her with me to Mission San Jose."

"Rose meant her no harm, I promise."

"How could you know?" he demanded. "She lied."

"To protect me," Thomas said. "Rose and I are, well. . .we are acquainted. I hope someday to make an offer of marriage to her. But that will be after this war is over—if we survive it."

Clay shook his head. "She was going to lure Ellis out into the night. She told her to be prepared to go at a moment's notice."

"Because she would be taking her to me." Thomas shrugged. "I had to make arrangements. It took time. And I certainly couldn't meet her at the mission, considering. . ."

"Considering what?"

"Considering Rose's father does not approve of me. I've been ordered to stay away." He nodded toward the exit. "If you think the men out there have it in for us, that is nothing compared to how Rose's family feels about me. Not that it'll matter when the time comes. We will marry one way or another."

"I see."

"However, I think an exception could be made for my sister," he said. "My suggestion is we move her to Mission San Jose, and then we leave her in Rose's care. When she can travel further, Rose will get her to safety."

Clay managed a nod of agreement but nothing else. Thomas clapped his hand on Clay's shoulder. "She will live to torment us both again. I promise."

At this, he did manage a smile.

Ellis opened her eyes to a room filled with color. And flowers. Were they real? She narrowed her eyes and tried to focus. Perhaps. Or perhaps they were merely carved into the surface of the wood. They moved, swirling in and out until she had to close her eyes to make them stop.

The air was cold, but beneath the blankets she felt warm. Her arms were filled with lead, or so it seemed, and she was completely unable to do anything other than hold her eyes open for a few brief moments. Until the flowers began swirling again.

The next time she opened her eyes, the room looked completely different. The walls were white, and the sun blazed down upon a quilt that she had seen before. Somewhere. A lifetime ago.

A crucifix hung on the wall just beyond her. She looked into the face of Jesus and closed her eyes. Feathers. Something about feathers.

"Ellis?"

Someone called her from far away. She opened her mouth to respond but could not. Instead she fell into the silence and dreamed about feathers. Lots of feathers. And then just two of them.

"I think we should stop giving her that sleeping potion," someone said.

"It's helping her," another voice argued.

"Yes, but she has to wake up sometime."

Feathers. Two feathers.

"Wake up, Ellis."

The words were insistent almost to the point of rudeness. She opened her eyes to say so but found her mouth so dry she could barely form a sound.

Water found its way to her lips and she drank. A woman stood near-by. "Not too much, Marianna. She's only just coming out of her sleep."

Rose. Yes, she remembered her. The other woman, younger and rounder of face, came into view holding a brightly colored pitcher. Marianna, yes.

"Your daughter, how is she?"

Rose translated as Marianna grinned. "She is good," the young woman said in heavily accented English.

"How did I come to be back at Mission San Jose?" she asked as she struggled to sit up until an overwhelming pain forced her to allow Rose to help.

The women exchanged looks and then Marianna slipped from the room with a worried expression. Rose moved a chair near the bed and sat down.

"You were shot," she told her. "Do you remember any of it?"

"Shot? No," she said, although she did recall an afternoon when she strayed too far while gathering herbs. But too far from where?

"The Alamo," Rose was saying, and then she began to cry.

"Am I that bad off?" Ellis said. "It seems as though I will recover."

Rose nodded and reached for the handkerchief she kept in her pocket. Once she dabbed her eyes dry, she began again.

"The surgeon was able to clean your wound. He insisted you be moved here and not be disturbed until the healing was successful. Marianna and I have been using your herbal medications the way you taught us and seeing to you since. . ."Tears sprang fresh, and this time the handkerchief could not contain them. "Oh Ellis. . ."

"What is it?" Ellis demanded. "If it is not me, then what?" She paused as a feeling of dread coursed through her. "Then who?"

"All of them," she managed. "He took all of them."

She leaned forward, ignoring the pain that it caused her. Grasping Rose's hand, she shook it. "What are you talking about? Please tell me."

Through the tears, she gasped a cry and then shook her head. "The Alamo. They let the women and children live, but they killed the rest."

Ellis shook her head as the words swirled around in her mind. They formed and then scattered, refusing to become a clear thought.

Finally the idea of what she'd heard took hold. "The Alamo has fallen?" At Rose's nod, she felt the breath in her lungs freeze. "When?"

"Nearly two weeks ago now. Sixth of March, it was."

"Thomas?" she managed.

"Gone. Clay too. And your papa. Thomas had only just written of his arrival and now this."

Ellis wailed then, giving vent to what she could no longer say. She closed her eyes. Feathers. Two feathers.

CHAPTER 28

Two months later

Ellis barely recalled how she got from Mission San Jose to the ship that took her home to Mama. To New Orleans. Grandfather had come for her, that she knew, though she'd never thought to ask how he found her.

Only later would she recall the letters she had written, for her memories of those days in San Antonio de Béxar were fraught with loss and unreliable at best. The man who shot her had barely missed killing her instantly, a fact that Grandfather Valmont reminded her of far more than she cared to hear.

Upon his arrival in New Orleans, her grandfather had commissioned three of her able-bodied cousins—men who had wished to join up with the Greys but had been dissuaded by family—to sail to Velasco and take over Valmont Shipbuilders until the war ended. Thus he lovingly plagued her waking moments with the same attention that she once lavished on him.

And to think she used to worry over his coughs and lack of sleep. The fact that the tables had been turned did not sit well with Ellis.

Nor did she think she could tolerate another day spent sitting in the parlor stabbing her fingers while attempting embroidery or some other activity that her aunts felt was ladylike.

The home on Royal Street that had been passed down from

generation to generation showed no sign of age. Rather, the elegant decor that had likely greeted her great-grandfather when he returned from his privateering missions was the same decor that Ellis was looking at right now.

Glancing up at the fire-haired female in the portrait over the fireplace, Ellis smiled. If the stories about Maribel Cordoba were true, the aunts wouldn't have approved of her either.

"That is the first smile I have seen from you in far too long." Mama set her embroidery aside to regard her with a curious expression. "To what do we owe the honor?"

"To her, I suppose," Ellis said, nodding toward the portrait. "I wonder how she was with embroidery."

"Hopeless," Mama said as she shifted position. "She claimed she had never successfully completed a piece of embroidery in her entire life." She nodded to the basket and the piece she had just set aside. "I am hoping to remedy that. I found one of her unfinished pieces in the attic and I am determined to have it finished before the baby comes in a few weeks."

Ellis glanced down at the baby gown and shook her head. "Better to plan to have that finished for the next generation of Valmont babies. I doubt you'll finish it in three weeks."

"Maybe four by my calculations," Mama said.

"Three," Ellis said. "Plus maybe a day or two."

Her mother grinned. "Well, aren't you the expert now?"

"I learned from the best," Ellis said.

"Yes, I will be in good hands for the birth." She paused, her eyes downcast. "This one will be bittersweet."

"Oh Mama."

Tears threatened but she refused to give in. She'd cried her weight in tears over the last six weeks, and she certainly would not be responsible for making Mama cry too. So she rose and went to stand in front of her, motioning for her to follow and then having to help her out of the chair.

"Where are we going?" Mama asked.

"Anywhere but here in this parlor." She nodded at the portrait. "I don't blame her for hating that painting. It's stuck inside this parlor all day."

Mama laughed. "Well now, I hope you're not planning some kind of outing that requires I walk anywhere. Not that I have done anything but waddle for the past month."

They both knew Mama's size was likely due to carrying twins, though neither wanted to discuss the matter. The one time Ellis had tried to talk to her mother about the possibility, Mama had refused to hear it. The fact that both of Mama's sisters had sets of twins spoke almost as loud as the expanding girth that her mother was carrying.

The bell rang downstairs, indicating a caller. Mama froze. Ever since her arrival back in the fall, old friends and family had made it their business to stop by to greet the newly returned Sophie Valmont.

Through Christmas and the spring the constant stream of visitors had continued. Though Ellis hadn't been here nearly as long as Mama, she was in complete agreement.

Nodding to the back stairs, she grinned. "You know, Mama, we could sneak out of here and hide from whoever thinks it's a good idea to interrupt our adventure."

She giggled. "Adventure? Is that what we were about to have?"

"It was," Ellis said, her enthusiasm rising for the first time in a very long time. "Let's slip away and have an adventure. And I promise, you won't have to do much walking."

"Yes, let's." Mama pressed past her to begin the arduous trek down the narrow servants' staircase. "As long as our adventure includes Antoine's Restaurant for lunch. I haven't had Antoine's since I came back, and I am absolutely starved for a—"

"So that's how it is, is it? Your husband leaves for a little while and his wife goes off to Antoine's without him?"

"Papa!"

Ellis whirled around to see her father standing in the foyer on the other side of the parlor. Though he was a little slimmer than when she last saw him, his smile was still the same. Thomas stood behind him, his grin matching Papa's.

"Boyd?" Mama called as she made the laborious climb back up the stairs.

"Where are you, Sophie-girl?" he demanded. "Your husband is home and you are taking your sweet time welcoming him. I brought your son with me, if that makes any difference. But if you truly were glad we. . ."

"Hello, Boyd," Mama said as she stepped into the parlor. "Welcome home." When he froze, apparently speechless, she continued. "Say something."

"Sophie?" he managed. "How did that happen?"

"The usual way, Boyd," she told him as she closed the distance between them to wrap him in her arms. "Oh Thomas," she said as the dam broke on her tears. "You're home. You're all home."

Not all of them, Ellis thought as she joined the family. And though her tears were mostly happy tears because her papa and her brother had survived, sad tears mingled with them for the man she had lost.

"Mama," Thomas said gently as the sound of Lucas and Mack echoed in the stairwell outside the parlor. "I would like to introduce you to someone special to me. If you'll excuse me just a minute, I will go and get her."

"Well, of course," Mama said. "Although I don't know why you would assume I wouldn't want to meet her," she called as he exited.

"Could be because her family wasn't so keen on Thomas," Papa said, his arm still around Mama. "We might have been home a week ago except that Thomas wouldn't leave Texas without her and I wouldn't leave Texas without Thomas."

Mama smiled up at him. "Thomas?" she said. "Am I thinking. . ."

He pressed his index finger to his lips. "Let the boy tell you," he said.

Lucas and Mack poured into the room with Thomas a step behind them. Trailing but holding tight to his hand was a very familiar face.

"Rose?" Ellis said, and Rose giggled then nodded.

"Mama," Thomas said. "I would like to introduce you to my wife, Rose Valmont."

"Your wife," she said on a whisper. "Why, Thomas, I don't know what to say." She paused only a second. "Except to say to Rose that I am so very glad to meet you and thrilled that the balance of males to females is returning."

"So I see," Thomas said as the two little boys whooped and danced around their newly returned father. He grinned while Papa knelt down to gather both little ones into his arms. "But there is more to tell."

Clay. Had he come with them? Ellis's smile rose but she dared not interrupt Thomas to ask.

"Rose and I have been married for a few months. After Ellis was shot, I knew I couldn't risk missing my chance to ask this woman to be my wife. So while I was at the mission, we had the padre marry us."

Mama's smile broadened. "Thomas, that is so romantic," she said.

"More romantic than you know," Papa said as he tossed Mack onto his shoulders.

"You're one to talk," Thomas said as he nodded toward Mama.

"Wait," Ellis said to Rose. "Are you, that is, you and Thomas are—"

"Going to have a baby," Thomas said. "Yes. And it doesn't take an expert to determine that he or she should be arriving nine months after the wedding."

Ellis hugged Rose. "I finally have a sister," she said with a genuine smile. "I am so very happy for both of you. This is the perfect happy ending to your story. He was lost and now here he is."

"I am so sorry you cannot have the same end to your story," Rose said softly. "I prayed every night that he could come home to you. Marianna, she sends her love and says she prays now too, in English and Spanish."

Ellis grinned through tears that rose once again. "She's a very good student."

"And a good healer too. She is shy, but she knows much of the healing ways thanks to you. She says she will write when her English is better."

Mama clapped her hands, and the room fell silent. Even the little boys ceased their chattering. "With only a month until my time arrives—"

"Three weeks," Ellis corrected.

Mama shook her head. "As I was saying, with only a month until my time arrives, I propose to throw a party for the newlyweds the likes of which New Orleans has never seen. What do you say, Boyd?"

"Is Boyd home?" Grandfather called from the stairs.

"Yes, Grandfather," Ellis said. "Papa and Thomas. And Thomas's wife." She grinned. "And Thomas's future son or daughter."

Grandfather arrived in the parlor and had to hear every detail of the story all over again. "So you were both at San Jacinto, then?" he said. "The newspapers appeared to exaggerate. Surely the battle was not over in such a short time."

"Eighteen minutes," Papa confirmed, "and Santa Anna tried to escape dressed as a common soldier."

"There will be time enough for talk of war," Mama said. "Ellis, Rose, and I must talk of parties right now. So if you will excuse us, we have so many plans to make and so little time."

"Just three weeks," Ellis said.

"Hush." Mama swatted her playfully and then led them out of the parlor and down to the kitchen to break the news to Cook and her crew that they had a party to prepare for.

In the days that followed, the entire house was in an uproar over the newly returned soldiers, the new Valmont bride, and the big party that would celebrate it all. While Ellis was thrilled that her friend Rose was now related by marriage, she did allow the slightest tinge of jealousy at the happily ever after that Rose and Thomas would have.

What began as a sit-down dinner for three dozen in the formal dining room soon became a ball with dinner and dancing. Ellis shook her head as the guest list continued to grow.

"You're not going to believe who is coming now," Rose said three days before the event as the seamstress was letting her new dress out once again.

"Who?" Ellis sat in the window seat casually turning the pages of the swashbuckling novel that had once belonged to her great-grandmother.

"The president!"

"Of what?" Ellis said as she turned the page and followed a young sailor up the mainmast to watch for sails on the horizon.

"Of the United States, Ellis!"

She shook her head. "Andrew Jackson?"

"Yes, can you feature it?"

"Well, he has friends here," she said. "Namely a few of my aunts, though none of them will admit to more than a flirtation in their youths," she said, imitating the society ladies.

She looked over at Rose, who was now crying. Rising, she went to hug her, shooing the seamstress out of the way. "Why are you crying?"

"Because my mama and father will not be here but the president will."

"Oh honey," she said as she patted Rose's back. "You cannot change them, but God can." She paused. "God and the news of a new grandchild. Just you watch."

Rose sniffed and smiled. "Do you think so?"

"I do," she said. "Just give them time."

But time was something that seemed to flow forward even though Ellis willed it to go backward. Back to the moments she spent with Clay.

She held that thought close and did not share it, even with Mama or Rose.

The day of the party, though chaos reigned downstairs, Ellis stayed up in her bedchamber in the eaves of the house until the very last minute.

Though she allowed for the maids to dress her and situate her hair just so, she refused any invitation to join the party until after the guests had begun arriving.

Finally her father knocked at the door. "You're very much missed downstairs," he told her as he sat on the bed beside her. "People have asked where you are."

"I don't mean to be rude," she said. "I just don't feel much like attending a party tonight."

"I know you don't, sweetheart," Papa said as he wrapped his arm around her. "You're heartbroken, and that is never an easy thing to remedy, even for a healer."

She smiled to keep the tears from flowing. "You always did understand."

"I still do." He stood and offered his hand to help her to her feet. "This is for Thomas and Rose," he said. "And I know you'll manage to feel like attending a party for them, won't you?"

"I will," she said, "whether I feel like it or not."

"That's my girl," he said. "Oh, by the way. I have something for you." He reached into his jacket and pulled out a small leather pouch and handed it to her.

"What is it?"

Papa shrugged. "Came by delivery a few minutes ago. Open it and see what it is."

She loosened the strings and poured the contents into her palm. One wooden cross on a leather string and a feather.

"Where did you get this?" she demanded.

"Go see for yourself," he said with a shrug. "The fellow who brought them is waiting outside in the courtyard."

Ellis fairly flew down three flights of stairs, ignoring the greetings of half of New Orleans high society and likely shocking all four of her aunts beyond their current state of disapproval of her. Throwing open the door, she stepped out into the courtyard and left the noise of the party behind.

Out here the only sounds were the splash of the fountain and the occasional laughter from the party upstairs. At first she thought she was alone. Then she saw the man in the shadows.

"Who is here?"

Clay stepped out then, moving toward her without a word. Ellis fell into his embrace, tears blurring the handsome face of the man she thought she would never see again.

"I thought you were—"

He stopped her with a kiss. And then another.

And then she lost count.

Later Clay would explain that Andrew Jackson had offered a job in his cabinet and he turned him down. That the money stolen from his rooms over the arcade had been found and delivered to its new owner courtesy of the United States government and the guards who had been secretly posted around Clay while he was in New Orleans.

He would tell Ellis that the Gallier treasure still lay hidden steps away from the tree near the San Antonio River and that he had plans for them to dig up that treasure together someday.

He would tell her about the pirate grandfather he was learning about through President Jackson's personal recollections and the family in Tennessee who would descend on them soon. He might also tell her that one of the memories he'd recalled included a visit with his uncle to this very home where he snuck into the parlor on a dare alongside a certain red-haired girl who looked very much like the woman in the painting over the mantel.

And then he would tell her about the hope he had that they would make a life together somewhere, be it in New Orleans, Texas, or Timbuktu. The hope that had kept him alive when he tried and failed to get through enemy lines to defend the Alamo alongside his men. About the mission that had taken him away from the garrison in time to save his life but to cause him to lose those same friends.

About the guilt that nearly drove him mad and the prayer about feathers that brought him back here to her door.

Later. But not now.

Now he would hold the green-eyed woman in his arms until he could find the words to ask her to be his wife. Which might take some time since he far preferred kissing over talking at this moment.

But he would tell her all of that.

And more.

Later.

BENT HISTORY:
THE REST OF THE STORY

As a writer of historical novels, I love incorporating actual history into my plots. As with most books, the research behind the story generally involves much more information than would ever actually appear in the story. In truth, I could easily spend all my time researching and not get any writing done at all!

Because I am a history nerd, I love sharing some of that mountain of research I collected with my readers. The following are just a few of the facts I uncovered during the writing of *The Alamo Bride*, and a few historical facts I have "bent" to fit the story. I hope these tidbits of history will cause you to go searching for the rest of the story.

We first meet Clay Gentry at an establishment on the corner of Magazine Street and Natchez Street owned by Jim Hewlett. Hewlett's Exchange, as it was sometimes called, was a multipurpose endeavor with fine dining and all the trappings of luxury on the second level and high-stakes gambling and gaming going on a floor above. The first floor was reserved for all manner of business transactions, including slave trading.

Moving to Velasco, Texas, there is a conversation in chapter 2 regarding the Battle of Velasco, which took place on June 26, 1832. In this battle, the Texians under Henry Smith and John Austin were engaged in battle when they attempted to pass the fort in a vessel that contained a cannon meant for use against the Mexican forces at Anahuac. The battle ended when the Mexican forces inside the garrison ran out of ammunition and were forced to surrender. Terms of the surrender included a return to Mexico by all who wished on a vessel supplied by the Texians.

The New Orleans Greys were mustered into action in October 1835 on the ground floor of a three-story building called Banks Arcade, which incidentally was more of a combination market and coffee shop and not anything like what we know today as an arcade. The men were divided into two units, each with a different commander. A few days later after being fitted with uniforms and weapons, one group headed north to Nacogdoches, Texas; the other went south to Velasco. Historians say that upon their arrival in Velasco, the men were indeed welcomed as citizens of Texas and took an oath like the one given by Judge Edmund Andrews— the name he shares with the real-life judge—in the book. Each Grey was also given a certificate of citizenship before signing the roster that was sent on to General Sam Houston, commander of the Texas army. I'm not certain if, when the Greys left New Orleans, they realized they would not only fight for Texas but also become official Texians, but history says that is exactly what happened. I don't know how the citizens of Velasco and Quintana greeted these soldiers, but I would like to think they made them feel welcome. Thus, I have bent history to show that they came down to cheer their arrival. The scene the next day where the whole unit of New Orleans Greys—minus one—floats past on a steamboat, however, is based on historical fact. The day after the Greys landed in New Orleans, they were shipped upstream to Columbia to meet such dignitaries as Jane Long and to be feted with parades and political speeches.

Meanwhile, in the fall of 1835, much was happening in Texas. Skirmishes occurred in several places, all pitting the ragtag volunteers of the Texian army against the well-trained soldiers of Santa Anna's Mexican army. In October, battles were fought in Gonzales and Goliad, and then on November 1, the siege at Béxar occurred. On December 9, General Cos surrendered the Alamo to the Texian army, and two days later he negotiated a peaceful surrender that allowed his troops passage back to Mexico. Certainly no one expected on that cold December day that less than three months later on March 6, 1836, after a siege lasting thirteen days, the Alamo would return to Mexican hands and the Texian army would be soundly defeated. This defeat, coupled with the Goliad massacre that happened three weeks later, made it appear that the dreams of a free Texas republic were swiftly dying. Then on April 21, 1836, on a battlefield just a few miles from where I now live, General Sam Houston defeated the mighty army of Santa Anna in a battle that lasted a mere eighteen minutes!

Much is made of the battles that led to the Texas Revolution, but we often forget that those who fought those battles were regular folks just like us. Though they were almost all men, there were women settlers in 1830s Texas, and their lives were anything but boring!

When I created the image of Ellis's home on the Texas coastal prairie, I imagined her family would have a home known as the dogtrot style, a type of log cabin that was popular during this period in Texas history and particularly suited to the environment there. The home usually started as one square cabin. When the family grew, another cabin of the same size was built a few feet away and the two structures joined by a wooden porch that wrapped between them and often around on all sides. The two squares also shared one roof, giving the porch a covering that helped in summer and during rain. As the need for more space occurred often, many of these dogtrot homes had a second story built to span the two structures. Sometimes the staircase to access the upper floor was contained in the parlor side of the home. Other times, the stairs were built in the covered porch area between the buildings. Due to the risk of fire, the place where the cooking was done—sometimes called a summer kitchen—was located in a separate building away from the home.

Another aspect of Ellis's life on the Texas prairie involved the healing skills she learned from her mother. The art of using medicinal herbs is an ancient one, so it is no wonder that women who could not run down to the local CVS Pharmacy would school themselves in the use of the plants around them to cure coughs, bring down a fever, or, as in the case of poor Clay, promote a sound sleep. The most interesting fact of all is that scientists are now proving that our ancestors were on to something!

During the writing of this story, I had to do research on many things. One of my most eye-opening finds was in regard to horses. Did you know a horse can travel forty miles in a day at a comfortable pace? They can do much more if pushed, but forty miles was a good average to maintain the health of the horse, especially when traveling long distances like the two hundred miles that Ellis and Clay were traveling. Can you imagine? The cars in our driveways would cross that two-hundred-mile distance in hours rather than the five days it took my characters. Life has definitely sped up since 1835!

And speaking of speeding things up, steamboat travel was definitely the way to cross the miles faster. A number of steamboats plied the waters of the Brazos River in the 1830s, delivering supplies and picking up crops destined for markets up and down the river. They also carried passengers, including animals. The river was far different than it is now, with many impediments to safe travel. A steamboat captain had to negotiate tight turns, avoid fallen trees and shallow sandbars, and still make good time. From firsthand reports I read in the diaries of travelers during that time, the trips were nothing if not harrowing.

When Ellis and Clay travel to San Antonio de Béxar in search of her brother Thomas, they take a steamboat to the town of Washington—soon to be known as Washington-on-the-Brazos where the Texas Declaration of Independence was signed on March 2, 1836—to the place where La Bahia Road crossed the Brazos River. Today this scenic drive is known as Texas Scenic Highway FM 390 (the first in the state to be designated as a scenic highway), and it winds through—among others—Washington and Fayette Counties. Originally an east-west Indian trail, the road goes through such picturesque Texas towns as Independence, William Penn, and Burton and is a favorite spot to see the famous Texas bluebonnets in the spring.

Among all these facts, I do have one "bent fact." That is, in order to make the time line work for the story, I had to play with history just a little. In reality, General Cos surrendered the Alamo to the Texian troops on December 9, 1835. He and his soldiers retreated and were given safe passage back to Mexico. In the story, however, I have that happening a little sooner.

During her time at the Alamo, Ellis befriends Susanna Dickenson, wife of Captain Almaron Dickenson. Susanna is a real person who indeed was at the Alamo during the siege and lived to tell the story. Her account of the battle is fascinating and makes for an interesting read for any history buff with an interest in the topic.

Amos Pollard was chief surgeon at the Alamo. He came to the Alamo with John York's company of soldiers and was responsible for seeing to the medical needs of those garrisoned there. He died a hero's death during the siege on March 6, 1836.

If you've read this far, thank you! That means you're a history nerd too! I can't wait to share my next novel with you very soon—and to delve into history all over again.

And maybe to bend a few facts, but only the ones that really need bending.

Bestselling author **Kathleen Y'Barbo** is a multiple Carol Award and RITA nominee of more than eighty novels with almost two million copies in print in the US and abroad. She has been nominated for a Career Achievement Award as well a Reader's Choice Award and is the winner of the 2014 Inspirational Romance of the Year by *Romantic Times* magazine. Kathleen is a paralegal, a proud military wife, and a tenth-generation Texan who recently moved back to cheer on her beloved Texas Aggies. Connect with her through social media at www .kathleenybarbo.com.